He made a

He lusted after the wrong woman. Let his need take over. Cassius "Cass" Striker knew that he should have never touched the sexy FBI agent, but he gave in to temptation and had the best one-night stand of his life with Agnes Quinn. It should have meant nothing. He should have been able to walk away...

He can't walk away. If he does, she's dead.

His enemies know about Agnes, and they plan to use her against him. He's the leader of one of the most notorious motorcycle clubs in the US. His name stirs fear into the hearts of nearly everyone...and he has a giant target on his back. Those who want to bring him down have been looking for a weakness to use against him—they think they found that weakness in the form of Agnes. Now he either saves her or he watches her die.

She doesn't need saving, but it's super sweet of him to try.

She fell for the bad guy. Not something that typically happens given her occupation, but Agnes couldn't quite help herself. She'd been drawn to Cass from the first moment, and now the world—uh, the "underworld" thinks that they are hot and heavy, that she's a way to break the unbreakable leader of the Night Strikers. Cass is vowing to protect her, but the only way to do that?

Enter his world. Accept his claim. Eliminate all the threats that exist to them both.

She has to go in undercover, continuing to pose as Cass's lover as they embark on a cross-country trip. She has to follow his rules. She has to seemingly sever her ties with the FBI. In other words, Agnes has to go deep and hard in an undercover mission as she and Cass take out some seriously bad guys. No worries, though. Agnes does love an undercover mission, so this should be fun.

The case is a nightmare. It is not fun. And if Agnes flashes her sexy smile at him one more time...

Cass is sure that he's lost his soul, and he's not even sure where his criminal life ends and the real man that he'd once been begins. He knows one thing, though. Agnes is trouble —and he wants her. Wants her so badly that maybe he'll let the dark side of his nature off the careful leash he holds. And he'll take what he wants as he damns the consequences. Threaten her? Try to use *her* against him? Worst mistake his enemies could ever make because Agnes is *his*.

Cass was never meant to be a protector, but he sure is one hell of a hunter.

When He Guards

A Protector And Defender Romance
Book 5

Cynthia Eden

HOCUS POCUS
PUBLISHING INC

v3

If you've ever wanted to ride into the sunset with a hot biker...ahem, this one is for you.
Ride hard, my friends. Read hard, too.

Chapter One

THE SEXY LITTLE FBI AGENT HAD NO BUSINESS walking into the packed bar as if she owned the place. A notorious dive, the place catered to motorcycle club members. The rough and the tough. The dangerous predators.

Not sweet-ass redheads in screw-me heels.

There was no way she should come strolling in, her thick hair loose around her shoulders, her heels too high, her skirt too short, and that top of hers far too tight as she ambled through the dangerous crowd and locked what were truly incredible blue eyes on him.

And she should not, absolutely should *not*, wink at him as she approached.

But she did.

Sonofabitch.

She winked at him, right before a crowd of far too eager and far too big MC members closed in on her and completely blocked her from his sight.

Cassius "Cass" Striker grabbed his beer bottle. He barely felt the cold glass beneath his grip. All he'd wanted was one night to just relax. Time to drink a freaking beer in peace. But was he gonna get that peace? Oh, hell, no, he was not. Because now he had to go and rescue the FBI agent who should've had more sense than to seek out the seediest bar in Atlanta. Everyone knew this was MC territory. You did not stroll in like you were—

"Hi, there." She was right in front of him. All electric blue eyes and dark red hair. Full, sexy lips smiling.

He blinked. Looked over her shoulder. The crowd of bikers had dispersed. Mostly, anyway. A few threw curious glances his way. One even gave him a thumbs up.

What. The. Hell?

She reached out and put her hand on the battered sleeve of his black, leather jacket. "So, I am truly curious…" Her voice was very clear. A little husky. Definitely sexy. Also, a wee bit too loud because he knew every ear in the place was probably straining to hear them. "Just what does a woman have to do in order to get fucked by the leader of the baddest motorcycle club on the East Coast?"

He slammed down the beer bottle. It clinked against the bar top.

Her eyes gleamed, dancing with amusement. Because, what, she thought this was some kind of joke? Did it look like he was laughing? "You're playing with fire, princess."

Instead of having some common sense and backing away—running away would be the smart choice—she leaned even closer, and her seductive, feminine scent wrapped around him. "Absolutely fantastic," she told him. "I love getting hot."

His back teeth ground together. "Agnes…"

"You remember my name. So good to hear. Delightful, in fact. I was a bit afraid that you'd forgotten me. I don't want to be forgettable."

2

She was not. She was a pain in his ass. A sexy pain in the ass, granted, but still a pain. He'd met her at the FBI's main office in Atlanta a while back. And the FBI office? That was a place that the leader of the Night Strikers did not want to be, ever. But he'd been there because he'd been making absolutely certain that individuals who'd hurt *his* people paid the price, and FBI Agent Agnes Quinn had just strolled her hot self right up to him in the middle of that Bureau hellscape. She'd stretched out her hand to him and said, "I'm Agnes Quinn." As cute and charming as you please. Like they were meeting for tea or something.

He had not introduced himself back to her. He also had not touched her hand. Feds and MC leaders did not shake hands. They did not mingle in public for fun.

They did not *fuck*.

But Agnes hadn't been put off by his refusal to speak or touch her at the Bureau. Instead, she'd just asked with a bat of her long eyelashes, *"Are you really as bad as they say?"*

Oh, he was. Much, much worse, actually.

The woman should've had the sense to stay away from him. Instead, she was in his favorite dive bar. Right the hell in front of him *now*. Talking about *fucking*. He rose from the bar stool and towered over her. "I'm gonna have that sexy ass thrown out of here." Deliberately, he kept his voice low, for her ears alone because he was *trying* to give her the chance to leave on her own accord. Look at him, being a semi-nice guy. That niceness would only last for about one more minute. "If you don't turn around and get out of here in the next sixty seconds, I will have my men carry you out and toss you onto the street."

Instead of appearing intimidated, she shook her head. Then she put her hand on his chest. She leaned close, too,

Cynthia Eden

so that it probably looked as if they were about to kiss. "I don't think so," Agnes told him, way too confident.

He blinked.

"I don't think you're the kind of man who would let someone else do the dirty work for him. If you want me out, I think you'd do it yourself. You'd put those big hands of yours on me, and you'd carry me out all by your—" Her words ended on a sharp gasp because he *had* just put his hands on her.

He'd wrapped his hands around her waist and lifted her onto the bar's top. Now they were eye to eye, and any amusement that he might have momentarily felt fled. "You don't want to know about me and the dirty work I do." He did not have time to screw around with a Fed.

Though screwing with this Fed would be incredibly fun. Fucking the ever-so-hot Agnes? Hell, yes.

No, no. Hell, *no.* It was not going to happen.

"Did Gray send you?" Cass demanded, referring to her supervisor at the FBI. Grayson Stone, FBI mastermind, mind fucker, all-around asshole. And...

The closest thing to a brother that Cass possessed. They were actually cousins. They'd grown up more as brothers, though, but that relationship was something that the majority of the MC did *not* know about. If you wanted to stay in power, you didn't advertise the fact that you'd kill to protect an FBI agent. That just wasn't the way shit was done.

"Gray has no idea that I'm here," Agnes returned. Her hands had flattened on the bar top, one hand on either side of her body. "I don't exactly run potential lovers by my boss. That would just be weird."

What?

Her words had been a bit hard to hear because there'd

been a flurry of sudden shouts behind him. The crew always got rowdy the later it became.

Her head cocked to the side as she looked beyond him, toward the noisy crowd. "I don't want to tell you your business..." With one hand, she reached for the beer bottle that he'd put down on the bar top moments before. "But I don't think this is a friendly group."

No shit. He snorted. "If you wanted friendly, then you should have stayed the hell out of this bar. Only MCs come here." Not just the Night Strikers, either. The Bottomless Pit was supposed to be a neutral zone, of sorts. Only things had a way of not staying too neutral the later it got and the drunker the crowd became.

"You were here, so I had to be, too." She raised the bottle.

So now the woman was drinking his beer? Drinking his beer, and, apparently, she'd been stalking him, too? Should that flatter him, terrify him, or annoy him? Maybe all of the above?

Her words definitely should not interest him. Should not. And why in the hell was he still holding her waist? Why was his gaze still locked on her face as he waited to hear whatever bullshit story she was about to spin for him next?

Random fact, she had a few freckles across the straight bridge of her nose. Oddly cute.

Dammit.

"Someone should really be watching your six," she murmured as she scrunched her nose in what was an oddly adorable way.

Not that he thought she was adorable. Adorable and sexy didn't go together. She was sexy. Way too hot. As for his six, he had a whole team who watched his six,

"Good thing I'm here," she added, and then she *threw* the beer bottle over his shoulder.

What in the hell?

Even as he heard the thud of the beer bottle connecting with *something*, Cass whipped around. The beer bottle crashed to the floor. Shattered. But it wasn't the only thing that crashed to the floor.

A knife did, too. The knife that some tricky bastard had been intending to *stab* into Cass's back. The bastard was just a few feet away, and the expression of utter fear and *horror* on his face was almost priceless.

"He was going toward your back," Agnes explained in a casual voice. "I saw him pull the knife from the inside of his coat. Everyone else seemed busy fighting or drinking or... you know, making out in dark corners. So I had to intervene."

She'd intervened...?

"You really should have better protection," she chided.

"I can protect myself." Deliberately, he turned to fully face the man who'd frozen. The prick who'd intended to stab Cass in the back.

"You weren't doing it this time," Agnes piped in from her perch on the bar behind him. "Thus, I stepped in like the amazing girlfriend I am."

Girlfriend? Since when? They barely knew each other. Had they even exchanged more than a full minute of conversation before this night? Cass didn't think so. But he'd deal with his *girlfriend* later. At the moment, he had a conniving jerk who needed to be handled.

Cass scanned the tats on the man's arms. His hands. Cass grunted as he recognized the ink of a rival MC. All those skulls with thorns twined around them. But no sign of a tat that would show a position of power in that MC.

"Seriously? You think you'll jump ranks by plunging a blade into my back? Aren't you precious?"

The creep's eyes darted to the left. To the right.

The fighting and the music and the laughter and every damn thing else in the dark bar stopped.

Things tended to stop when Cass used that particular tone of voice. And when people knew he was about to kick ass. He was so ready to kick some ass. Dark tension had been riding him hard. Hell, the darkness always pulled at him. Lately, that pull was even more intense. The idiot before him had just given Cass the perfect excuse to let the beast within off the leash that normally held him in check.

For a beat of time, he studied the dumbass who'd come to the bar in order to attack. Shaved head. Long beard. Nose ring. Beady eyes. Those eyes made the mistake of darting to the discarded knife.

Cass sighed. "You don't telegraph your intent, dumbass. You just attack. When you telegraph, that lets people like the cute redhead behind me..." He reached back. Maybe he gave her thigh a pat. Fine, there was no *maybe* about it. He did pat her thigh. Then his fingers lingered. The touch was supposed to be a sign for her to stand down. Not like he wanted her to fly into the fight that was moments away from occurring.

Yet...

His fingers lingered a little longer than necessary.

And stroked. Stroked right beneath the edge of her skirt. Touched smooth skin. Dammit.

Her skin was way too soft. "You should fucking cover up," he growled at her. "It's cold outside."

Amused laughter greeted him. Her laughter. "You should focus on more immediate problems."

He'd never taken his gaze off the immediate problem. So

when the bald biker before him lunged for the fallen knife, Cass was ready.

The fool never made it to the knife. His face *did* connect with Cass's boot, though, as Cass kicked the prick hard and sent him flying back. The would-be attacker slammed into a nearby table.

Cass's crew cheered.

The table wasn't meant to hold the jerk's weight, clearly, and it broke with a loud creak and a crash. The attacker's ass landed on the floor.

Did the jerk have the sense to give up? To turn tail and run?

Of course, not. The idiots who came, trying to take down Cass so they could claim the glory of killing the leader of the Night Strikers, never had that sense. Instead, the attacker grabbed a broken table leg, and, with a roar, the SOB was back on his feet. He drew back the hunk of wood, holding it behind his head, and he barreled toward Cass.

"Uh, tell me you've got this..." Agnes began, her words sharp with tension. "*Cass? Cass!*"

He had this. He launched forward, going in hard, and he rammed into the idiot before the biker could take a swing. Cass's shoulder hit the guy's torso, all of the breath *whooshed* from his prey, and Cass took that prick down.

Thunderous cheers broke out. The crowd closed in. Very, very tightly.

Cass kicked away the broken table leg.

"*Strike! Strike! Strike!*" The chants filled the air.

Hell. He was gonna have to give the crowd what they wanted.

Cass rose to his full height. He rolled back his shoulders. Shook out his hands. Got loose and ready. "You want to come at me?" Cass challenged the creep who thought the best way to attack was from behind. "Then you come at me directly. You don't sneak up behind me like a coward. You hit me, face to face." Cass smiled.

"Strike! Strike! Strike!" His MC members stomped their feet. Whistled.

The bald biker rose to his feet. Fury twisted his face. The golden nose ring gleamed.

Cass let his smile stretch. "You hit me face to face," he repeated. "Just like I'm about to hit you." Then Cass drew back his fist and attacked.

SHE COULDN'T SEE a damn thing.

Agnes Quinn huffed out a breath even as she rose to her feet—on the bar. Yeah, she was standing on the bar. Not dancing on it or anything cool like that. Just standing in her high heels as she craned to see around the crowd and make sure that Cass Striker was not, in fact, getting his ass kicked.

Because, sure, he was supposed to be big and bad.

But the jerk who'd been sneaking up behind him—with a knife—had been *bigger*. As in, while Cass clocked in at six-foot-three—yes, she knew his exact height, she'd done her recon work on him, after all—the biker with the shaved head and dark skull tats looked to be around six-foot-six. Maybe six-seven with his boots. And the dude was *big*. Not big as in muscled, but big with lots of extra weight and padding on him.

Since both men were so tall, she should have been able to see *something*. Especially from her high perch. But the crowd had closed in, and Agnes was pretty sure the fighters had to be on the floor.

Please, please, don't let Cass be pinned on the floor.

Her jaw locked. Okay, enough of this bullshit. She was a Fed, after all. Things had moved helluva fast, and she'd already shouted *twice* for everyone to stop. She'd been ignored both times. Agnes didn't enjoy being ignored. She also was not going to just stand there while a major assault went down. Time for her to call a halt to this mess, now.

She put her fingers to her lips and blew. Loud. Hard. Unfortunately, her whistle didn't really cut above the crowd. When she grabbed a bottle of whiskey from the stunned bartender and smashed it onto the floor, well, her continued whistling *and* the crash finally drew eyes to her.

Stunned gazes to which she yelled, "*Stop, now, because I am a—*"

"She's mine," Cass snarled before she could tell everyone there that she was an FBI agent.

Her breath shuddered out.

"Mine," Cass repeated gutturally.

And she could see him again. Finally. As if he'd spoken some magic word, the crowd parted around him. He rose to his feet, fisted hands at his sides, while his much bigger opponent remained groaning and slumped on the floor.

Uh, oh. "Does he need medical attention?" It certainly appeared that way to her.

Cass grunted. He also began stalking toward her. The place had been so loud moments before, but now, she was pretty sure that if you just strained the tiniest bit, you'd probably be able to hear a pin drop.

Agnes feared her heaving breaths were far too loud, and, oh, crap, she was still standing on the bar's top. Awkward.

What else was awkward? The absolutely predatory look on Cass's handsome face. Handsome as in...dangerous. Gorgeous. Knee-weakeningly sexy.

If you went for the type.

She normally didn't. True story. She did not normally think bad guys were hot. However, there was not anything particularly *normal* about her response to Cass. From the first moment that she'd seen him at the FBI Atlanta office, she'd felt as if an electric shock had gone through her entire system. She'd been working another case, and he had not exactly been enthused to meet her.

He was tall, broad-shouldered. He knew how to perfectly fill out a battered leather jacket and how to seriously work some faded jeans. His dark hair was thick and tousled, his jaw covered by the dark scruff of a light beard, and his intense eyes *glittered.* Not completely dark eyes. Some gold lurked deep in that darkness. And such a fierce glower currently covered his hard and chiseled face.

Oh, yeah. I'm hot for the bad guy.

But she did have a few other concerns at the moment other than just his incredible hotness.

She craned her head and looked behind Cass as he continued his intent stalking routine. The man on the floor was starting to rise. Agnes cleared her throat. "Uh, Cass…"

He lifted his right hand. "Throw his ass out."

That was it? Just throw him out? After an attempted murder?

Cass was in front of her now. Glaring up at her.

Agnes wet her lips. "He tried to kill you. You don't need to throw his ass out." She kept her voice soft. "You need to press charges." Obviously. "Should I arrest—*Cass!*" The last of her words ended in a shocked yelp because he'd hauled her off the bar and just tossed her over his shoulder like that was a normal thing.

She would admit, it was a fairly hot thing, if you went for that sort of alpha behavior. *Maybe I do.* But, it was not normal. And there had just been an assault, an attempted murder honestly, and Cass should be pressing charges, not carrying her around on his shoulder as if—

"Mine," Cass said again.

He was referring to her. Sighing, Agnes shoved her right hand against his back and levered herself up a bit so that she could see the crowd.

A whole lot of people were glowering at her.

So she sent a friendly wave with her left hand. "Delighted to meet you all."

Cass growled. Then he began marching through the crowd—well, more stalking again, really. The assembled bikers parted even more for him, and she saw that the attacker had already vanished. Wow. Talk about fast. Apparently, when the leader of the Night Strikers said *jump,* everyone bounced. Or, in this case, they all threw out an unwelcome visitor.

No one waved back to her which was, quite simply, rude. Before she could tell them all her opinion, though, she was outside. Cass had carried her outside of the dingy bar, and for a moment, she very much feared that he was just going to dump her on her ass on the sidewalk and walk away. Then he'd strut back in the bar and tell everyone that she wasn't supposed to be allowed inside and that would be problematic. "Uh, Cass..." Agnes cleared her throat. She tried to sound charming instead of worried as she continued, "Cass, my awesome new friend, how about you calm down—"

His growl cut through her words. "We are *not* friends."

Oh, ouch. "Someone's extra pissy after a fight. Good to know. I—*ah!*"

He'd hauled her off his shoulder.

But he hadn't plunked her ass on the ground. Instead, she was...

Her brows snapped together. "Is this your motorcycle?" She shifted her position, adjusted her legs so that she straddled the massive bike, and her hands flew to grip the handlebars. "Because I love it. One hundred percent *love it.*" She did. Agnes was not just blowing smoke up his cute, jean-clad ass. "I bet it feels like you are flying when you drive this thing." A blissful sigh escaped her. "Any chance you'll let me go for a spin? I promise to be very, very careful."

"You will drive my bike over my dead body." Flat. Nope, more guttural than flat.

She shrugged. "Your funeral then—"

"*Agnes.*"

She blinked. She also did a careful sweep of the street. Ah...*there* was the would-be attacker. Slumped outside. "Excuse me!" Agnes raised her voice as she shouted toward the bald and bearded biker. "You tried to kill a man tonight!"

He scuttled away. A fast scuttle for someone so large.

Sighing, she let go of the handlebars. She swung her body so that she no longer straddled the beautiful beast of a bike. "Excuse me," Agnes signed because Cass was in her way. "But I am going to have chase after that man and arrest him." She hated having to chase fleeing perps. So exhausting.

"For fuck's sake," Cass rasped. He reached out for her hips. Repositioned her on the bike so that once more, she was straddling the thing. "I'm not filing charges. You aren't arresting him.

"You *should* press charges against him," Agnes told Cass.

His jaw dropped. Then...booming laughter swept from him.

Her eyebrows snapped together. "That was not a joke."

His hand slid across her thigh. "This skirt is too damn short." He tried to haul the skirt down a few more inches.

It would not be hauled.

He swore.

She smiled. "Thanks for noticing the shortness. That was the whole reason I bought it."

Because of the nearby street lamp, she could see that hard jaw of his as it locked.

"When you're straddling me," he continued in his rough and deep voice, "it's gonna hike up way too far."

When you're straddling...Her mouth must have dropped open.

"Scoot back, Agnes," he ordered. "Then lock your arms around me."

Oh, he meant straddling him...*on the bike*. Not in bed. Sure. Check.

She'd hired a rideshare driver to drop her off at the bar, so she didn't have her own transportation home. A deliberate choice because parking in that neighborhood could be a challenge. Unless, of course, you had a motorcycle. Like he did.

But she didn't scoot back yet. "Do you seriously not want to press charges against your attacker?" Agnes asked. The attacker was gone, but if they gave chase right then—

"I just kicked the shit out of him. MC justice. It's over."

She wasn't so sure. "That was an attempted murder, an assault at the very least."

He grunted. "Scoot. Back."

Fine. She scooted back. After all, she did need a ride

home. This would save her from having to use her app to get a driver back to the bar for a pickup.

Cass didn't immediately settle in the seat in front of her. He glared more at her.

Agnes decided to keep talking. "Once you two got in that fun circle and started fighting, things got confusing, as least as far as who was the vic and who was the perp—"

"He came at me with a table leg. I defended myself. Case closed." He bent and unlocked the helmet that had been hooked to the motorcycle's frame. A big, dark helmet. With his jaw locked, he plunked that helmet down on her head.

She smiled. "Safety first, huh?" She secured the chin strap. "I can appreciate that, but do you want to go borrow a helmet from someone else? That way, you'll be covered, too?"

He took the small purse that she still had over one shoulder. She'd had that bag the entire time. Mostly because it contained some very necessary items. *Like my gun.* Though she hadn't pulled the gun because Agnes hadn't wanted to escalate the situation more than necessary. Cass took the bag and tucked her purse into one of the motorcycle's saddle bags. Then he straddled the bike.

Cass just hopped right in front of her. Took up a whole lot of space.

He also had the engine roaring and revving, and the seat vibrated beneath her legs with a rumble that took her by surprise and had Agnes's hands flying out to curl around Cass's waist.

"Hold on," he ordered.

Her fingers fluttered around his waist. Then pressed a little harder. Before they flew off into the night, Agnes realized she should probably explain to him *why* she'd gone to see him in the first place. Why she'd deliberately worn the sexy outfit and prissed inside the most dangerous bar in town even as she kept her gun stored in her cute purse. "Ah, Cass, about tonight..."

"You're gonna get exactly what you wanted."

What she wanted? But she hadn't told him yet. She hadn't mentioned the partnership that she was hoping he'd make with the FBI. With her. "I am?"

"Yeah, baby, you are. You are gonna get fucked long and hard by the leader of the Night Strikers."

Her jaw dropped. She had zero words.

The bike leapt forward, and as it raced through the night, with her body plastered to his, Agnes held on to Cass for dear life.

* * *

"THE SONOFABITCH JUST LEFT." Rage seethed in the words. "And he's with some woman. A hot redhead. Called her *his*."

The motorcycle was already gone from sight.

"Hell, no, he wasn't taken out." His grip tightened on the phone as he slouched in the shadows. The wood of the building behind him pressed into his back. "Cass flattened the jerk in like, two seconds, then he carried out his lady."

"He carried her out?"

"Uh, yeah." Hadn't he just said that?

"In front of everyone?"

Again... "Yeah."

"And he fucking called her *his*?"

He nodded. What was the big deal? "Cass hooks up with women all the time. No one stays long with him." The dude had zero permanency in his life. No connections. No big ties. No weaknesses.

"Follow them." The order came through the line, loud and clear.

Uh...

The rumble of the motorcycle filled the air, but Cass and the mystery woman were long gone. "That could be a problem."

"Follow them. *Now.* I want to know who the woman is. I want to know where she lives. I want to know every single thing about her."

The goal had been to eliminate Cass. Not to take out some random hookup of his. He didn't particularly like hurting women. Not his thing at all. As far as following them...

Shit. That's gonna be impossible. He fired up his ride. A much less impressive motorcycle than Cass's, second hand, and not very fast.

But he'd do his best. He'd try to find Cass. Find the woman.

And figure out who the hell she was.

Chapter Two

He braked at a red light.

And heard her laughter. Sweet, musical. Utterly delighted.

What. In. The. Hell?

Cass pressed a foot to the pavement even as he turned back to look at her.

She flipped up the visor on the helmet. He didn't know exactly when she'd flipped it down, but she had. And now she was beaming at him. A beautiful grin lit her face as the street lamps illuminated them. "That was amazing!" she gushed. "My whole body feels alive! Like, seriously, I'm vibrating. I have to confess that I've never ridden a motorcycle before, though I always wanted to give it a try. Sensational. Five stars. Highest recommendation ever."

He just stared at her.

She kept smiling. Then she dipped her head toward him. "The light is green. Vroom, vroom."

What? He growled. He was growling a lot with her. "What in the hell am I supposed to do with you?"

"I thought you had a plan. You know, you told me about

it not too long ago. Right before we began our fabulous ride into the dark. Don't go being a tease now."

He had to get her alone and in a secure location. *Not* so he could fuck her. Fucking a Fed was a bad idea. Something he'd told himself at least ten times already during their fast and furious ride. Such a bad idea.

And yet...

And yet...

Focus. "I want to know your game." No way did a Fed just sashay into his favorite bar without a reason. What was it this time? Was he under investigation? Did the Feds think they could use him? Blackmail him? Screw that shit.

Not happening.

He whipped back to the front, drove fast, and, fine, maybe it felt good when she curled her hands around his waist and pressed her body against his. Maybe it felt better than good. Maybe something about Agnes was making him a bit delirious. Or, hell, drunk. And he tried to never get drunk. Getting drunk would make you sloppy. Weak. In his line of work, there could be no weaknesses.

Since he didn't know where the hell to take her—not like he could drop a Fed off at her *door*—he drove to his home. On the other side of town. Actually, beyond town. An old scary-as-hell-from-the-exterior place that someone else had begun renovating and Cass had scooped up the property when that guy had decided to relocate to Texas.

Private, secure, with lots of sprawling space, the old house was perfect for him. The fact that it looked like something from a horror movie? Bonus points.

She didn't speak until they were inside his home. The garage door had lowered behind them. He'd killed the engine of the motorcycle, and he was trying to figure out a tactful way to say...

"Do people often try to kill you?" Agnes politely inquired. "I'm curious. Was wondering if tonight was a one-time situation or just a typical night out for you?"

He turned to look at her. Agnes no longer had a fierce grip on his waist. Pity. She had also taken off the helmet and now held it with one hand.

The lights were on in his garage so he could see her perfectly.

Those damn freckles were gonna be the death of him.

"My vote is for a typical night," Agnes declared, as if she'd pondered the matter extensively. "You're way too cool about everything. When someone tries to stab me in the back, I am not cool. At all."

He growled again. Dammit. He should stop that. Why in the hell was he down to making animalistic sounds with her? "People try to stab you in the back a lot?"

A sigh had her slender shoulders falling. "More than I'd like." She scooted back a bit on the bike, putting some distance between them. "You trust a fellow agent one day, and then...boom, betrayal the next moment. Life sucks that way, you know?"

Yeah, he knew. Betrayal was the name of the game in his world. Cass shoved down the kickstand and climbed off the motorcycle.

She kept straddling the bike but handed the helmet to him. "I believe this belongs to you."

He reached for the helmet. His fingers slid over hers and damn if a bolt of molten lava didn't seem to surge through his veins. Hell, hell, *hell*.

"Apparently..." Her head tilted. Her wind-tousled, thick red hair trailed over her shoulder. "Apparently, I do, too? Or else maybe I misheard that guttural 'Mine' bit you were throwing out at the bar. Got to tell you, it very much gave Eric Northman vibes from *True Blood.*"

His brows shot together.

"Tell me you got the reference? No, then I'd suggest you watch or read yourself some *True Blood,* like, stat. It's seriously hot. Or, Eric is, anyway. Most definitely, Eric is. I was always rooting for him in the show. Anyway...about me belonging to you..." She still straddled the bike. "That was new."

Cass locked his jaw. He was finding that he did that a lot around her. Just as he was growling a lot with her. Slowly, Cass backed up a step. "I was protecting you."

Agnes swung one leg over the seat. She angled her body so that she faced him as she continued to sit—sideways now—on his bike. That skirt was about to give up the battle because it could not rise much higher. "Is that what you were doing?" She put one hand to her chest. Against those pert breasts that had been pushing into his back as he drove them through the night. "How incredibly chivalrous of you, but...I don't really remember asking for protection." Her hand fell. "In fact, what I remember was me, protecting *you.* After all, that broad back of yours was incredibly vulnerable. Had it not been for my amazing throwing skills, you could have found a blade shoved deep into you, and wouldn't that have sucked for your night?"

He tossed aside the helmet. "What do you want? A medal?" Cass surged back toward her.

She sucked in her lower lip. A sexy lip. *Dammit.*

"You flash warm and cold, don't you?" Agnes suddenly challenged. "Promising to fuck me one moment and then offering me a medal the next. I think—" Her words abruptly ended.

He'd just leaned in close to her as Agnes carefully

Cynthia Eden

perched on the motorcycle. Cass knew his expression had to be helluva hard. His hands went to either side of her body, pushing down onto the seat, and maybe his thumbs brushed against the outside of her thighs. That stupid, short skirt might be the death of him. "What is it that you think? Don't leave me in suspense."

Her hand rose and pressed to his chest. "I think..." She tilted her head back a bit. "I think you want to kiss me right now." Surprise tinged her words.

She was right. He did want to kiss her. But... "I want to know what the hell kind of con you think you're running."

"I want to kiss you, too. That's not a con. It's the truth." Then she rolled her eyes. "Fine, you want some deep, dark confession from me? I did come after you tonight because I was hoping to team up."

This could not be happening. The woman was just spinning and spinning him with her words and confusing the hell out of him.

"I kinda threw out the line about fucking you because I knew other people were listening at the bar, and I didn't think you'd appreciate me just loudly saying something like, 'Hi, Cass. Do you remember me? I'm FBI Agent Agnes Quinn. We met when you were working a secret deal with the Feds not too long ago.'"

He could feel another growl building in his throat. Cass choked it down.

"You do remember our first, exciting meeting, don't you?"

It had not been exciting. But, yes, he remembered it. She was pretty hard to forget.

"I introduced myself back then, tried to shake your hand but you..." She *tut-tut-tutted.* "You left me hanging. Hardly the appropriate thing to do with a lady."

He made a mental note to never leave this woman hanging. "How did you know I was in that bar tonight?"

"Because The Bottomless Pit is a known hangout for the Strikers?" Her hand kept pressing to his chest.

"If I hadn't been there, you would have walked into a world of trouble."

"This may shock you to the heels of those bad-ass, black boots that you are wearing, but I know how to handle trouble."

"Do you?" A dare.

"Try me and find out."

He should not but...

"Kiss me," she breathed. "You know that you want to do it."

He did want to do it. He should *not*. He should send her on her merry way, but... "I am not partnering with you. I'm done working with the Feds."

"Really?"

"I kiss you, and it will mean nothing."

"Wow. Rip my heart out, why don't you? You haven't even put your lips against mine. Could be that when you do that, it will mean everything." A pause. "Why don't we find out?" Her hand suddenly fisted around his shirt as she yanked him closer.

And his mouth locked onto hers. Her mouth locked onto his.

It should have been just a kiss. He'd had plenty of good kisses in his life. Plenty of hot, passionate kisses. He knew kissing was great foreplay. Kissing was great for pleasure. Kissing was great for—

A fucking eruption of need and wild lust. A torrent that drove through his whole body.

Because her taste was insane. Sweet and heady and it

23

hit him harder than four shots of tequila. Yeah, four. It blew through his entire body, electrifying his bloodstream and sending lust surging in every pore of his body. His dick went rock hard. His hands grabbed for her waist and curled possessively around her, and he yanked her up and off that motorcycle. Off the motorcycle and into his arms even as her tongue met his.

She moaned into his mouth. Kissed him even harder, more passionately. Agnes wrapped her legs around his hips. Her body rocked against his, and he had a flash of how easy it would be to rip away her panties. To yank open his jeans and drive his dick into her right then and there. He could take her. Take and take and take and if kissing her was this phenomenal, then fucking her had to be absolutely mind-blowing.

She tore her mouth from his. Her hands were on his shoulders. Clinging on for dear life. "Wow." Her eyes were wide and stunned as they searched his. "Did you feel that?"

Uh, did she feel the giant dick shoving against her?

"It's like my whole body just caught on fire." She laughed, delighted. "That has never, ever happened to me before." A decisive nod. "I want to do it again."

So did he.

Their mouths collided. Open. Hot. Fierce. Her tongue slid against his. Her moans urged him on. She was rubbing her body against his. Those round, lush breasts pushed against his chest as he held her in a tight grip.

There wasn't anything controlled or muted about their kiss. It was pure fire. An explosion. And he'd never, ever had a reaction so intense *to a kiss* in his entire life.

She broke away a second time. "Wow." A heaving breath.

She'd said that before.

Her bright blue gaze pinned him. "Please tell me that you feel the same way. Because if I'm the only one feeling like the whole world is realigning, then that is just going to be awkward."

Her honesty floored him. The woman was staring straight into his eyes.

The whole world is realigning...

No, no, he could not afford for his world to realign. He had plans. Schemes. Hell to wreck on his enemies. One kiss —two kisses would not change anything for him.

Would not.

Her legs slowly lowered. Her gaze stayed on his. Cass wasn't sure he'd ever seen blue eyes quite her shade before. Those blue eyes of hers were currently filled with stark need and lust as her hands continued to grip his shoulders.

Her lips were plump and red from his mouth. She licked her lips, and whispered, "Is it about to get awkward? Am I the only one who just ignited?"

Like his giant dick wasn't answer enough for him. "You do not know me, Agnes."

Her breath caught. A delighted smile curled her lips. "I love the way you say my name."

He'd basically *growled* her name. Snarled it. How could she love that?

"And I do know you." Her feet were on the floor of his garage again. Those high heels had touched down. Her hands remained on him.

He liked for them to be there.

"You're Cassius Striker. Big, bad, infamous. You strike fear into the hearts of your enemies. And, ah, you *did* see what I did there, yes? *Striker striking fear.*"

Yes, he'd seen it. Her delighted grin made his chest ache.

"Anyway..." She rolled her shoulders. *And kept right on touching him.* "You lead the Strikers MC. Pretty sure that either your father or your uncle led the motorcycle club before you. But you didn't just inherit the leader title. You had to work your ass off for it." Her hands fell away.

He wanted them back on him. Because he wanted it so much, Cass backed up a step.

"I suspect you work your ass off for everything that you want in life." She reached out and took his right hand in hers.

His brows snapped together.

She lifted his hand up. "Your knuckles are callused and hard."

Every part of him was hard. But, yeah, he had calluses on his knuckles. The calluses came from pounding the hell out of a heavy punching bag each day.

"Despite the calluses, you might still bruise a bit from all that hitting you were doing to your attacker tonight." Her fingertips were soft, not callused at all, as they skimmed over his knuckles in the most careful of caresses. "But it's not like that will be anything new for you, am I right? You did street fighting when you were a teen, then moved your way up to some underground cage fighting. That's where your reputation for being such a fierce and dangerous predator began. No losses. Ever."

"I like violence." Gritted. "That probably means you should keep the hell away from me."

Another soft caress. "I don't think that's it. I don't think it's about *liking* anything. I think it's just about you needing to win." She let go of his hand. "You're working undercover right now."

The fuck?

26

"Did I tell you that I studied art in college? Well, it was my minor."

What in the hell did that have to do with anything? Had he *asked* what she'd studied in college?

Agnes waved toward him. "Sometimes, you get really quiet and this super intense look comes on your face. I guess you always have to be careful with what you say and do, huh? Makes sense that you'd slip into silence so you didn't trip yourself up with the wrong person." She bit her lower lip.

He could totally bite that lip for her.

A sigh eased from her as Agnes let her lip go. "But I'm not the wrong person. I'm the person you need. I can help you."

No one could help him. No, scratch that. He didn't need help. "Sweetheart..." He used the endearment deliberately and made it mocking. "I'm the leader of the most feared MC on the East Coast." Maybe in the entire US. "I don't need help. Not from you. Not from anyone."

"Sweetheart..." Agnes returned without even a single hesitation. "You need my help. You're walking a tightrope, and you will fall soon."

The hell he would. But he needed to get the woman to back up and focus on something she'd said a few moments before. "What does you taking art have to do with any damn thing?" Why the hell was he so curious about her? He needed to stop asking her questions. "And how in the world did an artist become an FBI agent?" Shit. Another question. No more. Dammit.

He needed to figure out a way to get her sweet ass out of there and permanently away from him.

Why did I even bring her here?

Oh, but he knew. Deep down, he knew exactly why he'd brought Agnes to his home.

Her words from the bar replayed n his head... *"What do I have to do in order to fuck..."*

"Being an artist means I notice things that others might miss," Agnes informed him.

He waited.

She smiled at him. No dimples. Just a wide, slow smile that made her eyes even brighter.

She looked cute, harmless, sexy.

How in the world was this woman an FBI agent? Why did she want to track down killers when it looked like she should be playing with puppies somewhere? Baking cookies or some shit like that?

His gaze dropped to the short skirt.

Okay, fine, not like she looked *sweet*. Definitely sexy, and instead of puppies, she could play with him all night if she wanted.

"Grayson Stone is my supervisor at the FBI."

Ah, finally, she'd added more info that was actually relevant. Though she'd just said something he already knew. Grayson—or *Gray* to his friends and his enemies—Stone was hard as nails. A real bastard who never stopped. A whiz when it came to mind games and general mind fuckery. The man lived to profile, and he was one of those annoying do-gooder types who wanted to make the world a better, safer place.

Cass enjoyed watching the world burn. Or, starting the fires.

"You worked with Agent Stone not too long ago," Agnes added.

He shook his head. "I *used* Agent Stone not too long

ago. He had connections that I wanted." *Because I needed to catch a killer.*

"Uh, huh. Right. You used him, and he used you. Sure. But you did all of that because you're family."

The beating of Cass's heart suddenly echoed in his ears. *She needs to watch what the hell she says.*

Agnes tapped one high heel. "Like I said, I notice small details that others might miss. Like bone structure. You and Gray have the same cheekbones."

He suddenly wanted to yank a hand over one cheekbone.

"You're the same height, share the same build, too, yes, but it's the similar facial structure that really caught my attention." Her head cocked to the right as she studied him. "Same hair texture, but the color is a bit different. Yours is a little darker. I definitely can see the family connection when I look at you both."

Nope. Not happening. He laughed.

She sighed. "Really? Gonna lie to my face and tell me that I'm wrong?"

He lied to people's faces all the time. Why should she be special?

But his laughter slowly faded. "You said Gray didn't send you."

"I came on my own. Because I think we can help each other."

Screw that. "I only help myself in this world."

But Agnes shook her head. "I don't believe that."

And why the hell not? "Lady, you don't know me. You think my *cheekbones* have told you some bullshit about me. You have no clue who I am, deep inside." He needed to scare her. Get her to run away and never come back. "I'm a dangerous man."

"I have no doubt about that." Agnes nodded. "If it makes you feel better, I'm a dangerous woman."

He blinked. Shook his head. Refused to be derailed. "You have to know about all of the crimes that have been linked to my MC."

"Oh, yes. Murders. Robberies. Thefts. Drug-running. So many stories circulate. I'm pretty sure if you believe all the tales, your MC is responsible for every single crime that happens every single day in the United States." A roll of one shoulder. "But I'm not one to believe the hype."

He did not speak. She was as cool and casual as you please, and he had no idea what he was supposed to do with the little Fed. Except, well, maybe fuck her. He really, really wanted to fuck her. Talking to her wasn't making his dick settle down any. In fact, hell, he was finding himself more and more curious about her with every single word that she spoke.

"You spend too much time in the darkness," Agnes suddenly told him.

Yes, he did.

"Gray has profiled you, you know. I mean, Agent Stone has."

"Of course, he has. Because the guy lives for mind fuckery." Maybe he should have a drink. Not like he'd even gotten to finish his beer at the bar. Not before she'd started throwing it at his attacker. "Guessing you do, too, huh?" Cass challenged. "What are you, like a Junior Mind Fucker? A Mind Fucker in Training?"

Her nose scrunched again. Damn cute freckles. "I don't know if that is the professional term..."

He had to fight a smile.

"But I did decide to make my own profile on you after our paths crossed at the FBI office."

His muscles tightened. "You made a profile on me... after a one-minute meeting?"

"I studied you for more than just one minute." No humor. No scrunched nose. Just all seriousness.

"And what did you discover in your studies?" He wanted to kiss her again.

He'd been so deep in the darkness with the MC. Agnes was right on that count, he spent far too much time in the dark. So much that he sometimes forgot what the light even was.

Darkness. Pain. Betrayal. Violence. Over and over again.

The adrenaline from the fight tonight still churned in his blood. He'd beat the hell out of a man, and Agnes wasn't so much as batting an eye about the events of the night.

Maybe she does understand me.

No, no, impossible. No one understood him. He wasn't looking for understanding. But maybe he was looking for two bodies slamming together in the dark. Her soft skin. Her moans. Her body opening for him as he drove in deep. And made all the demons that tormented him go silent for just a little while.

"You're a highly protective individual," Agnes noted. "If someone belongs to you—if you consider them *yours*—then you will do anything necessary in order to defend the individual. Or to get justice for them." A decisive nod of her head. "You'll even work with the Feds if that is what it takes to get vengeance. You're old school like that. The eye-for-an-eye type straight to your marrow. Someone fucks with you, then you fuck with them harder. You wreck them *harder*."

Okay, she was not wrong.

"I can relate to that," the cute, delicate FBI agent told him. "I enjoy wrecking my enemies."

"Be still my heart," he muttered.

She plowed right on, telling him, "You're a dirty fighter. Skilled but dirty. You don't follow rules."

Ah, but now he had to clarify a point for her. Cass cleared his throat. "I just prefer to make my own rules. I'm not a good little FBI agent who has to toe the line all the time."

She smiled. Not a sweet smile. A bit wicked.

Seriously, be still my damn heart.

"If I were a *good* little FBI agent, I wouldn't be here with you tonight."

Yeah, okay, done. He was fucking her. "You have five minutes," he said.

"Five minutes?" A little furrow appeared between her brows. "To do what?"

"To get out. To call for a ride." Nah, that wasn't wise. Not like he wanted a trail that tied her to his place. "To get me to take you home." He'd make sure he wasn't spotted dropping her off. "To get some sense and get the hell away from me." There, better. "Otherwise..."

She crept toward him. "Otherwise, what?"

"I'm not in the mood to be *mind* fucked all night, but I am in the mood to fuck." To fuck her, specifically. Heavy tension poured through him. "So..." A dare. A challenge.

Her eyes narrowed. He could practically see the wheels churning in her head.

Ah, she was trying to manipulate him. As if he didn't realize she'd been attempting to do that all night long. Fun side story, he was rather skilled at mind fuckery, too. Not like Gray was the only one in the family with that talent.

Yeah, he's my family. She was not wrong.

At least, she hadn't been wrong on that particular detail.

But if the gorgeous FBI agent thought that he was *good*

like Gray, that he shared the annoyingly noble trait of wanting to help the whole world...

So very incorrect.

Whatever good had been inside Cass, it had died long ago.

She turned away from him. Her heels tapped on the garage floor as she walked around the motorcycle. Tap. Tap. Tap. She ran her hand over the handlebars. "I haven't been with anyone in a long time."

Okay...so, this would be the part where she fled.

And why was jealousy rising inside of him?

They were strangers. *Strangers.* He shouldn't care about any lovers she'd had. Yet, he did. He wanted to obliterate anyone who'd fucked her before him.

"I don't have one-night stands, but, I can see where you probably won't believe that, considering that I'm here with you."

Uh, huh. His hands fisted. *She's going to leave.* That was what he wanted.

No, what he wanted was to shove that short skirt of hers up higher and *take and take* what he wanted. "Then you're ready to go home? You've had enough of your walk on the wild side?"

Her hand trailed over the gleaming handlebars one more time. "No." She turned to face him. "I'd like to stay on the wild side longer, if you don't mind."

That had to be the most polite way that someone had ever—

Agnes cleared her throat. "Just what does a woman have to do in order to get fucked by—"

He was on her. Cass lunged forward, closed the space between them, and his mouth crashed onto hers.

Chapter Three

MISTAKE. MISTAKE. MISTAKE.

Like she didn't know that this was a colossal mistake. Like Agnes wasn't aware of the fact that she was way out of her safety zone and flying blind.

Cass wasn't some by-the-book accountant. He wasn't some buttoned-down Fed who would toe the line. He wasn't some arrogant stockbroker who'd tell her all about his big trades for hours on end...

All men she'd dated in the past.

Men she'd dated and had *not* fucked.

Because what she'd told Cass was true—she didn't have one-night stands. She hadn't been with a lover in years. She was never the type to just let go. To be wild.

Except...

Tonight, she was. With him, she was.

A moan slipped from her as he carried her through his house. He'd started kissing her in the garage. When his mouth touched hers, electricity had poured through her veins. It was the kind of off-the-charts reaction you saw in movies but never found in real life. Her knees had gone weak. Her toes had curled. Her body had ached.

Yes, she could have walked away from him. Played it safe. But...

She'd never felt this way before. Not with any of the men she'd dated. She'd wanted to feel a spark. She hadn't.

What I feel with Cass isn't a spark. It's an inferno.

She'd been used to loneliness. To pain. To sadness that snuck up on her late at night.

This time, this night—she'd feel something different.

Not like it was forever. After all, as she'd tried to explain to Cass, she'd done her research on him. Very, very careful research. She knew him better than he might know himself.

He wasn't looking for commitment. Happily-ever-after wasn't in his vocabulary. Fair enough. It wasn't in her vocabulary, either. She'd tried that route before, then wound up standing at a gravesite.

Her arm had curled around Cass's neck. Her hold tightened as she tried to draw him closer and push away the sorrow from the past that wanted to sneak its way into her present. Not happening. She was going to take this moment, this time. It wasn't about love. Or about a future with some silly picket fence. It was just need. Sex.

She was pretty sure, based, ah, on her detailed profile of Cass, that he would be amazing in bed. Since she wasn't quite sure how *she'd* be—it had been way too long—Agnes was counting on his amazing self to make this night outstanding for them both.

He lowered her onto the bed.

She bounced. Once. She also shoved her hair out of her eyes as she peered up at him.

He stood on the side of the bed, in a very dark and

Cynthia Eden

intimidating bedroom. He was just a big, dangerous shadow, and what could have been a faint quiver of unease slid through her. "Turn on a light," Agnes ordered.

"Why?" Deep. Rumbly. "Do you think you'll be less afraid in the light?"

Great question. "Yes, actually, I do."

He reached out and turned on the lamp near the bed. Not a whole lot of illumination, and, if she'd hoped the light would make him less intimidating, then that hope had been in vain. The soft light just spilled around the bed. Half of Cass remained in shadows. So she had one illuminated side of him, and one dark side.

Like that probably wasn't the story of his life. A struggle between darkness and light.

She kicked off her heels. They hit the floor with a very loud clatter.

"This is your chance to say no," he rasped. "To run right out of this bedroom."

Not happening. Instead of running, she reached out for his belt. Her fingers trembled a bit, but she ignored the tremble. Not like she could really help that little shake. She was running on nerves and adrenaline, and even FBI agents had shaky fingers every now and then.

She unhooked his belt. Unsnapped his jeans. Lowered the zipper. Surprise, surprise, Cass wasn't the type to wear boxers or briefs. Commando only. As if she hadn't already guessed that about him. What she *had* not guessed was exactly how, uh, big he would be. The heavy, full length of his arousal thrust into her fingers. Way more solid than she'd expected—and she'd had high expectations. So, maybe this was the part where she should warn him that when she'd said that she didn't have a lot of experience, she'd meant...

36

It's been years. We may need to go slow.

Except she didn't want to go slow. If she went too slow, she might change her mind. She might lose this wonderful sense of anticipation and hunger that filled her.

No, forget being slow. She'd go fast. Two hundred miles an hour? Would that be fast enough?

She shimmed forward, her head bent, and she put her mouth on the head of his dick.

"Agnes." His hands clamped around her shoulders.

She opened her mouth wider. Took him in deeper. Licked and sucked, and she loved the way he tasted. Cass tasted good, and she wanted to see if she could push him to the edge, then beyond. Wouldn't that be something? Agnes Quinn, making the big, bad biker go wild for her—

"Cass!" His name broke from her because he'd just pulled away. And pushed her back. Back and down on the bed. Her shoulders hit the mattress as he loomed over her.

"You go straight for what you want, don't you, sweetheart?" he asked her.

"Life is too short…" And far too fragile. "To do anything else."

"Fair enough. Then it's my turn to get what I want." One of his hands smoothed up the inside of her thigh. He pushed the edge of her skirt up higher. Higher…

She realized that she was holding her breath. When he touched her, rubbing her core though the soft silk of her panties, her breath left her in a heaving rush.

"How long do you think it will take you to come for me?" Cass asked.

She had no clue, but her hips were eagerly pushing down against those stroking fingers of his. Her panties were in the way. If he could just tug them down or drag them to the side and get them out of the way, that would be outstanding.

"What do you like, FBI Agent Quinn?" Cass demanded.

Who knew? She didn't. They could find out together. "Ah...this is good." Breathy.

"Good isn't what I'm going for. I want you screaming."

Was that a possibility? "Then you should really get my panties out of the way."

He did. He didn't tug them down. He ripped them. The sound was overly loud, and her eyes widened.

Laughing softly, he tossed aside the scrap of silk. "Aw, sweetheart. That the first time you've had your panties ripped away?"

Yes, it was. Were her panties supposed to get ripped away every day or something? Was that normal for some people?

"You've clearly been around the wrong men. Let me show you what it's like when a bad guy fucks you."

He shoved her legs apart. Her skirt gave up the fight and exposed her completely.

"Pretty," Cass whispered.

Was she supposed to say "thank you" for the compliment? She was clearly thinking and worrying too much, and she needed to switch off the over-thinking and turn on the *feeling,* but she had no idea how to do that and—

His mouth was on her.

Right. On. Her.

Licking her clit. Sucking her clit. Then even thrusting *inside* of her.

She jerked and tried to heave up on the bed, but his hands clamped around her hips. His head lifted.

Oh, wow. Savage desire marked the side of his face that she could clearly see.

"Do you want me to make you come?" Cass rasped.

Yes, please. She nodded.

"Good. Then you take everything I give you." His mouth went back to her. Merciless. Demanding. He stroked her with his tongue. He sucked her clit. Cass had her shaking, crying out, and arching toward him. One big finger worked into her. Then another. He kept licking. Tasting. Taking.

She shattered apart for him. Her hips pressed to his mouth. Her hands fisted in the bedding, and she came on a long, hard wave of release that left her thighs quivering and her whole body feeling as if it had just broken into a thousand pieces.

He kept licking her. "So sweet..."

Aftershocks rolled through Agnes.

His head slowly lifted. "Now that you're ready for me, I'm going to fuck you until you scream."

She'd have to catch her breath before she could scream. And that was gonna be very hard due to the way that she was panting like crazy.

"The sexy top has to go, sweetness."

Now she was sweetness? Hadn't she been sweetheart a moment ago? Or...FBI Agent Quinn? Maybe even princess once? Yes, yes, she distinctly remembered him calling her—

"I'll help." He yanked the top over her head and tossed it to the floor. His hands slipped beneath her, and a moment later, her bra fell aside, too.

His mouth immediately closed around one tight nipple. He licked. Sucked *hard.* And her eyes nearly rolled back in her head. His right hand caught her other breast. Plucked the nipple. Teased. Pinched lightly.

Cynthia Eden

Arousal flooded through her. Again.

Especially because...

His left hand had gone back between her thighs. Two fingers were *in* her. Stretching her. Thrusting. Making her quake.

She was completely out of control. Her body didn't seem to be her own. She was lost to need and sensation and everything he was doing...*More, please. Don't stop. Do not dare stop.*

"Grab the headboard."

He'd pulled away.

Why had he done that?

She blinked and saw his shadowy form near the side of the bed. He opened the nightstand drawer. Her eyes narrowed, then she realized he was pulling out a condom packet.

This is happening.

He held the packet in his hand. "You aren't going to forget me anytime soon."

No, she doubted that she would.

"The headboard," he ordered. "Lock your hands around it. Hold on tight."

Um...

She rolled. Scuttled for the headboard. Damn, that probably had looked horribly unsexy. She just wore her skirt, and it was hiked way high at her waist. She should probably ditch the skirt. Quickly, she did. A fast shimmy that left her naked.

Her hands reached out and clamped around the wooden headboard. Her head turned when he climbed on the bed behind her.

He'd stripped completely. She had a fast impression of

40

rippling, powerful muscles. A whole lot of strength. An insane amount of sexiness.

His right hand curled into her hair, twisting it around his grip. Not pulling her hair. Not hurting her. Holding her.

And his other hand smoothed over her ass. "Spread your legs for me."

They were spread. But she spread them a bit more. Her grip tightened on the headboard. She leaned forward a bit, arching her hips toward him. The broad head of his cock nudged against her core. Her breath sucked in as she prepared for him to—

His left hand moved to her waist. Clamped on her as he drove inside. Filled every single inch. Stretched her. Claimed her. *Owned* her.

"Cass!" His name burst from her in a wild cry. Both of her hands clamped harder on the headboard. He was so big, so thick, that she was on the verge of pain. A weird pleasure-slash-pain combo, and her body wasn't sure which one of those two forces would win. Every muscle tensed.

Yeah, okay, it had been a *while*. She should probably have told him that fun fact with some specific time included.

"You're so damn tight."

Uh, yes, she was *aware*. Her breath heaved in and out. In and out.

He didn't get any smaller. If anything, Cass got *bigger*. And she stayed way too tense.

"Your last lover must've been—"

"It's been years since I've been with a lover, and you could have warned a woman that you were gonna be this damn big!"

His hand tightened on her waist. "Years?"

She hadn't stuttered. She was sure of it. "Years," she bit out.

"Fuck," he growled.

They were in the process of that, yes. But the wonderful, wild excitement she'd felt before was quickly evaporating as uncertainty and fear crept through her veins. So much for grabbing onto pleasure and not letting go.

Her hands began to lift from the headboard.

"No." A low order from him. "Hold on. Do not let go."

He released her hair. That big, strong hand of his flew around her body. Went between her spread thighs, and he began to stroke her clit. His mouth slid along her neck, licking and sucking and kissing her in places that she hadn't realized were so hypersensitive even as those rough, callused fingers of his kept stroking her clit again and again.

Some of the fear fled. Her body began to relax. Not in fear or panic mode any longer. And she was pushing into his wicked fingers. Moaning.

"That's better," he rasped.

Yes, it was. It was better.

He pulled back. Drove deep. Slowly, inch by inch, until she'd taken all of him again.

She tensed again, but there was no pain. Just a tightness that was now pretty wonderful.

He pulled back.

Her white-knuckled grip held onto the headboard.

He sank inside of her. Slowly, inch by inch.

Her heart drummed in her chest.

His fingers knew exactly what she wanted as he worked her clit. A fever pitch arose within her again.

He pulled back.

"Cass!" A demanding cry broke from her.

He thrust into her. Again, slowly. Inch by tormenting

inch. His big dick pushed hard into her even as her head tipped back against him.

"Don't hold back!" Agnes pleaded. Not anymore. There was no reason to hold back any longer. "Give me everything."

"Not sure you can handle that."

Oh, what a taunting bastard. And maybe, like, two minutes ago, she hadn't been sure herself. But now... "Give. Me. Everything."

He pulled back.

"Cass!"

He drove deep. Not inch by inch. Not this time. There was a barely controlled savagery in his thrust this time, and she loved it. Her own control seemed to snap as her hips began to buck wildly. He withdrew, only to pound hard into her. Again and again.

A second orgasm hit her. A fast and consuming avalanche that was the strongest blast of pleasure she'd ever felt in her entire life. Agnes opened her mouth to cry out, but she couldn't. The pleasure—the release was too strong. All she could do was gasp and shudder, and she could feel her inner muscles clamping and contracting around the long length of his dick.

"Oh, fuck, yes." He thrust into her again and again. *"Fuck, yes."*

Then his hands were flying over hers. Holding tight. The whole bed was rocking and shaking, and the headboard hit the wall again and again. *Thud. Thud. Thud.* His thrusts were merciless. So strong. So hard. So consuming. And she loved it. This was what it was like to be fucked. To have pleasure wipe away everything else.

The release battered at her. The same one? Another

43

climax? Agnes could not tell. She was just holding on for the fabulous ride.

Then he stiffened behind her. And Cass *roared* her name.

* * *

HE'D JUST FUCKED an FBI agent. Probably—nope, definitely, *definitely* a colossal mistake.

So why was he holding so tightly to her hands and thinking that had been the best fuck of his life?

She was soft and warm in front of him. All silky skin. Tousled hair. His dick was still inside of her. *She is so freaking tight.* And as he tried to get his racing heart under control, his cock decided it wanted to start swelling.

Again.

Because he wanted to fuck her again.

That would be a colossal mistake. Just like the first fucking.

He didn't give a shit.

I want to fuck her again.

And why not take what he wanted? Why not take her?

Her head turned. She glanced over her shoulder at him. The lamp light fell on part of her. He'd really prefer to have full, blasting overhead lights on them because he would love to see every single inch of her.

She was staring at him all solemnly. Her face very, very serious. He should say something profound. Deep. Not just have her thinking he was some menacing jerk who— "Years, huh? Why the hell did I get to be the lucky bastard tonight?"

Okay, shit. That had not been profound. Or deep. It had been very assholery. But the question had just slammed out of him because he damn well wanted to know why she'd picked him.

Cass had never been particularly lucky a day in his life.

So, he'd typically followed the mantra of...*Screw luck. Live hard. Take what you want.*

He had just taken what he wanted. And he'd do it again, too.

But, first, he needed to ditch this condom and grab another one.

She was also not responding to his question, so he took that moment to carefully pull out of her.

A soft gasp came from her lips, and he froze. "Did I hurt you?" Gruff. Hurting her had never been on his agenda. He made it a habit not to hurt delicate things in this world.

Despite the fact that she routinely carried a gun and could toss a mean bottle in a bar fight, Cass still considered FBI Agent Agnes Quinn to be one of the delicate things in the world.

"No, you didn't hurt me. Though I wasn't quite sure there for a minute. Things were a little, um, tight."

Tell me about it. She'd been so tight and hot that he'd nearly lost his mind. All he'd wanted to do was slam into her. Again and again and—

I had to make it good for her. So he'd held onto his control with a death grip, until he'd felt her come around his cock.

He climbed from the bed. Stalked into the bathroom and ditched the condom.

You just fucked an FBI agent.

One who had, apparently, not been with a lover in years.

Yeah, he was gonna need to get an answer to his question. *Why the hell did she decide to fuck me?* Naked, he marched back into the bedroom, and, this time, he flipped on the overhead lights.

Illumination immediately flooded in the bedroom. Bright.

She grimaced and blinked from her pose on the bed. Not holding tight to the headboard any longer. Instead, Agnes had flipped around. She'd been crouching in the middle of the bed, as if she'd been about to jump *out* of the bed, and he could see her perfectly now. Every single inch. Those gorgeous breasts. Those silky legs.

The...

Knife wounds that rained across her stomach and abdomen.

His breath shuddered out. "What. The. Fuck?"

"Oh, you're going to be difficult about this, aren't you?" She grabbed the cover and hauled it over her body.

She had no idea. In two breaths, he was across the room. He yanked the cover off her and glared at the old scars. Stab wounds. He should know. He had some, too. But he slowly and carefully counted the thin, white lines that cut into her soft skin. He touched each one.

Seven. She'd been stabbed seven fucking times.

His breath sawed in and out as a killing rage filled his blood. Slowly, his gaze rose.

Her eyes widened as she took in his expression. "Uh, Cass?"

"Tell me his name." All he needed was a name. He would be able to find the bastard. Put him in the ground. "And I'll kill him for you."

Chapter Four

She had the naked leader of the Strikers offering to kill for her.

Not exactly what Agnes had put on her bingo card for the day but...

She'd take it, thanks.

Holy hell, but the man is hot. The overhead light poured plenty of illumination on them, and her gaze kept darting over his chest. His very broad chest. Powerfully muscled. A chest that also had its share of swirling tats. A tiger with razor-sharp claws. A skull with burning eyes. A big phoenix over his left shoulder, with its black wings spread.

And...maybe her gaze also dropped. Went down, down to see his—

"Name," Cass bit out. "You think I don't know the marks left from a knife's blade when I see them?"

Her stare whipped up to lock with his blazing eyes. With her left hand, she also tugged the bedspread up to cover her body.

As to the marks on her, he was correct. They had come from a blade. One that had been driven into her a very long time ago. A horrible night that had changed everything for her.

She'd stopped wanting to be an artist. She'd stopped seeing the beauty in the world. All she'd seen had been darkness. Especially when she watched as the man she loved be buried in that rainy cemetery. She hadn't been able to tell the difference between her own tears and the rain.

She'd just stood there, crying, staring at the flowers on the grave as they got soggier and soggier, and her brothers had been so worried about her. They'd said she was too injured. Too weak. That she had to go. That it was time.

They'd finally carried her away from the gravesite. Until the day she died, Agnes was sure she'd remember crying into Ryan's neck as he cradled her.

"Agnes." Cass put his hand on her cheek.

She flinched.

He immediately began to pull back, but her right hand flew up to curl around his. She pressed his fingers to her cheek, harder, even as her left hand kept clutching the bedding to cover her body. "That's really sweet of you to make the offer."

"Sweet? You think it's sweet to want to kill a man?"

She thought it was sweet that he'd offered to put someone in the ground for hurting her, yes. But... "I'm an FBI agent. You aren't supposed to just casually talk about killing in front of me."

His eyes gleamed. Darkness but...warmth.

She'd been in the darkness for years. Ever since the night that had changed her life. She'd come to enjoy the dark. And being with Cass, well, he was like darkness personified.

Was that the reason she was so drawn to him? She had no clue. But, when he'd asked his question...

Why the hell did I get to be the lucky bastard tonight?

Agnes hadn't exactly had a response to give him. Saying that he'd made her feel alive for the first time in ages probably would come across as, uh, maybe far too over the top? Saying that when he touched her, her blood ignited? Nah, she couldn't go with that one, either. Not like she wanted to inflate the man's ego too much.

But both statements would have been the truth.

"Where is the sonofabitch?" Cass asked. His head tilted.

Cass made no move to cover his naked body. His very, very muscled, naked body. And his very big dick.

Apparently, talking about potential murders did not lessen his enthusiasm. Interesting point.

"Is he rotting in a jail cell?" Cass wanted to know.

"I suspect you have reach, don't you?" she murmured. "Bet you can get to people in jail."

He winked. *Winked.*

She took that as confirmation even as her lips pressed together. That wink of his was way too sexy. So was his muscled body. Those abs that just went on and on and on.

And the big, thrusting cock that went on and—

"Is he already in the ground? Did you put him there, sweet Agnes?"

No, not yet, she had not. But she was working on the goal "There really isn't anything overly sweet about me. You shouldn't be fooled on that one. Appearances can be deceiving." It was the freckles. Or at least, she figured the freckles threw people off. They saw the scattering of freckles over her nose, thought she was all cute and innocent and, bam...they never saw her attack coming. Not until it was too late.

She'd had a trainer at Quantico who said she should

always use her size, her appearance, and even her freckles to her advantage. If people wanted to underestimate her, that would just be their fatal mistake.

Cass's hand slid down a bit. His thumb brushed over her lower lip. "Appearances are deceiving. But when it comes to you not being sweet? Ah, on that, I completely disagree." Deeper. Rougher. "That mouth of yours was very sweet when it was on my dick."

Was she blushing? Now? Yes, she was. The curse of being a redhead.

"And when my mouth was between your legs...oh, yes, talk about *sweet*."

Her thighs squeezed together. She was still feeling wonderful little aftershocks every now and then.

His hand pulled away. "So...?" His arms crossed over his chest as he backed up. One step. Two.

"So...what?" Was she missing something?

"Is this the part of the night where you run away? You fucked the villain. You walked on the wild side. Now you can rush back to your safe world, and this will just be our secret."

"Our secret." She nodded. Not like she'd expected the guy to ask about dating her. This was a one-night stand. Sure, she'd never had one until this very moment, and, honestly, she was delighted by the results so far, but that part about running away didn't sit too well with her.

She glanced toward the window just as a strike of lightning flashed. She caught the flash through the curtains that didn't completely block the outside world. Agnes sucked in a breath.

Thunder boomed.

"Seems like a storm is coming." Her head tilted as she

focused on Cass once more. "And the night isn't over. Isn't the point of a one-night stand—isn't the point that it lasts for a whole night? Not like it's a one-hour stand. It's a one-*night* stand." Judging by that eager cock, he was certainly ready to go again.

So was she.

"You're too sore for more."

Oh, was she? "Then I guess it's your job to make me forget any pain. Think you're up for that challenge?"

His hands fell to his sides. He took a surging step toward her. Then caught himself. "This is your chance to run."

Cute. She tossed aside the covers. "I thought this was my chance to fuck the villain." His words from earlier. "The night is young." Another strike of lightning. "Some people are scared of storms," she said as her nipples tightened and she remembered how utterly amazing he'd felt inside of her. "But, me? I like the rain. It washes away the pain." Sometimes, she thought a part of her had died in the rain at that cemetery. Then she'd been born again—born with the goal of getting vengeance. "I'll dance in the rain and laugh while the lightning strikes."

He climbed into the bed with her. Didn't touch her, not yet. "That's dangerous."

She reached out to touch him. Her fingers slid over the powerful muscles of his chest.

"You like dangerous things, don't you, Agnes?"

Yes, she did. The good girl that she'd been long ago would have run from danger. These days, all she did was run *to* it.

"Get on me," he ordered. "Get on my dick, now."

Her eyes widened.

He didn't wait for her to comply. He caught her hips.

Cynthia Eden

Lifted her up. Settled her on top of him. Her legs were spread, one knee going down on either side of Cass.

"Grab a condom. Put it on me."

Her hand reached out. On the second try, she opened the nightstand. Retrieved a condom. With more fumbling, she succeeded in actually getting the packet open. Yes, she was exceedingly clumsy and halting with the whole process. Not like she put condoms on guys all the time.

She pumped his dick. Slid her fingers over him. Very, very slowly, Agnes rolled that condom over his thick cock.

He hissed out a breath. "Don't play."

She wasn't playing so much as trying not to tear the condom. But she bluffed with, "Why not? We have the rest of the night."

"Get on my cock."

"Tsk. Tsk. You could try asking nicely."

He didn't ask nicely. He did put his hand between her thighs where he proceeded to absolutely own her clit. Stroking and rubbing and pinching feverishly until her breath choked out and she moaned his name over and over again. She got wet and ready again, and she didn't care if she was sore or if that big cock was going to stretch her when he drove deep into her.

She heaved her body up. She rose onto her knees, and she got onto his cock. She pushed down, and she took him inside of her. Not inch by inch. Not the slow way he'd done before.

All the way inside in one surge. Until he was as deep as he could go. Until her heart raced and her breath caught and she was precariously balanced on that tightrope of pain and pleasure again.

One of Cass's hands stayed on her clit. His fingers stroked her more.

His other hand caught her right nipple. Played and tormented.

"Up, FBI Agent Quinn."

She went up on her knees.

"Down," he gritted out.

She was already surging down. Going up. Coming down. Moving fast and frantically because need blasted through her, and she loved the rake of his fingers on her clit and the way his dick pushed so deep inside of her.

Her hands fell onto his chest as she leaned forward, changing the angle of his penetration, and, oh, that was even better. Even stronger. Even—

She came. Bam. Detonation. Just exploded and she could barely choke out a breath.

"You feel incredible when you come for me. I feel it. Your pleasure squeezing me…"

Her inner muscles were clamping greedily around him.

In the next breath, he'd tumbled her back onto the bed until her shoulders slammed into the mattress. "My turn."

Yes, fine, he could have all the turns that he wanted.

Lightning flashed again.

A hard roll of thunder.

He caught her legs and draped them over his shoulders.

She gasped as he went in her even *deeper*.

His thrusts were fierce and fast. Uncontrolled. He pounded into her again and again, and she caught the tangled covers and her hands fisted on them.

This wasn't nice sex. Not easy. Not gentle.

It was body-churning. Soul-stealing. Heart-racing *fucking*.

He fucked her hard, and she shoved her hips back up against him with every maddened thrust because she absolutely loved it. She didn't need to think about the future or the past. It was just their bodies, colliding together. Insane sex. Earth-shattering pleasure.

He erupted into her again.

And she was right there with him, riding that blast of pleasure as the storm raged around them.

* * *

"You NEED to stay out of my bar."

Oh, yes, that was hardly the...*You're the best lover I've ever had and please, please stay with me* plea that Agnes had maybe, sorta, kinda hoped she'd get when morning dawned.

Her eyes opened.

Surprise, surprise, Cass was fully awake. Fully dressed. Standing beside the bed, glowering at her while she was naked and tousled and probably looking super, super scary. Mornings were never her best time. Especially when she hadn't gotten her coffee. So she squinted at him.

"Do not come slumming on my side of town. Stay *out* of all the bars I frequent. Out," he emphasized. "I won't be able to save that gorgeous ass again. You don't jump into a brawl. That should be, like FBI 101."

"Coffee," she croaked. She'd done a fair amount of screaming during the night. His fault, one hundred percent. The man should not have been so incredible.

His dark brows shot together. His hands were on his jean-clad hips. He wore a faded gray shirt, and he looked almost disgustingly good with the hard stubble on his jaw.

Someone is gorgeous and all chatty in the mornings. A mental note she made about him.

"Coffee before conversation," she rasped. "Pretty...ah, please." Because her mother had taught her manners.

Granted, her mother never needed to know about this awesome one-night stand, but...still.

Manners.

Her mother and her brothers. They should never know.

Some things would just stress them out unnecessarily.

"I don't have coffee here. I never drink it."

She gasped. The sound held utter shock. Maybe some betrayal, too. "You monster."

He frowned at her. "What?"

"Mon...ster." So her manners had gone out the window.

"Agnes, I'm being serious."

She was, too. She was also increasingly awake, aware, and realizing...*I have no idea how to handle a morning after with him.* She'd been way too open and vulnerable with him during the hours of darkness. She hadn't slept with anyone —like, actually slept in a bed with another human being—in years. And as far as the sex was concerned...

Years. It had been years.

Apparently, when she decided to jump back in the sex pool, she went straight for the deep end. Without any sort of floatation device.

She glanced down at herself. At least she was covered up. Mostly. "Is this the walk of shame portion of the event?"

"*Agnes.*"

"In the bright light of day..." Her voice wasn't quite as husky, but she could *seriously have used some coffee.* "I don't quite want to prance around naked in front of you."

"Why the hell not?" Cass demanded. "I had my mouth on every inch of you last night."

As if she needed the reminder.

She held out her hand. "Would you please pass my shirt to me?"

He did not. He did put a big sweatshirt in her extended hand. Big, black, soft.

"It's cold outside," he said gruffly. "That's better than the thin shirt you wore last night. It will give you way more coverage."

"Fine. I'll, ah, bring it back to you."

"Keep it."

She sat up in bed, still clutching the shirt in her grasp. "Have you seen my panties?" Her voice was prim. How could she be prim when she asked about her panties? Yet, she was.

"They were ripped to pieces, sweetness."

Oh, right, they had been. "And my bra?"

He dangled it from his fingertips. She snatched it from him and nearly fell from the bed.

A ghost of a smile lingered on his handsome lips. "I wish I was a different person," he said.

Wait, what?

"Because in another life, I'd never, ever let you the hell out of my bed, Agnes Quinn."

Had she just imagined those words?

"I'll give you privacy to dress since you don't want to be prancing around naked in front of me." With that, he turned on his heel and marched for the door. "By the way, your purse is on the chair over here. Thought you might want it, so I got it out of the saddlebag for you this morning." Cass shut the door after he exited.

She dressed. Quickly. With knees that shook and thighs that trembled. She put on her skirt, her bra, her shirt, and then *his* sweatshirt. His sweatshirt swallowed her, falling past the hem of her skirt. It was warm and carried a crisp, masculine scent. His scent. Wearing it was like being wrapped in him.

Nope. Stop the thought.

She put on her heels. Used his toothpaste on her finger for a quick brush and then tried to smooth down her wild hair. An utterly failed effort. Agnes grabbed her bag. Checked inside it. Yep, her gun and ID were there. Her phone, too. She used the phone to schedule a pickup with a rideshare driver, and then she dumped the phone back into her bag. After inhaling a few deep, steadying breaths, she hung the purse strap over one shoulder.

When she could hesitate no longer, she opened his door. She strode very purposely down his hallway. He was waiting in the kitchen. A very modern and gorgeous kitchen. One that had no sign of coffee. How did one even function without caffeine in the morning? What was he, superhuman?

He stared at her. She stared at him. She had to bite back the words, *"Thank you for a very good time."* That was her wanting to be polite again, but she didn't know if you were supposed to actually thank your one-night stand for all the orgasms that he'd given to you.

Someone should write an etiquette book on the matter.

She also didn't think that she should ask him about a partnership. Not right then. It would just look as if she'd tried to seduce him into cooperating with her. She hadn't. The seduction-slash-sex had been its own thing. Its own truly glorious thing.

"Stay out of my bars," Cass told her, voice grim. "Stay away from my MC. You will get hurt in my world."

Oh, he was back to singing that tune. As far as getting hurt, he'd been the one in danger the previous night, not her. "If I see you in danger, I will have to step forward," she said. "Whether it's in your world or mine, I'd help you when you were in trouble."

His eyes narrowed. Those eyes were so deep and dark and consuming. "You offering to bend the law for me, Agnes?"

Whenever he said her name, it made butterflies swirl inside of her. Growing up, she'd hated her old-fashioned name. But now...

I love the way it sounds coming from him. "I'm not bending anything. I'm just saying that if you're in trouble, I'll step in. I'm not going to let someone drive a knife into your back. I helped you last night, and I'm pretty sure that you never even gave me a thank you for my outstanding effort with that flying beer bottle."

He stalked toward her. No shoes. Still way too tall. "You don't consider the six orgasms a thank you?"

Had it been six? "You thanked me by fucking me?" She shook her head. "I don't think I like that idea." She grimaced.

"I fucked you because I wanted you. End of story."

Fair. She liked that far better. "That's the reason I fucked you, too." *Not* because she wanted a partnership with him. Just because need had swept through her and destroyed every other thought.

What could have been regret flashed for the briefest of moments on his face. "This *is* the end of our story, sweetness. Stay out of my world."

She put a hand to her heart. "You're so very charming. How do you keep the women away?" Her hand fell. "I mean, jeez. Why don't you just say I should hurry up before the door hits me in the ass?"

His eyes narrowed.

"You think we have to be enemies?" Now she was truly curious. And more than a little sad. "Because I'm a Fed and you're..."

"The villain?"

"I don't think that's what you are."

"Then you would be wrong. Better go back to the profiling board and see what you can come up with on your second try."

"Are you trying to piss me off?"

"I don't know. Are you getting pissed off?"

Yes, she was.

"I like you in my sweatshirt." A roll of one big shoulder. "I like you better in nothing at all."

"I like you better that way, too." Her chin lifted.

His hand reached out. Curled under her chin. An oddly careful touch. "Watch your back, FBI Agent Quinn." A soft rumble. "I'd hate like hell for anything bad to happen to you."

No way. No way could he be... "Are you threatening me?"

"Hell, no. Just saying...no one had better ever fucking hurt you."

That was sweet of the man who claimed to be the villain. "Guess what you're saying is...if you see me in danger, you'd step forward too, huh?"

A faint incline of his head. His touch lingered.

"Maybe we're more alike than you realize." She needed to get out of there. Because this wasn't just about hot sex. Something else was stirring within her the longer she stayed with this man. "For the record, I'd hate like hell for anything bad to happen to you." Then, unable to help herself, she rose onto her toes. Her mouth brushed against his. "Goodbye, bad guy." She stepped back, turned from him, and blinked quickly.

Those are not tears in my eyes. They can't be.

Weird, though, because they certainly felt like tears.

59

She hurried through the monstrosity that was his house.

He trailed after her. "I'll take you wherever you need to go."

"Nope. I already arranged for a ride to come and pick me up. Don't worry, the pickup location is a few blocks from here. Not like I'd leave a trail that led straight to your door. I get that I can't be seen getting picked up from your place."

"I can take you—"

She spun around. "I'm good." Her purse was still over her shoulder. "I have a gun in my bag, and believe me, I know how to use it."

"You are good." He nodded. His hands fisted at his sides. "Thanks for some truly stellar fucking."

Oh. Maybe you *were* supposed to thank someone for orgasms. Her head inclined toward him. "Thank you for the best climaxes I've ever had." Way better than the ones she got with her vibrator.

His jaw dropped.

"See you in another life, Cass." She left him. Deliberate steps. With her shoulders thrown back. Her head up. Her high heels clicking. She walked out of his place. Careful, unhurried steps. She crossed the street. The sidewalk. She dipped between buildings.

After a short walk, she found her ride waiting.

She got inside and when she glanced over to the right, just before the car pulled away...

Cass was watching her from the side of the road. Hands shoved in his pockets. Dark sunglasses over his eyes. But she *felt* his stare. He'd followed her. Watched over her until she got into the car. Such a protective thing for a bad guy to do.

Her hand lifted toward the glass of her window.

And she left him.

* * *

HE'D FOLLOWED HER. Fuck, yeah, call him a stalker, but he had. Not like it was the best neighborhood in Atlanta, and she'd been wearing those too high heels and the short skirt, and so what if it was barely six a.m. and most people weren't out?

He'd wanted to make sure she got to her ride safely.

Even villains could do a random good deed every now and again. And it wasn't even *that* good of a deed. He'd just shadowed the woman a bit. After all, when a lady gave you the best fucking of your life, you at least made sure she got to her car safely.

You held onto her. You didn't let her go. You chained her to your bed, and you kept her there.

He swallowed. FBI Agent Agnes Quinn was not for him. He wasn't looking for commitment. Not forever. Nothing permanent.

She was gone. He'd get back to business.

And...

Who the hell took a knife to her? The scars on her bothered the hell out of him. Seven times. Seven stabs with a knife. He'd kissed each scar during the night.

She hadn't told him who'd hurt her. She also hadn't told him if the prick was in the ground.

Not his concern. Check, but...

Would doing a small bit of digging hurt anything? He didn't think so.

The car was gone. Time for him to move on. He had deals to make. Payback to dish out. Rivals to trample. The same old, same old.

And yet...

He could still smell her on his skin.

He would not be forgetting his night with Agnes anytime soon.

Chapter Five

HE SAW THE WOMAN LEAVE CASS'S PLACE. WEARING A sweatshirt that was far too big. A sweatshirt that had to belong to Cass.

He'd lost them the previous night. But instead of admitting defeat, he'd just gone and had himself a stake-out at Cass's place all night long. Because he'd had a hunch...

That sonofabitch took her home.

And she'd stayed there, all freaking night long.

When she left, he followed her. Staying against the edge of buildings. Lurking in the shadows. She slipped into a waiting car, and he hightailed it for the ride that he'd stashed nearby. He also made a point of getting the license plate of the car that picked her up, just in case he lost her again.

But he didn't lose her. He *did* make sure that Cass didn't catch sight of him. Not like he wanted to deal with that big bastard right then. Or, honestly, ever. At least not in any kind of fair hand-to-hand situation. The leader of the Night Strikers would totally kick his ass.

He stayed out of Cass's sight, and he followed the

woman to the high-end condo in downtown Atlanta. He got her address. He got her name.

And within the hour, he also knew...

FBI agent. Cass Striker had just fucked an FBI agent all night long.

He whipped out his phone. "You are not going to believe this shit." Because he knew pay dirt when he hit it.

And, oh, but this dirt was *good.* It might just be the key he'd been searching for—the key to wrecking Cass's entire world.

Chapter Six

HE GRIPPED THE POOL CUE IN HIS HAND, SURVEYED THE table, and then Cass called his shot, "Eight ball, corner pocket."

The other men around the table leaned in.

He took the shot. Tipped the cue ball. Sent it rolling straight to the eight ball, worked the angle, and it sank perfectly into the corner pocket. Done.

A faint smile curved his lips There was some grumbling from the others. But a bet was a bet, and the beers were about to be given for free to every single member of his MC—

"I hear that you're fucking Feds these days, Cassius."

The smile on his lips froze. Taking his time, Cass stretched to his full height, then he turned to face the sonofabitch who'd just spoken.

Bayne Hendrix stood about five feet away, flanked on each side by his two lieutenants. The Western Mavericks had no damn business being in that pool hall. At least, not unless they wanted trouble. Clearly, they wanted it.

The Western Mavericks weren't even supposed to be in Atlanta. They belonged on the other side of the US.

"I was just driving through town, and a fun little rumor swept its way to me..." Bayne had taken control of the Mavericks a few months back. After the previous leader had been killed in a motorcycle accident.

A suspicious accident? Hell, yeah. Super suspicious. The brakes had failed. Then the bike had ignited. That shit didn't happen every single day.

"Seems that you've taken to sleeping with Feds." Bayne's voice was overly loud. As always. His eyes glittered at Cass. Not quite as tall as Cass, a few inches shorter, and with a stomach that was going soft. Soft from too much booze. Too many drugs. Or maybe from too much time being a straight-up asshole who loafed around and let other people in the world do the hard, grueling work that had to be done. As always, he wore his beat-up, ancient leather jacket. A jacket that was a little too big and hung past his wrists. "What's the game plan there, Cass? You selling out the MCs? Getting in that nice, FBI pussy so you can—"

His words stopped, mostly because Bayne could not speak any longer. Cass had broken the pool cue in two. He dropped one piece to the floor, grabbed Bayne, and in a flash, Cass shoved the prick to his knees. Cass positioned the broken piece of pool cue he still held underneath Bayne's chin, holding it horizontally across his neck. Cass yanked back hard on the pool cue, one hand on each side as he pulled it against Bayne's throat.

Bayne's head whipped back as far as it would go, and he grabbed at the cue stick.

Too bad the jerk wasn't strong enough to actually take it from Cass.

Bayne's two lieutenants immediately reached for their weapons.

"Yeah...no." A slow drawl from Cass's right-hand man, Javion Booker. He might enjoy a slow drawl, courtesy of his Mississippi roots, but Javion moved helluva fast. He already had his own weapon out and aimed. "I think these two got things covered without us interrupting them."

Oh, Cass had things covered. He'd just sort of lost his sanity a minute there and seen red when he'd let Bayne's words get to him.

I don't like anyone talking about Agnes. Especially not her pussy.

Because that is mine.

Wait, wow. He seriously needed to calm down.

Two days had passed since he'd fucked her all those endless hours. Two days.

And he'd thought of her way, way too much in that time.

Cass released a long, slow breath, and he lifted up the pool cue.

Bayne immediately surged away. He whirled to face Cass, and the guy's hand flew up to press against the long, red mark that was clear to see on his throat.

Cass might have been applying a whole lot of pressure with that wooden cue.

"Gonna..." A wheeze from Bayne. "You gonna tell me that I'm wrong?"

No, he was not. Because, obviously, the rival MC leader had gotten his intel from somewhere. So, Cass would roll with it. "Yeah, I fucked a Fed." He shrugged. "She was fabulous, too."

"You're selling us out to some—"

He extended the broken pool cue and put the jagged,

cracked edge against Bayne's jugular. "I'm not selling out anyone. I'm fucking. Didn't realize I needed to run a list of my fuck-mates by you." He tapped the jagged edge against Bayne's skin. "Got to warn you, man. You are way too involved in my *fucking* business."

Javion laughed.

"You're telling me the woman meant nothing? Just a fuck buddy?" Bayne sneered. His sneer was brave, but the man was sweating. A lot.

"One-night stands happen." Cass thought he sounded well and truly bored. "Deal with it."

And Bayne began to smirk.

Cass didn't like that smirk.

"Then you don't care..." Bayne leaned into the pool stick. "If anything happens to her?"

Cass did not let his expression change.

"Because, see, she threw a bottle of beer at an...associate of mine. Someone who might be looking for membership in the Mavericks."

That prick who'd tried to stab Cass in the back was a Maverick wannabe? Figured. "Thought he was a Backstreet Phantom." All those skull and thorn tattoos on his arms had marked him as a Phantom.

"He *was* a Phantom. But the guy was looking to switch his allegiance. Only your pretty Fed stepped in. She embarrassed him."

"And I kicked his ass." Flat. "If he wants payback, he can come at me." But the dick wouldn't. Because he was too scared of Cass. So...

Is he really going after Agnes?

The stretching smirk on Bayne's face said that the jerk was. "The man is gonna take the bitch out. He was real, real pissed to find that a Fed had gotten involved in his business.

68

In fact..." Oh, but that smirk needed to be punched off Bayne's face. "He might even be closing in on her, right this minute."

Every muscle in Cass's body turned to stone. "The hell he is." Bayne's words replayed through his head. *He'll take the bitch out...Take the bitch out...*

Bayne blinked. "Why would you care what happens to her? She's just a casual fuck, right? And what's one more dead Fed? Not like there's any sort of attachment there. Not like you care about the bitch." He spun away. "Even though some assholes were swearing you were saying she was *yours* at The Bottomless Pit."

Cass's hand clenched around the pool cue.

"The heartless leader of the Strikers has no weaknesses. You even killed your own uncle. Your old man, too, if the stories are true. You never have any attachments." Laughter rolled from Bayne. "But you could still send flowers to the bitch's funeral. That's a nice thing to do and—"

"No one fucking touches her." The words ripped from Cass. Low and lethal and pouring with savage fury.

Bayne's laughter died away as he slowly turned back to face Cass.

He knew every eye was on him. Every ear. For years, his enemies had been looking for a weakness to use against him. Now they had it—or at least, they thought they did. They had it in the form of one small FBI agent.

A woman he'd fucked.

He should have acted like he didn't care. *But I can't let anyone hurt her.* The very thought of someone hurting Agnes sent fury spiking in his blood.

"Thought she was a casual screw," Bayne muttered.

"No one touches her." Loud. Clear. "She belongs to *me*."

Javion sidled closer. "Uh, Cass, you just told everyone she was a Fed."

He was aware.

"Do you know what you're saying right now?" A low rasp from Javion. Meant only for Cass's ears. "Do you know what you are *doing* by claiming her?"

He did. Since there was confusion from Javion, then Cass would just repeat himself. Very clearly so every person there would understand. "No one touches her."

"I think the guy is gonna do more than touch her." Bayne swept a hand over his sweaty forehead. "Pretty sure he's going in for the kill." A shrug as his hand fell. "Right the hell now. Poor, dead Fed."

"*Call him off.*"

"He's not mine to call off. Not like I paid him to do the deed." Bayne's brown eyes gleamed.

Screw this shit. Cass surged forward and wrapped his hand around Bayne's throat. "Call him off," he barked.

Bayne clawed at Cass's hand.

Cass eased up, just a bit. Enough so that Bayne could wheeze out a breath and say, "You going to war with me over a Fed?"

"Not war." Cass shook his head. "I'll just end your ass here and now, *unless you call him off.*"

* * *

SHE WAS BEING FOLLOWED. Agnes knew she had a tail, mostly because the guy was a piss-poor stalker. She'd caught his image four streets back, reflected in a storefront window. Maybe he thought that, because it was night—just after 10 p.m.—that the darkness hid him.

The fool had clearly forgotten that *street lamps* existed.

So he tailed her through the city. He annoyed the ever-loving-hell out of her, and she casually put her phone to her ear as she called for her backup.

"He still tailing you?" Malik Jones wanted to know when he picked up the phone on the second ring. They'd chatted before, when she first noticed her unwelcome follower.

"He is indeed," she confirmed to her primary FBI partner as she stopped at the street corner. "About six-foot-six, two hundred and sixty pounds, shaved head. Bushy beard. Lots of piercings." As if she hadn't recognized the jerk from The Bottomless Pit. The attacker who'd thought it would be fun to come up from behind Cass with a knife. Quite obviously, the man preferred attacking from the back.

She figured he was going to try and drive a knife into her spine in the next few moments. He'd been drawing closer and closer to her in the last half hour. *Coming in for the kill, are you?*

That was fine. While he'd been edging closer to her, Agnes had been setting up a trap for him.

Did the dumbass not get that there was a bar right on the corner that was frequented by cops and Feds? It was *her* hangout place when she wanted to go and blow off some steam with her friends. She'd been slowly and deliberately leading her stalker straight to that place. The better to surround him.

Well, once she was done with him, anyway.

"My eyes are on you," Malik told her. "I can see you now. You...and him."

Ah, steadfast Malik. She did adore her quiet, intense Fed buddy. The man didn't say much, but he had a core of pure courage. You could always count on Malik. He was

Cynthia Eden

very much the true-blue type, much like their boss, Grayson Stone. Defending justice. Protecting innocents.

Following the law.

Malik didn't bend it occasionally the way she did.

The way she was about to do again.

"Hang back a bit," she told Malik. "I want a Q&A session with him."

"You want a what?"

She wanted a chance to grill the prick. But—

"I think he's making a move," Malik suddenly groused. "Coming on your left, watch out. Watch—"

She spun around, one hand on the phone, the other clutching her mace. Sure enough, the jerk was running hard and fast at her. He also had a knife gripped in his hand.

Someone was a one-trick pony.

She sprayed her mace, aiming right for his eyes, and he screamed. That scream was loud and desperate, and, instinctively, he dropped the knife as he moved to cover his eyes.

"FBI agent, you asshole," she snarled at him. "You don't *stalk* and attack an FBI agent unless you are looking for a world of pain."

He blinked over and over as his eyes streamed. The street lamp glowed over him as his lips twisted into a snarl. With a shout, he barreled right at her. He was way bigger than she was. Nearly twice her size, and his bear-like hands grabbed for Agnes.

She stepped to the side. Those teary eyes of his weren't going to provide him with the best vision. Maybe that was why he didn't see her leg slide out in a quick glide. Her gliding foot hooked him, and he went crashing down on the pavement before her.

Before he could leap to his feet, she was on him. Agnes

shoved her phone into her pocket, and she put her gun to the back of his head. "Freeze." Then in case he'd somehow missed this ever-so-important point of... "FBI Agent. You just tried to *stab* an FBI agent!"

Malik would be coming in, despite her polite request for him to hang back a bit. Not like Mr. True Blue would hang back when she'd nearly been stabbed. The Fed and cop hangout was about twenty yards away. She was about to be swarmed as "help" burst out of that bar. But first...

"Asshole, who sent you after me?" Agnes demanded. Like she didn't know a targeted attack when one came stalking through the dark after her.

His hands slapped onto the pavement. "Cass!"

Her heart just stopped. Pain knifed through her. No way, no way could Cass have done that to her. She'd profiled him. She'd been so sure that he was the one she needed. That she was—

"That prick is gonna pay!" A vow from her would-be attacker.

Her gun pressed harder against him as she tried to make sense of his shout. He was saying Cass had paid him to kill her? No, that could not—

"He'll pay for fucking me up!"

Oh, wait. Her breath left in a relieved rush.

"He'll pay because I'll kill his girlfriend!"

His girlfriend? "Uh, I think you have the wrong idea," she began. How did one tactfully explain to an attacker that he'd just gone after a one-night stand and not some emotionally involved and invested girlfriend? "Cass won't give two shits about what happens to me."

The guy heaved up. His hands had pushed hard against the pavement, and he levered onto his knees. She eased the

73

gun back an inch or two because it wasn't like she wanted to accidentally shoot him in the head.

Or...not so accidentally do it.

Nope, not me. I'm a good FBI agent.

Even though the jerk had been sneaking up to stab her in the back. Such a dick move.

Footsteps thundered nearby. "Agnes!" Malik shouted.

Right. The cavalry was there. Good guys, at full attention.

"Turn around," Agnes ordered the perp. "Slowly. And keep your hands up every second."

Slowly, he turned. He also rose to his feet. Towered over her. As if she'd be intimidated by a guy with constant tears streaming down his cheeks and dripping into his bushy beard.

Malik stopped a few feet away. He had his gun out and aimed. "You good?" he demanded of Agnes.

Not really, she wasn't. And sometimes, she did get tired of pretending that she was. *When I get really tired, I like to go out and have hot hookups with MC leaders.*

Nope. Not multiple MC leaders. Just with one.

Cass.

But that would be far too much info for poor Malik, so she simply replied, "Absolutely. I'm good. Always good."

A phone began to ring.

Some cops wandered out of the hangout bar. They weren't wearing uniforms, but she could always spot a cop from a mile away. Detectives, with loose coats and wrinkled pants. They stiffened when they saw the scene unfolding, then began to rush toward them.

The phone kept ringing. It was coming from the assailant in front of her. Curious...a call right after he'd been slicing at her with his knife. A knife that was still just a few feet away. "I can't help but wonder, is that someone calling to confirm the hit? To confirm that little old me is as dead as can be?"

The phone rang again.

Agnes waved toward the perp. "Why don't you answer that call?"

"You do it, bitch!" he snarled. "You answer it!"

Oh, well, if he was going to give her permission, then she definitely would. "Keep your gun on him, would you, Malik?" As if she had to ask, though. Malik never lowered his guard.

She closed in. She plucked the phone from the pocket of the biker's battered jacket. She swiped her finger over the screen. Turned it on speaker so they could all hear the conversation. "I'm sorry," she began, voice friendly and warm, "but the would-be killer you're trying to contact is unavailable at the moment..."

"Agnes?"

She blinked.

"Agnes, is that fucking you?" Cass demanded.

"Uh, yes. It's me. Hi." Oh, he was growly. She'd missed that growly voice.

"You're in danger." A snarl.

She surveyed the scene. Lots of cops. Her partner at the ready. The perp with his hands up and his knife no longer heading for her. Hmm. She should really frisk him now to make sure there were no other weapons on him. She'd bet the guy had other weapons. "I'm kinda busy right now. How about we talk later?"

"He wants to kill you."

"Already tried. No worries. I stopped him." How had Cass gotten the number for her attacker?

"I'm coming to you," Cass said. Flat. Hard. "On my way."

Nope. He probably did not want to do that. Not with all the police around. "This is not really your scene—"

He hung up. Incredibly rude. She shrugged.

But she realized the perp was watching her way too closely. "Weakness," he whispered. Then he smiled.

She wasn't afraid of much in this world. But that smile... that one word...A shiver skated down her spine.

Her gaze darted over the jerk who loved to slice with his knife. A knife was her least favorite weapon of choice. Mostly because she'd never, ever be able to forget what it felt like to have a blade plunging into her again and again. Her gaze went to the big hands that were still up in the air. The sleeves of his shirt and jacket had fallen down, and she could just make out a tattoo swirling around the perp's right wrist.

Her breath caught. She stepped closer to him.

A snake tattoo. Black ink. Intricate scales on the snake. And...two heads. She was staring at a two-headed, snarling cobra. Both heads showed razor sharp fangs ready to bite. The tattoo was clearly visible beneath the glow of the street light.

"See something you like?" the bastard mocked.

Her grip tightened on her gun. She held his phone in her left hand. The gun in her right. "Where'd you get that tattoo?"

He laughed.

She stared harder at the tattoo. The faint lines. The details on the snake. The tail that disappeared into the sleeve of his jacket. Not quite the same, not exactly as she remembered. A bit larger, actually. The two-headed snake from her nightmares had been smaller, closer to her attacker's wrist.

Not the same tattoo. But close, so close.

A knife slashing down. Screams. Blood.

A two-headed snake with fangs bared, black eyes staring at me...

She put the gun to the perp's forehead. "Where did you get the fucking tattoo?"

He wasn't laughing any longer.

He also wasn't speaking.

"Uh, Agnes." Malik touched her shoulder. "I've got him. Put the gun down."

Her whole body was shaking.

A knife slashing down. The blade going into me again and again. Blood...

"I've got him," Malik said again.

Her breath heaved out.

"*Agnes*," Malik's voice sharpened.

She lowered her gun.

Chapter Seven

"WHAT IN THE HELL JUST HAPPENED?" FBI AGENT Grayson "Gray" Stone demanded. Gray was not just a run-of-the-mill FBI agent. He was someone who had flown up the ranks in record time. His fancy new title—because it always seemed to be changing with Gray—was *Executive Assistant Director*.

The man held a whole lot of power at the Bureau.

And he currently looked extremely pissed...with her.

Probably because it was a Monday night. He'd expected to be home in bed with his lovely wife. His lovely *pregnant* wife. And, instead of being with Emerson...

He was at the FBI office. Glaring at Agnes.

She shifted a bit in the exceedingly uncomfortable chair that had been positioned directly across from his desk. Gray didn't sit in his leather desk chair. He stood behind the desk. The better to glare down at her.

"What just happened..." Agnes nodded. She kept her voice brisk as she told him, "A sneak attack, sir. That's what happened. The attacker came up behind me. Luckily, I thwarted his attack." *Thwarted.* That was a fun word. It kind of swirled around in her head. She had *thwarted—*

"Agnes." Flat. Zero amusement. Typical Gray. "I'm talking about when you shoved the muzzle of your gun against his forehead. What the hell possessed you to do that?"

Oh, yes. That part of the night. "He wanted to kill me."

"So you arrest him. We lock his ass away. When we stop a perp, we follow the rules. We don't nearly shoot an unarmed man in the street, with half a dozen cops nearby."

"I didn't nearly shoot him. My finger *never* got even close to pulling the trigger." Time to just get real with Gray. "We both know that if I'd wanted him dead, he would be dead. I wouldn't have just sprayed mace in his eyes. The perp was coming at me with a knife. I could have shot him there and then and had a solid self-defense case."

He swore.

"Yeah, exactly," she agreed. "I didn't. I didn't shoot him. He's under arrest, cooling down in holding. I did everything the right way."

"*You're a Fed.*"

She knew that fun fact. She carried the badge. She hunted the monsters.

She saw the victims who'd been left behind. She buried the dead. She...

Wanted vengeance.

"You think I don't understand?" Gray's voice lowered even as his face tensed. "You think I don't have a profile on every single member of my team?"

Her hands gripped the chair's armrests on either side of her body. "Judas Long had four open arrest warrants." They had ID'd the guy not too long ago. "Because of me, he's now behind bars. I think that makes for a pretty good night's work." As far as Gray having a profile on her...

She wasn't sure she wanted to know what his profile would say.

"You're still hunting," Gray charged.

Aw, damn. She shrugged. Maybe she slumped a little in her chair.

"Agnes." Flat. "You're still hunting."

Guilty. True story, she would be hunting until the day she died. *Or until the day I bury the bastard who hurt me and killed my boyfriend.*

"You know I'm looking for him, too," Gray added. Because, of course, he was. This was Gray. "I'm searching for the perp based on the profile *we* built," Gray added, because, yes, they had worked together to create a profile on the man she was after. She'd wanted Gray's insight as she tried to understand the killer. *Understanding him isn't my goal. Eliminating him is.* "We know the perp was most likely an MC member," he continued. "Based on the tattoo work you described, he was more than just a regular MC. He was a Twin Cobra. Because they are the bastards who use the two-headed cobra tat to mark their members. But when you were attacked, you only saw the tat. You never saw the face of the man who hurt you. Hell, you really didn't see anything but his tatted wrist..."

His wrist, yes, because she'd stared up as the knife had plunged down at her.

But she had seen more than just that.

The black helmet. The dark visor that completely covered his face. The dark, battered, leather coat that he wore. The coat I grabbed with my blood-covered hands. The black t-shirt. The jeans. The boots as he walked away and left me bleeding beside the dead body of my boyfriend.

"Agnes?"

She blinked. Her breath shuddered out. "He spoke to me."

"The perp tonight? Uh, yeah—"

"No. The man who attacked me all of those years ago." As if she'd ever forget his voice or his words. "You know he did. If I could just get an *in* with the powerful MCs, if I could just get close, I could—"

"That shit isn't going to happen. We are talking about the Twin Cobras. They're freaking shadows, Agnes. You know that. The Twins—if the stories are true—they are actually *in* the other MCs."

She was aware. "The Twins are supposed to be the most vicious, hardened bikers out there. They are chosen because they show extreme potential." Potential for violence and destruction. "But they have to prove themselves to get inside that secret, inner circle."

"Some people are wannabes." Gray kept his stare on her. "They heard the stories about the two-headed cobra tat. They get the ink to pretend that they are the most dangerous bastards out there."

"Yeah, and then they wind up in the morgue because no wannabes are allowed in the Twins." As if she didn't understand this. She'd gone to plenty of morgues to look at bodies supposedly belonging to the notorious group. She'd never found a match for the tattoo on the man who'd come after *her*.

"The perp tonight could just be a dumb wannabe."

Judas could certainly be. "Maybe. But he also tried to kill Cassius Striker a few nights back. Pair that up with the fact that Judas just tried to take out a Fed, and, to me, you're talking Twin Cobra level work."

Gray blinked. "He tried to kill Cassius?"

81

Um...

"How do you know about that?" Gray thundered.

Oh, the usual way. "I might have been in the bar at the time." Did she need to say more? Hopefully not. Time to redirect her boss. "The inner circle of the Twins," she said deliberately. "If I can get access, I know I can find the killer I'm after. No, more than that, I can help take down the whole group. They're the worst of the worst. Criminals. Murderers. I just need to get—"

"No." He pushed his hands down on the desk as he leaned toward her. "You're not going to just sashay into the MC world and somehow infiltrate the secretive Twins. That shit does not happen. Ever. Don't you understand? No one has gotten in undercover with them. We've had agents who tried. The Bureau has been attempting to infiltrate the Twins for years. Any agents who get close are unmasked. Those agents vanish completely, or else we find pieces of them."

Not like she wanted *pieces* of herself to be discovered. Agnes swallowed.

Gray was not done. Nostrils flaring, he fired, "There have been explosions that we believe are linked to the Twins. Actual bomb detonations because these perps are freaking extreme. They don't just destroy their enemies. They often obliterate them. That's not happening to you. Not on my watch."

They'd had this talk before. Whenever she mentioned going undercover in an attempt to reach the Twins. And, frankly, the very fact that the group was so extreme just meant that they needed to work harder in order to take them down. She wanted in that group. She wanted to rip them apart from the inside.

But when she brought up the Twins, Gray always put

roadblocks in her path. So maybe she'd decided to take a different path.

"I want to get back to Cassius." Grim determination underscored Gray's words.

Sure. Because no way would Gray be redirected so easily.

"You were in the bar when Judas Long attacked Cassius Striker?"

"Well..." Modest. "I actually saved Cass's life." She rolled one shoulder. "No big deal."

Gray's jaw dropped.

"You can't go in there!" A raised voice. One from just outside of Gray's inner sanctum. "You can't—this is the *FBI!*"

The door to Gray's office flew open. "Like I give a shit," Cass announced darkly.

Her head snapped toward him.

He filled the doorway. All big, bold, and furious. Cass jerked a thumb over his shoulder. "Tell your guard dog to back off," Cass ordered as he glared at Gray. "And get those agents of yours to stand the hell down. I'd hate to have to punch someone else."

Oh, no. *Someone else.* That pretty much implied that he had *already* punched at least one other person. At the FBI office.

She jumped to her feet and whirled to fully face Cass even as she heard Gray swear.

Wide-eyed, she gaped at Cass. "You just..." A shake of her head. "You should not be here."

"Tell me something I don't fucking know." He stalked toward her. Didn't stop until he was right in front of her. He reached out and caught her chin. He tilted her head from one side to the other, as if searching for injuries. "You're okay?"

She hadn't been sliced with Judas's knife. She had zero injuries. "He was trying to stab me in the back," she whispered. "That's his go-to technique. No worries, I maced him."

Gray marched out of the office. "Stand the hell down," he blasted to whoever waited outside of his office door. "Everything is under control. And I want you to erase all security footage that shows..."

She didn't catch what else Gray said because Cass grabbed her full attention.

"You maced him." Cass nodded. "Of course, you did." His mouth kicked into a half-smile. He began to lean down toward her.

Was he going to kiss her? Right there? Wait, bad idea. Wasn't it?

Yes, yes, of course, it's a bad idea. You don't make out in the office of your FBI boss.

The door to the office slammed shut. "What. The. Fuck?" Gray thundered.

Cass froze. His eyes glittered at her. Then his head turned toward Gray. "Hello, sunshine."

"I am not in the mood for your bullshit." Gray stomped closer to them. "You think it's easy making security footage of you just vanish whenever you decide to stride in this place? Dude, what in the hell are you thinking?" But his gaze jumped to Agnes. Or rather, to her chin. The chin that Cass still cradled carefully in his fingers. "No, no, no."

Cass let her go.

She backed up. Put her hands behind her back. The better to not reach out and grab Cass in front of her boss. Because that would be a very bad move.

84

"Since when are you touching *my* agent?" Gray demanded of Cass. *"Since when are you rushing in here to check on her?"*

Since they'd had wild sex two nights ago.

Gray stood right beside them now. His gaze swung from her to Cass, then back to her. "No." A shake of his head. His gaze returned to Cass. "No."

Cass's jaw had locked. "We have a problem."

"I noticed," Agnes assured him.

His head cocked as he studied her.

She sent him a weak, very brief smile. "It was hard to miss the man who came barreling at me with a knife. His name's Judas Long, by the way. Guess Judas didn't like that I stopped him from attacking you the other night."

"Shit." Gray squeezed the bridge of his nose. "You actually saved Cass's life a few nights back? That story was for real?"

"She didn't save my life," Cass growled. "She just threw a beer bottle."

From the corner of her eye, she saw Gray squeeze the bridge of his nose harder.

"A beer bottle that stopped a knife attack," she had to point out. Seriously, her throw had taken some skill. "Don't belittle my efforts. Not cool."

"Sorry, princess." Cass nodded. "Your beer bottle kicked ass."

Damn straight, but... "Technically, you kicked ass when you started that whole hand-to-hand fight in the bar with him. The guy is covered in bruises, FYI."

"For the love of—*dammit!*" Gray exploded.

Her head whipped toward him.

A muscle flexed along his clenched jaw. He wasn't squeezing his nose any longer. He was pointing straight at her. "I'm in charge here. I'm supposed to be *in the damn loop.*"

She hadn't planned to loop him in on her, uh, sex life. Kinda a need-to-know situation. She had not thought he needed to know.

"The near stabbing tonight wasn't about you," Cass told her.

"It felt like it was." Her attention shifted back to him. "Call me crazy, but when a man comes at me with a knife, it feels personal."

Cass pressed his lips together. Then... "It's because we fucked."

Her eyes widened.

"*Sonofabitch!*" An explosion from Gray. "This is not the shit I need to hear right now!"

Yes, well, she'd prefer not to be discussing this either but... "What does us having sex matter? What does it have to do with anything?"

"Weakness." One word from Cass. Gritted. Snapped.

She waited for more. He kept her waiting. Sighing, she told him, "You've got to elaborate. I'm all for a bit of suspense, but you can't just drop one word and be done. You leave too many unanswered questions that way."

"You're my weakness," Cass said, as if each word had been torn from him. "And they are gonna use you against me."

She wondered who "they" were. She also wondered how in the world she could possibly be his weakness. As far as she knew, the man had zero weaknesses. That was why he was the big, tough badass leader of the Night Strikers.

"My enemies know I fucked you. They know you are a Fed. They will line up to take you out."

Because she'd had a one-night stand with him?

"Me fucking a Fed didn't exactly go over well in the MC circles. Those who hate me have always been looking for a weapon to use against me. A weakness. They think you're that weakness."

How flattering. What woman didn't want to be called a weakness? Her eyes narrowed, and she realized that her hands had fisted.

"Oh, hell." From Gray. "You two really—jeez, *why?* How do you two even know each other well enough to do that crap?"

Cass never looked away from her. "A bastard named Bayne Hendrix came up to me tonight. He's the one who told me about the coming attack on you. Bayne said he'd picked up on rumors that I fucked a Fed."

A curse from Gray.

"He told me to my damn face that you were going to be eliminated. Said I should send flowers to your funeral."

And she had a flash of soggy flowers on a gravesite. But not her funeral. It had been Max's funeral. Her boyfriend. Her fiancé. She'd stood in the rain and felt as if she were drowning.

"What did you do to Bayne?" Gray wanted to know.

"I...convinced him to call up the prick who was going after Agnes."

Ah. That would be how she'd gotten the phone call. Or, rather, how Judas had gotten the call. "Where is this Bayne now?"

"Running." A bit out response from Cass. "Running and getting the hell out of my town. He was told to spread the word that you were protected. He was also warned that if he *ever* tried to hurt you or come after you in any way..."

She waited. He needed to finish that sentence.

Cass shrugged. "If he ever tries to hurt you, death will seem like a blessing compared to the hell I'll bring to him."

Well, okay then.

"When Bayne announced to everyone that I'd fucked a Fed—"

"How did he learn that," she cut in to ask, "exactly?"

"He learned it because there are too many pricks wanting to take me down. Too many eyes on me."

Did that mean that someone had been trailing them that night? Trailing him...her?

"It was either act like you meant nothing to me and let a line of attackers come after you..."

"That doesn't seem like a fun plan," she muttered.

"Or claim you," he finished. "Tell the world that you did matter. That you mattered more than anything."

Silence.

"I claimed you." Cass extended his hand toward her. "Agnes Quinn, from here on out, you are mine."

Chapter Eight

SHE'S NOT HURT. SHE'S NOT HURT. SHE'S NOT HURT.

More importantly, *she's not dead. She's not dead. She's not dead.*

The two refrains had beat through his head as he hauled ass across town and tried to get to her. Agnes had stopped the attacker after her. She was safe. She was alive. And Cass was going to keep her that way.

His hand extended toward her. Agnes peered down at his hand. She didn't take it. Just peered at it with a faint furrow between her delicate brows. "Yours as in...?" She bit her lower lip. "What, exactly?"

"*Mine.*" Wasn't that clear enough? Rage still wanted to choke him. The idea that someone would hurt her, kill her...

"*Ahem.*" From Gray. Followed up with, "Agnes, I need a minute alone with Cass."

Cass growled at Gray. Not like he was there for Gray. *I'm here for her.*

"I'm the senior agent here. I'm the one in charge, so stop growling at me. Agnes, wait outside a minute. Now." An order.

Cynthia Eden

She sucked in a breath. Nodded. Her gaze avoided Cass's as she stepped to the side and briskly made her way to the door. She opened it.

A moment later, it closed behind her with a soft click. His gaze remained on the closed door. He'd turned his head to follow her movements. Every single step.

He wanted her back.

"I didn't come here to talk with you," he told Gray.

"That's glaringly obvious." Gray grabbed his arm. "When in the hell did you fuck Agnes?"

"Two days ago."

"*Why* did you fuck her?"

"Because I wanted her more than I wanted breath."

The brutally honest answer seemed to catch Gray by surprise. His mouth hung open, then he snapped it closed.

The brutally honest answer had also caught Cass by surprise, but he wasn't as obvious about the shock as Gray.

"Feds and MC leaders don't become lovers." The faint lines near Gray's eyes tightened. "At least, they don't without someone winding up dead. In case you forgot, people in your sphere aren't exactly big on law enforcement."

As if he could forget. "That would explain the attack on Agnes tonight." He whirled away. Marched toward the desk. Files. A closed laptop. A picture of Gray's wife.

Because the guy had a wife now. A kid on the way. A normal, happy life. What did Cass have?

Death and violence. That was his life.

Was he jealous of Gray? *Yes, I freaking am.*

"I told you before, I can get you out," Gray said.

Death was the only way out. Not like he could easily walk away, not without hunters following him and everyone trying to get credit for taking him down.

He whirled to face Gray. His cousin. The man who was closer to him than any brother would ever be. Not that anyone knew that. Certainly not anyone in Cass's world. No one except... "You told her."

Gray's brows lifted. "Excuse me?"

"You told Agnes that we are family. Why did you do that? Did you think that would make me trust her?"

"I have no clue what you are talking about. I have never told Agnes Quinn about our relationship. Exposing that information to the wrong person would put a target on us both."

"Is she the wrong person?" What an odd thing to say. "Don't you trust your own agent?" But, then again, this wouldn't be the first time someone at this office had gone bad. Except he knew for a fact that Agnes had helped take down the bad guy in the previous case.

Instead of answering what Cass thought were very valid questions, Gray fired, "You've been to this office before. People think it's because you're pissed as hell at me and won't be intimidated by the Bureau. They figure you come in here to try and intimidate me and to look like the badass that you are."

"I'm not intimidated by the Bureau." And he was, generally, as a fact of life, pissed as hell. As far as being a badass...*Aw, thanks for the compliment.*

Gray just looked even more intense than normal as he added, "You having a vendetta against the FBI is one thing. But you fucking a Fed is another cluster altogether. You've put yourself at risk."

No, more than that... "I put her at risk." Because he hadn't kept his dick zipped up. "Now we have to move, quickly, and take out my enemies before they take out Agnes."

Cynthia Eden

Gray sucked in a breath. "Dammit."

"Yes, dammit to hell." He pointed over Gray's shoulder, toward the shut door. He kept his voice low because he did not want anyone outside the office to overhear his conversation with Gray. "We need the world to believe she's turning her back on the Feds. She needs to swear allegiance to me and only me. Because otherwise, there are too many assholes looking to get payback against me. Idiots who think they can take me down. Word is gonna spread like wildfire about my hookup with the Fed."

"And *maybe* you should have thought of that before you hooked up with her!"

"She came to me," he rasped. "She walked into my bar and..." His words trailed away.

Gray waited. And waited. And... "She walked in and you just did not have the physical strength to walk *away*?"

Actually, he'd carried her out, then driven away with her. "The prick who came after her tonight—"

"Judas Long."

He nodded. "Bear of a guy, bald, bushy beard, nose ring?" Just so they were talking about the same man.

Gray inclined his head.

"He tried to get the jump on me the night that Agnes came into my bar. She, uh, let me know he was closing in for the kill."

Gray crossed his arms over his chest. "Pretty sure she said that she saved you."

"Of course, she'd say that. I *had* it handled." But... "She didn't have to step in. She did. Then I kicked the prick's ass. Turns out the guy is a floater who was looking to switch MC allegiances. He thought that by going after me, he'd make a killer name for himself." A roll of one shoulder. "He thought wrong. But he learned exactly who Agnes was.

92

Word has now spread, and I don't want her getting zipped up in a body bag because she had the bad taste to—number one—save my life and number two—"

"To fuck you?"

"That wasn't bad taste. That was her lucky night."

Gray rolled his eyes.

Grim, Cass told him, "Because of me, she will be targeted, again and again. Tonight's attack will just be the first of many."

"Dammit," Gray repeated.

Yes, dammit. Dammit straight to hell and back. "Bright side," Cass gritted out.

Gray frowned at him. "Did you just freaking say 'bright side' to me? Since when do you ever have a bright side?"

Since I get to keep Agnes at my side. Wow. Hold up. He wasn't looking *forward* to this madness. Was he? Cass cleared his throat. "Bright side, you'll have a Fed embedded with me."

"Yeah, the whole problem is that I had a Fed *in bed* with you."

Smartass. "We'll take down some very powerful individuals. I'll finally wrap up the fucking mission…"

Those were words he'd *never* said, not out loud. But an end had to come…

The end would be on his terms. His way. And he'd raise as much hell on the way to the grave as he possibly could.

Silence.

"You're…wrapping up the mission," Gray repeated carefully.

He nodded. "My objectives have nearly all been reached."

"No, they haven't." Gray watched him with that intense, knowing stare. "You're still after revenge. Still looking to burn down the world." His mouth tightened. "So the hell is she. That's why this is a clusterfuck. The whole thing could explode in our faces."

He closed in on his cousin. "Why is Agnes looking for revenge?"

Instead of answering him, Gray let out a long sigh. "How did you and Agnes get together?"

She walked into a bar and asked what she had to do in order to get—"The usual way."

Gray waited.

Cass didn't share more. He'd already said that she came into his bar. That she'd intervened with that dumbass Judas. There was no more info that Gray needed. "Do I look like I kiss and tell?"

"Agnes isn't what you think."

"I think she's a sexy and smart FBI agent who is now in the crosshairs because of me. You gonna tell me that I'm wrong?"

"Agnes can handle threats. She's not going to turn and run just because some jerks are after her. She took out the attacker tonight without breaking a sweat."

Now uncertainty stirred within Cass. "You're saying you don't think she'll go undercover and follow my rules?"

"Oh, she'll go undercover. It's what she's been waiting for." Definite disgruntlement. "But she needs to fully explain what *you're* getting into."

He didn't like the sound of that. "We'll have to stage a public scene," Cass mused. "Word has to spread that she's separating from the Feds. When you pick a side, everyone has to know."

A quick knock rapped on the door. Then it swung open.

Agnes ducked her cute head inside. "Hi." She flashed a

slow, broad smile. "Are you done talking about me? Can I now enter the conversation that is about *me*?"

His gaze got stuck on her smile.

"Agnes." A long sigh of her name from Gray. "Come inside. Shut the door. Have a seat." He walked behind his desk and heaved down in his own chair.

Taking her time, Agnes came inside. She softly shut the door. She strolled casually across the small room. Took her seat. Even crossed her legs. One foot swung lazily.

Cass remained standing.

His hands did clench into fists, though. Rage still burned inside of him. *She'd been targeted. She could have died before I got to her.* He'd forced Bayne to give up Judas. Bayne had called the bastard. *After* Cass had delivered some brutal punches. And when the phone had been answered, Cass had been surprised as hell to hear Agnes's voice. Surprised—and relieved.

Agnes tilted her head toward him. "Stop fretting."

What?

"I didn't even get a scratch." She winked at him. "But I did leave a few, new bruises on that perp."

"You also put a gun to his head, Agnes," Gray groused. "And your partner had to pull you back."

She'd done what now?

Her shoulders lifted, then fell. "I wasn't going to pull the trigger."

Cass's gaze sharpened on her.

That left foot of hers kept casually swinging. He thought that might be her only sign of nerves.

"You have a choice to make," Gray announced.

The hell she did. Her choice had already been made. She was going to belong to Cass. End of story.

"What choice would that be?" Agnes inquired sweetly.

Gray opened his mouth to speak.

"You have to turn your back on the Feds," Cass said as he took a hard step forward. "Publicly. Very, very clearly. A fuck-you that all can understand. And then you swear allegiance to me. You can't be a Fed and be mine at the same time. So you choose."

A little furrow appeared between her brows as she glanced over at Gray.

"Undercover mission," Gray said.

Her hands gripped the armrests on either side of her. Hard. As if...as if she was trying to keep herself from jumping out of the chair. That bright, bright blue gaze of hers swung right back to Cass. "You're undercover."

He didn't say a word.

"*You're undercover.* You're not an MC leader—"

"Oh, I assure you, I am one hundred percent an MC leader. I bled for the title. I killed for it."

"*Cass.*" A warning note in Gray's voice.

What was new? Gray always liked to warn. And toe the line. And follow every rule in the book. Boring. So very, very boring. Cass could not help it, he had to flash his own smile at Agnes and his cousin as he said, "My world is shades of gray."

"That is not funny," Gray told him.

Cass thought it was a little funny.

"I'm not undercover," Cass stated, voice flat. "What you see is who I am."

"He is an MC leader. Cass just...ah, happens to be doing some work for me at the same time," Gray allowed.

Her tight grip remained on the armrests. "Undercover."

She did seem to like that word.

Agnes nodded. "And I'm going to be undercover, too." Now her stare lingered on Cass. "As your lover?"

"As the woman who is so obsessed with me that she threw away her badge, betrayed her fellow Feds, and went all in with a criminal. Yes." She'd be undercover. "Think you can handle that?"

Their gazes held. Tension thickened. He had a sudden flash of her as she'd been during that long, hot night with him. Tousled hair. Swollen lips. His hands tight on her waist as he heaved her against him and her warm, tight—

"Sounds like a dream job." She nodded and flashed that slow smile of hers again. "Pretty sure I could do it in my sleep."

Uh, say again?

"Consider me obsessed," Agnes told him. "When does the job begin?"

* * *

She was shaking on the inside. Her stomach was in so many knots that she ached, but Agnes kept her bright and shiny veneer in place until Cass left the FBI building.

They'd come up with a game plan. A dramatic one, granted, but desperate situations could often call for dramatic measures. She was aware that wasn't exactly how the old saying went, but, in this particular instance, she thought her version worked better.

"You'll have to trust him."

Gray's low, rumbling voice. Because she was still in Gray's office. Cass had vanished, but she still had her boss to handle.

Gray's expression was hard. His eyes intent. No emotion entered his voice, and that was a bad sign. Gray was quietly furious. She could *feel* his rage in the air around her.

"If you trust him, I trust him," she said.

"Cass says you believe we're family."

"Uh, you *are* family." That would be why she believed it.

"And how did you reach that conclusion?"

"Bone structure. Plus, the fact that I haven't heard a denial from either of you so far so, yeah...family."

He leaned forward. His chair squeaked. "Did you think he was an undercover Fed when you fucked him?"

She actually...had, yes.

"Because he's not." A muscle tightened along his jaw. "He is not following some secret rulebook. Cass is not going to make the good-guy choices when you are in the field with him. He is the leader of the Night Strikers. He has done things that will give you nightmares."

Those knots in her stomach got worse. "You don't know what my nightmares are like." She shouldn't have said that. She should have kept her mouth shut.

Because *sympathy* flashed in his eyes, only to be blinked away. "And is that the reason you went to him? Did you think that he was an undercover Fed who could help you get the revenge that you've wanted for so very long?"

Yes. "I hate when you profile me."

"I hate when you make profiling you so easy." An immediate return. "You've lived and breathed for revenge— you've done that for years, but, Agent Quinn, you just stepped straight into the fire. Where you are going..." A shake of his head. "I can't be your backup. Malik won't be your backup. It will be you and Cass against the world, and you are going to learn fast that he plays dirty and hard."

Yes, she was getting that impression. "I can play that way, too."

"Tell him about your past."

She had already told Cass some about her past. Filling him in fully on all the dark and twisted details was on the agenda. She just wasn't completely sure how he would react to everything.

Slowly, she rose to her feet. "Guess I have to get busy. Dramatic scenes to enact. New allegiances to swear. Busy, busy, busy." She turned for the door. Agnes exhaled slowly. Her words were flippant, but when she reached out to touch the doorknob, her fingers trembled.

Don't show fear. Do not hesitate. You are going to get what you want. Finally.

"If you go off the rails, if you cross the line while you are out there, you won't be able to come back to the FBI. You understand that, don't you?"

She stiffened.

"There are things that you cannot do. And one of those things? It's commit premeditated murder."

Gray...always profiling. And always...right.

Agnes glanced back at him. She used her bright and sunny smile on him. Most people never looked past that particular smile. Gray wasn't most people. "I have no intention of committing premeditated murder."

No, she'd make sure it never, ever looked that way...

"Agnes."

"I learned a great deal working with you, Agent Stone." True story. She had. "Thank you for the opportunity." But it was time for her to take the next step.

And the next step?

That was to sever all ties with the FBI. Because she had to choose...

And the world would believe she was choosing Cass.

Time to burn bridges. The fire would need to be very, very bright. Good thing she had a pocketful of matches.

Chapter Nine

"Is it true that hot redhead is a Fed?"

Cass sat at the bar, his booted feet on the floor, his ass on the old stool, and a cold beer bottle gripped in his hand. At the low question, his head turned to the right.

A biker was beside him. Not MC affiliated. At least, not wearing any obvious signs or sporting obvious tats. Cass didn't know the prick. Youngish, maybe early twenties, shaved hair on the right side. Dark hair. A patchy beard covering his jaw.

"Do I know you?" Cass asked bluntly.

The guy's Adam's apple bobbed. "Name's River. I, um, was here at The Bottomless Pit the other night. Saw you take out that SOB with the knife." A low whistle. "You're one hell of a fighter."

Cass grunted. "Had to be. Either I kicked the shit out of my enemies when I was a kid, or I would have been in the ground." Enough chit-chat. This River guy was a hanger-on. There for the fury. The second-hand adrenaline.

Hell, maybe River had picked up on the whispers. He'd heard that others were pissed at Cass because he'd screwed

100

a Fed. Maybe River thought he was about to see a serious battle go down.

"Is it true…" The kid leaned closer. "That you took out your own uncle? Your *father?*"

Did it *look* like he had the patience for this bullshit? Cass reached out and grabbed the little prick by his collar. "Ask me another question," Cass told him, "and I will put a knife in your heart. Sound fun?"

"OhmyGod." A whimper.

"Get the hell out of here." Cass shoved him back.

River jumped up from his stool and scuttled across the bar. He glanced back, twice, and almost tripped three times.

Cass took another swig of his beer. He did not have time to deal with idiots or wannabes. He had to get his head in the freaking game because the show was about to start.

Same bar, different night. Yep, he was back at his favorite crash site, The Bottomless Pit. The same bar he'd been inside when Agnes had first sashayed her sexy self into his world.

Come back to me, Agnes.

He was waiting for her. He hadn't seen her since the showdown at the FBI office. A new day—and now, *night—* had dawned. The big scene was about to go down. He was so ready for this scene to be done.

Members of his MC were there. Other groups. Lots of watchful eyes. The perfect, public place. And it was about to be turned into utter chaos.

I just want Agnes. I want my hands on her. I want her to be mine.

Because she wouldn't be safe, not until everyone knew that she didn't have allegiance to the Feds any longer. That her only allegiance was to him.

He turned toward the bar. Time ticked slowly past.

How the hell did I wind up here?

Maybe he could have gone down a different path, a lifetime ago. But that ship had long since sailed.

Whispers. Mutters. The faint *tap, tap, tap* of heels. Because, sure, why wouldn't she wear sexy heels again?

"Cass." Her voice. Husky. Warm. Seductive.

He took another swig of the beer. He didn't face her. Not yet.

"Cass." Urgency. "You need to leave this place. Now. They're coming."

Taking his time, he put the beer down. Then he turned toward her.

Black top. Black pants. High heels. A cute little bag on her shoulder. She looked sexy and feminine. Not the hard-ass FBI agent. Her hair had been pulled back into some kind of twist. Her features were delicate, beautiful.

"Don't think you should be here," he said. The words weren't rehearsed. There was no rehearsal. No script. He knew what was going down, yeah, but getting from point A to point B...

I'm gonna wing it.

He truly meant what he'd said, though. She shouldn't be there. She still had a chance to end this game. Now. Before it was too late.

But she rushed toward him and closed those few feet that had been between their bodies. Her hands lifted. Her soft palms pressed against the stubble on his cheeks. "This bar is about to be raided." A very clear announcement.

In response to her announcement, chairs scraped across the floor. Boots thudded for the exits.

He didn't move.

Her lips pulled down. "You think we don't know this bar is a front? That *you* own it, Cass?"

"*Fuck*," came from the bartender behind the counter. He slapped down his cleaning rag and stomped for the kitchen.

"They are closing in," she said as she stared straight into Cass's eyes. "They are after you. They've been after you for a long time. I was supposed to take you down."

He was still sitting on the bar stool. They were at eye level.

She leaned in and planted a fierce, passionate kiss on his lips. "I can't," she breathed. "I won't."

Uh, yeah. Right.

She grabbed his hand. "Come with me. Now."

The place had cleared out. Not like there was anyone to see the rest of her performance. All because of that one magical word. *Raid.*

But Cass let her tug him outside. A light rain had begun to fall.

Most of the motorcycles were gone, no longer lined up near the entrance to The Bottomless Pit. But...

He felt the eyes. Knew that watchers lingered. He'd already caught sight of Javion across the street. Casually, Cass made a quick gesture with his open hand. A bare flutter of his fingers.

"What are you doing?" Agnes demanded. "Did you just tell him to come closer?"

No, quite the opposite, actually. He'd just signed for the guy to wait. Not like he wanted Javion to get caught in the crossfire—

"FBI!" A voice blasted. "Freeze, Cassius!"

Oh. So it was gonna be a bold *outside* show. Interesting.

"No!" Agnes's shout. And she was suddenly between him and the FBI agent. The agent—a male wearing dark clothes and with his gun drawn. "Malik, no, *don't!*"

Cynthia Eden

"Get out of the way!" Malik yelled back at her. "We're taking him in!"

Cass climbed onto his motorcycle. "I don't think so." He'd had maybe three swigs of beer. Cass had known he'd need to be sober for the events coming. Besides, he usually believed that a drunk leader was a fool just waiting to get taken out.

The sound of revving cycles filled the night.

So did a gunshot blast. One, another.

His head whipped toward the sound. Had that Fed—Malik—just shot at them?

In response, Agnes had her gun out. She aimed it toward Malik.

He ran for cover.

"Fuck." Cass reached out a hand and curled it around her waist before she could start shooting. "On the motorcycle. *Now.*"

She got on the motorcycle. Dropped her bag. Kept the gun. And he got them the hell out of there.

Everyone was rushing off that street. Someone screamed. And when Cass looked back, he saw the Fed, rushing from his temporary hiding spot and trying to catch them.

Right. Good luck with that.

* * *

"I AM DYING TO KNOW..." Cass shut the motel room door behind him. He flipped the lock. A flimsy-as-hell lock that wouldn't keep anyone out. "Did you take acting classes in high school? Maybe college? Or do they teach Drama 101 to all new FBI recruits at Quantico?"

Agnes perched on the bed. The lone bed in the no-tell,

104

motel on the edge of Mississippi. They'd driven for hours and hours. Reached the motel just as the sun was rising. He'd traveled down winding back roads the whole time. Not like he wanted to make it easy for anyone trailing him.

Like the Feds.

Or his enemies.

His many, many enemies.

So he'd stuck to the less traveled routes. He'd been highly conscious of Agnes's soft body pressed against him.

She kicked off her shoes. "I've done undercover work before."

Really? "Do tell."

"I was a prostitute for three months."

He stiffened.

"Sorry. I *pretended* to be a prostitute. Received quite the number of offers, let me tell you..."

"I can imagine." Was that jealousy coiling in him? Like a snake ready to strike? Sure felt that way.

"I eventually caught the serial who'd been abducting and murdering women along the South Carolina coast. Things got a little dicey when he tried to drug me, but I just turned that needle right back around on him."

He could not *breathe*. "He's dead."

"No, but he is on death row. Is that close enough? I think it's pretty close. Anyway..." A bob of her head. "I was also an inmate at a women's prison for two months. Food was crap, by the way. Some guards there had been reported for taking advantage of the inmates. Forcing them to perform sex acts." Her expression hardened. "Rape."

She'd faced off with a serial killer who *drugged* his victims and then she'd gone into a prison with bastard guards who'd hurt women? *"Names."*

She blinked. "Excuse me?"

"Give me their names." They'd be dead in days.

"Uh, I got evidence on all the guards involved." She squared her shoulders. "I had them locked away. And let me tell you, other inmates don't react very kindly to former guards who are now trapped in cells with them."

No, he didn't think *kind* would be a word that applied in that situation. "No one hurt you." He needed to be clear.

"No one hurt me." A pause. "But I appreciate you caring."

And, sonofabitch, he did care. He cared that she'd nearly been drugged. He cared that she'd been locked up with monsters who hurt women. He cared that she'd ever been at risk for a single, solitary moment.

This was a clusterfuck.

Because he'd *cared* the entire time he'd been driving through the night, with her pressed to his back. All of those sweet, lush curves. He'd *cared* when the shots rang out back at The Bottomless Pitt, and he looked back, terrified for one, wild moment that she'd been hit.

Yeah, next time, he'd get a fucking script. "I thought Feds *cared* about innocent people getting hurt," he growled.

Her brows climbed. "We do."

"Then your FBI firing into a public street was...what? For shits and giggles?"

A shake of her head. "We made sure the street was secure. I had a transmitter in my ear. Malik did not fire those blanks until he was given the all-clear."

She'd what?

She reached into the front pocket of her black pants and pulled out a small device. Looked like a super, super tiny ear bud. "Gray told us when everyone was clear. We had some Feds out there, dressed in plainclothes, but those were all people he trusts implicitly. The street was secure."

Bullshit. "And the bikers who could have started shooting? Did he trust them implicitly? Is that the story you're spinning right now?"

"Most of them had moved out of range. A few lingered, but those were people who were loyal to you. And you gave the signal for them to stand down."

Tension knifed through him.

Sighing. She tucked the earpiece back into the pocket of her pants. Then she lifted her hand, and she fluttered her fingers. Almost looked like a "come here" gesture.

It wasn't.

"Wait," she said. She fluttered again. "Wait." A nod. "As soon as you gave the order, I knew that it was time. Gray knew, too. He was there, watching in the shadows. When he saw you sign, that was when he gave the order for Malik to shoot the blanks."

Check. The blanks. "You acted like you didn't know sign language. When I made that motion, you literally asked me if I was telling Javion to come closer." The woman had done recon work—he would bet his life she knew plenty about Javion. And about everyone else in the inner circle of the Night Strikers.

"Sorry. That was for show. You know sign language," she said. "So I made it a point to know it, too."

She would have needed a whole lot of time to learn sign language. He had the feeling that when she told him she knew sign language, Agnes wasn't just talking about a few gestures. "Gray told you." Fuck. Was nothing sacred these days?

"I've been...watching you for a bit," she confessed.

Well, hell.

"I saw when you'd use it. Don't worry, most people would miss it. I just made a point of studying you closely."

He hadn't been aware that he'd been under surveillance. "Gray doesn't trust me these days? He's sent Feds in to keep an eye on me? How the hell long has this been happening?" *And why didn't I see you?* He was usually good at spotting watchers. Was he slipping? Losing his edge because he'd been in this mess for far too long?

She nibbled on her lower lip. That ever-so-delicious lower lip. Then, "Gray didn't know what I was doing." A miserable whisper. "I was watching you on my own time."

Was he supposed to be flattered? Or super worried? "You watched me? And you decided to teach yourself sign language?"

"I'm *teaching* it to myself now. Not like I'm completely fluent. I'm learning. Gray doesn't know about that, either."

"I didn't spot you tailing me." That bothered him.

"I wasn't very close. I know to keep my distance. A good watcher can spy from a distance." She exhaled on a soft sigh. "I'm good at not being seen when I don't want to be."

Uh, huh. Cass finally stepped away from the thin door. He closed in on her with slow steps. "Someone has been a naughty FBI agent."

"Totally, you should spank me."

What?

Her eyes closed. "Forget I said that."

Never in a million years. The woman confused—and aroused—the hell out of him. "Who are you?"

Her eyes opened. "I'm Agnes Quinn. I...say kinda crazy, outlandish things when I'm nervous. I had this FBI shrink once who told me that it was a shielding technique." She remained on the bed. "It was after my very first officer-involved shooting. A man had a put a gun to his pregnant wife's stomach. He'd been screaming and raging, saying the kid wasn't his and that he wasn't going to put up with a cheating whore any longer. I knew he was going to kill her and the baby. I demanded he drop the gun. I yelled it three times. *Three times.* He didn't comply. And he was going to pull the trigger." An exhale. "I shot him in the leg. That got him to let her go. But then he raised the gun and aimed it at me as he screamed and screamed, and—when I fired a second time, I hit him in the heart."

Shit. He stopped advancing toward her. Halfway between the door and the bed. He just stared down at her, shaking his head. "So you look delicate, but you're very clearly not."

"She raged at me. The wife, I mean. She screamed that I'd left her baby without a father. I did, of course, but...I kinda thought it was more important that the wife and the baby got to live. That I got to live, too. I was a big proponent of me living." A roll of one shoulder. "So when I was talking to the shrink—see, you have to be cleared by the FBI shrink after a shooting. You don't just get to head straight back into active duty. She told me that I used humor and flippant statements as defensive and shielding mechanisms. She explained that I tend to say outlandish things to redirect." A nod. "Guilty as charged. I do that."

He could see that. "You're sharing an awful lot with me."

"Yes, well, considering that I have to trust you with my life for the foreseeable future, I figured a bit of sharing was necessary. Especially since we began our relationship with me...lying to you." Now her shoulders sagged. "Pretty sure you are going to be pissed."

"Our relationship?"

"Well, yes, we have one now, don't we? At least, I'm about ninety-nine percent certain you are going to declare me as your lady to the members of your MC. You're going to take me with you when we leave this motel. Where you go, I go. I'll be your ride-or-die. That whole situation is what we've got going, right?"

His back teeth had clenched. "Tell me about your lie," he bit out.

"I will but, promise you won't be furious?"

"You *just* said I'd be pissed."

"Yes. I did." A quick nod. "But I think, with you, there is a difference between being pissed and being furious." Her gaze searched his. "I think when you're pissed, you're scary. Intimidating. You'll make me feel super, super horrible."

He waited.

"But when you're furious, I suspect that is something quite different. I think that when a real rage takes you, it's like the devil walks on the earth."

His whole body tightened.

"So just promise you won't be furious. Try to see things from my point of view, would you?"

He would make no promises. "You lied to me."

"Know what? *Lie* might just be too strong of a word. How about...I misled you. *Misled.* I began our relationship by misleading you. Technically, I've told zero lies to you." A thoughtful hesitation. "Yet. Maybe. *Honestly,* I can't remember every single word I said to you...so..."

Enough of this bullshit. She wasn't going to spin her way into his life, throw him off guard, *charm* him, alarm him, and get him twisted into a million knots. He finished stalking toward the bed. Stopped when he was inches away from her.

He would *not* think of how easy it would be to wreck the bed. With Agnes. "How about you vow to always tell me zero lies from here on out?"

110

Her pretty lips pursed. "I don't like to make promises I might not be able to keep."

What? His hands went to his hips as he glowered at her. "*Agnes.*"

"You're really sexy when you say my name. Full disclosure, I always hated my name. Makes me sound like a maidenly aunt, and FYI, I actually did get the name from my maiden aunt. Though, if you listen to the stories, she was quite the partier back in the day."

His temples were throbbing. It had been a helluva night, and he'd just discovered that Agnes lacked the ability to answer a question simply. "The idea of spanking you holds definite appeal."

"Glad we're both into that."

A muscle flexed along his jaw.

"Sorry." Quiet. "That defense mechanism thing again." She huffed out a breath. "I deliberately sought you out."

Apparently, she'd also deliberately and secretly *stalked* him.

Her hands pressed against the bedding near her. "Once I made the connection between the leader of the Night Strikers being secretly related to my boss, I knew...I knew there had to be a lot more to you than met the eye. Sure, you seemed to be the big, bad guy."

"I *am* the big, bad guy." He gave nightmares to most of the world. There was no pretending on that point. He'd been born for the Night Striker MC. And, eventually, he'd taken leadership a bloody battle that had left a man dead.

Two men, actually.

She frowned at him. "You're working undercover. You need to be honest with me. I'm being honest with you."

He leaned toward her. Put one hand on either side of the bed. The old, sagging mattress dipped even more. "You think I'm some true-blue hero pretending to be MC? You think I'm playing by the rules and rolling over to deliver dirt to the Feds?"

Her gaze searched his. "Yes."

He laughed. In her face. Sorry. That was probably rude. His mother would have been horrified. Then again, his mother had been dead for a long time. "I thought you were way better at profiling."

"Tell me how I'm wrong."

He'd rather kiss her. Maybe spank her. Definitely fuck her. But...no. Not happening. Because he'd fucked her before, then a jackass had tried to kill her.

And...when Cass had fucked her before...

I let my guard slip. I wanted her too much. "Tell me why you're using me." Anger rumbled in the words. He didn't like being used. Not even when the user came in such a tempting package.

"I was using you." A blunt admission. "I'm sorry."

Well, damn. "Why?"

She bit her lower lip. His right hand flew up, and he lightly pressed on that lower lip. "Don't." Because when she bit, she made him want to bite, too.

She stopped biting her lower lip. Her tongue snaked out. Lightly touched the tip of his finger. Her eyes widened in horror. "I did *not* mean to do that." Her breath blew over his finger.

His eager dick was glad she had licked him. But his dick needed to calm the hell down. His hand moved to curl under her jaw. "Why were you using me?" He would get a straight answer from her.

"Because I need you to help me kill a man." A thoughtful pause. "At least one man, but maybe two."

Chapter Ten

THE BED WAS UNCOMFORTABLE. LUMPY. SAGGY. IT smelled faintly of old cigarettes. No bedbugs, though. Agnes was very happy that her fast and frantic search for bedbugs had yielded no results.

The room was dark. Almost pitch black, even though it was daytime. The lone window in the little room had been covered by blinds and by what had to be the thickest, roughest curtains she'd even touched in her life. They'd felt more like cardboard than fabric.

She was supposed to be sleeping. Cass had given that order in his gruff-as-hell voice. And then he'd...

Spread out on the floor.

The floor, not the bed.

She'd told him that she wanted to kill a man. Potentially, two men, and he'd responded by telling her to get her ass to sleep. *She'd* closed the cardboard curtains because she could not sleep with any light streaming at her, and he'd hunkered down on the floor. The *floor*.

The bed was bad, but the floor had to be a million times

Cynthia Eden

worse. "There's room up here," she mumbled into the silence that had stretched and stretched.

He didn't speak.

She rolled onto her side. Inch-wormed her way to the edge of the bed so she could try peering down at him. "Did you hear me?"

Nothing.

She reached out her hand and poked at him. Her poking finger touched what felt like his shoulder. "There is room up here with me. You can sleep in the bed." She waited a beat. "With me." *Duh, Agnes. It's obvious you meant he could sleep in the bed with you.*

But he didn't respond.

She poked him again. "Cass?"

A long sigh.

Her lashes fluttered. "Were you sleeping?" No way. Not on the floor. Not so quickly. Not when the adrenaline from the night's events had to be quaking through his veins. It was certainly quaking through her veins. She tipped a little closer to the edge of the bed.

He was on the floor, between her and the door. The bed was shoved up against the wall with the window.

"If I was sleeping," came his rasping response, "then I am certainly not sleeping any longer, am I? Because you keep *poking* at me. Literally, poking me."

Yes, guilty. "I'm not a murderer."

"No?"

"*No.*"

"You mean you don't just want me to help you kill for shits and giggles?"

Ah, there it was. She'd seen the anger flash in his eyes when she'd made her little confession earlier. That had been right before he told her to get her ass in bed and sleep.

114

"You fucked me because you wanted me to do your dirty work for you." Anger definitely burned in every single word from Cass. Maybe not just anger. Maybe he was skating toward rage. "I don't like being used, Agnes."

"Pretty sure most people don't like being used. Not like it's one of my favorite things." She sucked in a breath. "I fucked you because I wanted you."

"Liar." Almost a caress. If angry accusations of lying could be considered a caress. Oddly enough, from him, that was exactly what the single word had sounded like. *A tender caress. An endearment, an—*

Agnes shut off the thought. "You think I faked my response to you? Granted, I do have some fair acting talent, I thought that was on display during my dramatic performance at The Bottomless Pit. But I did not fake being turned on with you. And I certainly didn't fake all of those orgasms." Now she was getting angry, too. "I hadn't been with anyone since Max died. You are the first person who made me *yearn.* Who made me want to let go and be with a lover again. So don't think I faked anything. After years of not feeling anything at all, my body basically erupted for you. No faking involved. Just feeling so much that I couldn't control myself." She snatched back her poking finger. The better to grip the side of the bed.

"Who. The fuck. Is. Max?"

She blinked in the darkness. "He was my boyfriend. He, um, we were high school sweethearts." His image flashed in her mind. His curly hair. The dimples that appeared when he smiled, and Max had always been smiling. Everyone had loved him. He'd been so kind and easy going. He'd made the world a better place by being in it and then...

Then he hadn't been in it. He'd been gone. She'd been in the hospital bed, crying for him.

"We went to college together," she continued. She'd moved her body so that she clung to the edge of the bed. She was about to practically fall on Cass. *Why am I trying to get so close to him?* Her fingers dug into the mattress. "Austin, Texas," she whispered. "That's where we were from. That's where we planned to raise our future family one day." They'd had so many dreams. "And that's where, one summer night, when we were coming home late from a party..." *Right after Max proposed and slid a ring on my finger.* "It was where we were attacked. The man on the motorcycle circled around us. Over and over again. Riding a big, black bike. The engine howling and growling. A black helmet and visor covered his head and face. He jumped off the bike and came slashing at us with his knife."

"Fuck."

Yes, yes, fuck.

"That's why you have those scars on your stomach," Cass said. His voice was thick and hard.

She swallowed. "That's why I have those scars on my stomach." It could have been worse for her. It should have been. "He came at *me*." Agnes would never, ever forget that terrible moment. "He was slicing directly at me. Saying he was going to cut up the pretty girl." *I will always remember his voice.* Just as she would always remember the tattoo that she'd seen peeking at her on his wrist. That lone streetlight had hit it—and him—just right. "Max jumped in front of me. He fought with the attacker but..." *Run, Agnes. Run!* Her eyes squeezed shut. "There was a lot of blood. Max went down. I couldn't get away. The attacker was driving the knife into me, over and over, and Max was on the ground beside me. I thought we were both going to die right then and there."

Silence.

Her eyes opened. But she still didn't see anything but the darkness.

The silence stretched. Slowly, she became aware of faint sounds, from *outside* the room. The distant honk of a car. The occasional sharp cry of a bird. The growl of an engine, one that was quickly cut off.

"I woke up in the hospital. Some Good Samaritan had found Max and me in the street, where the attacker had left us."

She heard a squeak and rattle beyond the motel room door. Maybe...maybe a cleaning cart outside. Already?

The squeak stopped.

"I woke up," she said, picking up the story and trying to ignore the pain that pierced through her with the memories. "But Max never did. He died protecting me. And ever since then—"

"All you've wanted to do is get revenge. To send the bastard who hurt him and you to hell."

Yes, that summed things up nicely. "Glad you understand."

"Aren't Feds supposed to put bad guys in jail?"

They were.

"But you didn't ask me to help you lock him away. You said you wanted to kill him."

She blinked quickly because tears had filled her eyes. *You weren't there that night. You didn't hear me screaming and begging him to stop. You didn't hear him laughing. You didn't see him kick Max as he was bleeding out and then reach down and deliberately slit Max's throat even as I reached out to the man I loved...*

Right before the bastard came at me again.

"You don't want him locked up. You want him dead."

She wanted him in the ground. Him and his

accomplice. *Because I remember the bastard making a call. As he walked away, he'd flipped up his visor. I'd seen his hand lift. He'd had a phone and he said... "I got a redhead. She's bleeding out behind me."*

"You want him to die, don't you, Agnes? You don't want to catch him and put him in prison."

She waited a beat, then replied, "You sound awful judgey for someone who told me that you were a bad guy, like, ten minutes ago. I don't think bad guys should be so judgey."

"It was fifteen minutes ago. You've been tossing and turning and sighing loudly in that bed for fifteen minutes."

Okay. "So you...weren't asleep when I poked you."

"You want me to kill for you." Rough. Flat. "Fine. Done. Tell me the bastard's name, and I'll have him dead before sunset. I figure fucking you is worth killing a man or two."

"Lots and lots to unpack there." Her heart raced in her chest. Her nervous fingers plucked at the bedding. "Let's start at the end. The *last* thing you said—"

"We need *sleep*, Agnes. We have a lot of work to do. A lot of traveling ahead of us. A whole lot of enemies behind us because people are gonna be pissed that I hooked up with a Fed."

"But...I chose you." Very publicly and with lots of fanfare. "Won't they back off now?"

"No, I'll be tested. I have to be ready."

Sounded to her like *they* had to be ready. She caught the rattle of what she believed was the cleaning cart once more. Then the rattling stopped. Maybe at the room next to them, on the right? She vaguely remembered Cass slapping the "Do Not Disturb" sign on the paint-chipped door to their room before he'd slammed it shut. "I do really appreciate you saying that fucking me was, ah, worth killing for. You were fantastic, too, by the way. Definitely exceeded any and all expectations."

He growled.

She tensed.

"You're doing that defensive thing," he muttered.

Guilty as charged. She had been doing that defensive thing again. "I don't want you to kill for me."

"You said—"

"I'll do the killing on my own, thanks very much." Not like she wanted someone else doing the dirty work for her. She didn't mind getting her hands dirty. Or bloody. Besides, this was personal. Agnes sniffed. "I know how to kill, after all. Got trained at Quantico. This may shock you to the soles of those big, black boots that you like to wear, but I can handle myself pretty damn well."

"Then what the hell do you want me to do?"

Thanks for asking. "I want you to get me close to him." Killing close.

"Give me a name—"

"I don't have a name. If I did, if I knew who he was, I would have killed him long ago." That had been a big life goal for her. It had been the goal since, well, she'd been standing at the cemetery, and the rain had started to fall, and her brother Ryan had lifted her in his arms and carried her away. "I never saw his face. If I had, I would have drawn him out perfectly. I would have given his photo to the cops. I would have plastered it all over the internet. I would have hired every PI in the world to help me hunt him down so that I could slowly and painfully kill him." *The way he slowly and painfully killed Max. The way he tried to slowly and painfully kill me.* He'd left her to bleed out, confident that she'd die before help arrived.

She hadn't died.

"You never saw his face."

"Hard to see a face when the perp is wearing a motorcycle helmet and he has the visor down." As she'd told the initial cops, over and over, when they'd come to the hospital to interview her. All these years later, and the crime that had shattered her world was unsolved. "He wore black gloves. A battered jacket. Jeans. Black boots. The only part of him that wasn't covered was his wrist. When he lifted the knife up high..." *You're gonna die, pretty girl. You're my ticket in. Had to bag a redhead.*

No, no, she didn't like thinking of that night. Of remembering how he'd been so proud to target her. He'd followed her from the club, she'd pieced that together later. He'd seen her and stalked her and stabbed her because she happened to have red hair. "When he lifted up the knife, I saw part of the tattoo on his wrist. It was very unmistakable. Two cobra heads, sliding down toward one snake body."

"*Fuck.*"

That was...recognition.

"The killer was part of the Twin Cobras," she said.

"No."

"Yes," she threw right back. "I know what I saw."

"The Twins are fucking boogeymen used to scare the world."

"They are monsters without conscience. They hunt and they prey on those weaker than they are. They live in the shadows. A very, very select few individuals because initiation into their freak club is so rare." She ticked off the things she'd painstakingly learned about them. "The members are in other motorcycle clubs. That's how they are selected. Because they stand out in those other clubs as being the most powerful. Being the strongest. The baddest."

He didn't say a word.

So she kept going. "They all sport the twin cobras tat somewhere on their bodies. If you see that tat, then you are looking straight at the worst kind of killer." The kind of killer who'd ruined her life. "They are protected, and they are insulated. To find them, to hunt them, you'd need a way to get into the most powerful MCs in the nation."

"Sonofabitch. That's why you're using me. You want me to kill the boogeyman for you."

No, not exactly. He was not listening to her. "I'll kill him." With extreme pleasure. "I just need you to help me find him. You are my way in. If I'm at your side, then I can search. I can ask questions of the MCs. I can—"

"Get us *both* killed? Because a nosy Fed will damn well get hell raining down on us both—"

The motel room door flew inward. A blasting, shattering sound because someone had just *kicked* in the door, and the flimsy lock went flying even as the door banged into the nearby wall.

She fell out of the bed. *Leaped* out, actually, and landed on top of Cass as she covered him with her body. Gunshots rang out. *One, two, three.*

Bang.

Bang.

Bang.

Three fast hits that were all directed straight at the bed. Exactly where she'd been. Her hand flew up. The hand that now held her own gun. When she'd *leapt* from the bed, she'd grabbed the gun that she'd placed on the nightstand before settling in.

The shooter had now realized that she wasn't in the bed. *Missed your target, asshole.* He was jerking his gun down, toward her, adjusting his aim.

"Stop!" Agnes yelled.

Nope, he was not stopping. He surged forward and—

With zero hesitation, Agnes fired her gun.

She fired...even as Cass grabbed her hips and tried to spin her beneath him.

Her bullet slammed into the target. *The intruder's chest*.

Cass's fingers wrapped around her gun.

The man in the doorway tried to shoot again.

She and Cass fired once more. Together.

The bastard fell, slamming backwards and hitting the cement right outside of the motel room doorway.

Her breath heaved out. She stared at the door.

Cass lifted her up, then off him. She scrambled for the door.

Cass's hands wrapped around her waist again and he picked her up. Way up so that her feet just sort of cycled in the air, and she didn't go anywhere.

"Stay *the fuck* behind me," Cass snarled.

"Let me *the fuck* go."

He let her go, but only after he'd put her behind him. He went to the open doorway.

Someone was screaming from somewhere close by.

Cass had his own gun out. She wondered where he'd been hiding that thing. He'd yanked off his t-shirt and ditched his boots before bunking down on the floor. So he headed toward the perp wearing just his jeans with his back toward her. And she—

She flipped on the lamp near the bed. Then she stopped dead.

Absolutely dead in her tracks.

Because...she'd made love with Cass all night long at his place. *Not made love. Fucked. You fucked him all night long*.

She'd...she'd seen so much of him. Touched so much. And the lights had been on but...

122

But she hadn't seen his back.

The lights had been *off* the only time she'd kissed his back. The only time she'd...

Tattoos were on his back. A skull with fangs. A grim reaper. And...

A two-headed, snarling cobra.

Oh, my God.

The screaming outside abruptly stopped. Footsteps clattered. Wheels squeaked away.

"The maid is probably gonna call the cops," Cass said as he knelt beside the attacker. He put his hand to the guy's throat. "Still breathing." A muscle flexed along his jaw. "Maybe not for long, though."

"You're one of them."

Cass kicked the gun away from the fallen man.

Her breath shuddered in and out. She grabbed for the phone on the nightstand. She dialed nine-one-one. "Help," Agnes said as soon as the operator picked up. "There has been a shooting at the Grove Motel on—"

Cass snatched the phone from her fingers and slammed it back onto the cradle. "What in the hell are you doing?"

Damn. He'd moved fast. As far as what she'd been doing... "Calling for help. You said he was still alive." She still gripped the gun in her right hand.

Cass sucked in a deep breath. "You aren't a Fed any longer, remember?"

"I just *shot* an intruder who tried to shoot me, I—"

"You'd better get her the hell out of here."

Her gaze flew to the open doorway.

Javion Booker stood there, hands on the wooden frame, a twisted glower on his face. *Javion Booker, Cass's right-hand.* Agnes knew he had been a member of the Night Strikers since—

"Can't a man even get half an hour's worth of damn sleep," Javion grumbled, "without some prick getting his ass shot? Without gunfire waking everyone up?"

When had Javion arrived at the motel?

Javion's dark eyes locked on her. "She shouldn't be here when the cops arrive," Javion warned. "None of us should be."

"Tell me shit I don't know," Cass groused.

She looked back at the man sprawled on the cement. She lunged for him.

Cass locked an arm around her waist and hauled her back against him. "What are you doing?" His breath blew lightly against the shell of her ear. *Trying to help the man who just attempted to murder you in your sleep?*

Her gaze whipped back toward the bed. She could see the bullet hole in the pillow. Where her head had been. And the two holes in the sheets and mattress. Where her body had been.

"Good thing your ass fell out of bed," Cass added.

Her mouth dropped open. "I didn't fall! I leapt out! To save you! To cover *you!*" How dare he suggest that she'd fallen? She hadn't *accidentally* been protecting him.

He grunted and tightened his hold on her. "Good thing you fell."

The jerk—

"We're getting out of here. Now."

"Great plan," Javion praised. He crouched next to the man in the doorway. "Oh, yeah, he's dead."

What? "Cass said he was still alive! That he was breathing!"

Javion frowned. "That's a hole in his heart."

She jerked against Cass's hold. "Were you lying to me? Is he already dead?"

124

When he didn't respond, Agnes elbowed Cass and tore from his grip. In two seconds, she was on her knees next to the fallen man. She searched for a pulse. Didn't find one, dammit. Her hands flew over him. "We can help him." Absolutely, one hundred percent. Maybe? Potentially?

He wore a motorcycle helmet with the visor still down. Like that didn't play right into her nightmares. She grabbed the helmet and lifted it off his face.

Teardrop tattoos marked his cheeks. Two on the left. One on the right. A series of skulls and spiderwebs covered his neck. She grabbed his sleeves and shoved up the right one.

Two-headed cobra. Not the one from her nightmares, though. This was too high on his forearm. The heads were right at his elbow. And the heads were smaller than they'd been on the man who'd killed Max and used his knife on her.

Her breath choked out.

A siren wailed in the distance.

Her fingers went toward the shooter's chest. She could stop the blood flow. Get answers. She could—

She was yanked up before her fingers touched the bloody mess that her two bullets had made when they tore into him.

"*Hell, no, princess.* He's dead. You're not bringing him back."

She struggled, but Cass's hold was unbreakable.

"And he's a good message to leave for our enemies," Cass added.

Her struggles ceased. That was a brutal thing to say. She whirled in his grip.

He'd put on a t-shirt. His jacket. Someone had moved super fast.

125

"She needs shoes," Javion pointed out.

She still wore her pants. Her shirt. No shoes. She hadn't stripped before climbing into the sagging bed, but she had at least kicked off her heels.

"Get the shoes or leave without them," Cass ordered.

What?

The siren's shriek grew louder. Actually, it sounded like multiple sirens.

"Fuck it." Cass tossed her over his shoulder and rushed out of the motel room. She kept her grip on the gun because no way was she leaving that behind.

He carried her to his motorcycle. Dropped her on the seat. He glowered at her. "Give me the gun."

"You're one of them." Something he should have mentioned. And maybe...maybe her gun was aimed at him. "You told me they were boogeymen. As if they weren't real. Just made-up monsters. *And you have one of their tattoos on your back.*"

"I have a lot of tattoos. On my back. On my arms. All over."

Yes, he did have lots of tats. Only one both terrified and infuriated her. The two-headed cobra. "*Are you one of them?*"

The two heads...two allegiances. An allegiance to his main MC, the Night Strikers. And a secondary allegiance to the Twins.

The sirens were louder. Closer.

Javion ran past them and jumped on his motorcycle.

Cass stepped closer to her. Her gun pressed into his chest. "Either pull the trigger or scoot the hell back and let me get us out of here."

She didn't pull the trigger. She also didn't drop the gun. "How did that shooter know which room we were in?"

"He must've followed us."

She'd searched when they'd been driving on that motorcycle. Agnes had not spotted a single tail. "Why weren't you in the bed with me?"

His eyes narrowed.

"He only shot at the bed." A whisper. "I was in the bed. Not you. You were on the floor." She wet her lips and kept the gun pressed to his chest. "Why weren't you in the bed?"

He leaned in toward her. Completely ignored the gun pressing into his chest. "Because I was trying to be a gentleman and not *fuck you* into oblivion."

She snorted.

He snatched the gun from her.

"I let you take that," she said. Because, for the record, she thought it was important for Cass to know and deeply understand that important fact. If she'd wanted to keep her gun, she would have kept it.

He shoved the gun into a saddle bag. "Scoot the hell back."

She scooted back because they did need to get the heck out of there. "I need my purse," she said, sniffing. One did not leave a bag at a crime scene. "And my shoes would be really helpful."

Cursing, he bolted away. Cass returned in seconds with her shoes and her bag. She shoved on the shoes while he pushed her purse in a saddlebag. Then he slid in front of her.

"I don't trust you," she said, voice tight.

"Good," he told her. He plunked a helmet on her head.

No, it wasn't good. They needed to trust each other.

"I will never hurt you," he vowed. "Now hold on tight."

And the motorcycle flew out of the lot. She glanced back, toward their room.

The mystery shooter was still sprawled in the doorway. *So much blood.*

The story of her life.

And, even though she didn't trust him, Agnes held tight to the man in front of her. The lover who'd fucked her. The MC leader who bore the tats that marked him as being part of the mythical *boogeymen.* The worst of the worst...

But, no. I won't believe that. I can't. She'd profiled Cass. She'd fucked him. Her life was on the line with him.

If she was wrong...

Then she was dead.

Chapter Eleven

HE BRAKED THE BIKE. "AGNES."

She snuggled against him. All softness. Sweetness.

She'd killed a man hours before. Technically, his hand had been on the gun, too. So...*we killed a man hours before.* A bastard who'd broken into their motel room and tried to kill *her.*

"Agnes, you're falling asleep while *you're riding a motorcycle.*" Something that should not have been possible. He twisted toward her. Caught her shoulders and gave her a light shake.

She gasped.

He'd felt her slump against him moments before and been absolutely terrified. His hand had flown back as he held her in place long enough to stop the motorcycle.

It's been twenty-four hours since she appeared at The Bottomless Pit for the big, dramatic scene. No wonder she's collapsing on me.

But her body had stiffened now. She was awake again. Good. "We'll get you some coffee," he promised because he remembered how much the woman loved coffee. "But we can't stop yet. We've got at least an hour to go."

The helmet strap remained tight beneath her chin. "Where are we?" Slightly sleep slurred.

"Texas." A long, lonely stretch of straight road in East Texas. They'd be stopping soon, though, because he was as dead tired as she was. "Stay awake for me a little longer, understand?"

"I'm good."

"Are you?"

"You shoot one man who is trying to kill you...and suddenly the MC leader is questioning your life choices."

No, dammit, that hadn't been what he meant when he'd asked if she was *good*. "Agnes..."

"I'll stay awake. Promise. And it's not like I fell asleep. I was...just resting my eyes."

"Bullshit."

"I'm good," she repeated, stubbornness entering her voice.

He turned back to the front. Gripped the handlebars. A moment later, they were hurtling through the night.

* * *

GRAY DIDN'T ALWAYS GO into the field. Okay, fine, the truth was that his bosses didn't want him in the field. They kept promoting his ass through the ranks, and at this rate, all they wanted him to do was sit in the office, make profiles, and be a pompous dick who ordered other agents around.

He did have the pompous dick part down to an art, but...

Every now and then, he definitely liked walking back into the field.

Night had fallen. He'd hopped on a quick flight, then rented a car to get to his current destination. A crime scene at a no-tell motel. The local sheriff had been stunned that the Feds had any interest in the random motel shooting in the middle of nowhere, Mississippi.

But Gray knew it wasn't random. And he had to clean up after people some days. Such was life. And death.

He paused a moment outside room four at the Grove Motel. Gray surveyed the scene, then he cut through the crime scene tape on the broken door.

"I think someone died in there." A quiet voice to his left.

He turned. Saw the kid. Maybe seven or eight years old.

Hell. He had a soft spot for kids. Especially kids with big, scared eyes. Kids who were huddled in rundown motels.

Because I was one of those kids a long time ago.

"Nah, no one died in there," he assured the kid. Not like he wanted to give her nightmares.

Her breath expelled in a relieved rush.

Someone died in the exact spot I'm standing in. Right here. Not in the room. He could see the blood drops. Automatically, though, he directed his flashlight away from those blood drops. Not like he wanted the kid getting terrified.

"Naomi!" A woman's sharp cry.

Ah, that would be the mother.

She rushed out of a room about five doors down. She saw her kid talking to a strange man and immediately freaked the hell out.

Good for her.

"Naomi!" The mom broke into a run. She grabbed Naomi by the shoulders and yanked her back. "What have I told you about *never talking to strangers?"*

Cynthia Eden

"He has a gun, Mom," Naomi said.

"Oh, God." Naomi's mom shoved her daughter behind her back.

"I'm an FBI agent, ma'am." Gray flashed his ID. Even illuminated it with his flashlight. All while still making sure that he did not shine that light on the bloodstains beneath him. He was a master multitasker that way.

Despite seeing the badge, the mom still scuttled back with her daughter.

"Your daughter is safe with me," Gray assured her. His head angled to the side. "Your mom is right, Naomi. Don't talk to strangers. Especially not at night. In front of strange motel rooms."

The mom bolted with the kid.

Her door slammed seconds later. Gray was fairly certain furniture would be pulled in front of that door for extra security. Good choice.

"You just scared that woman to death."

His head turned to the left. To the heavy shadows that waited.

Malik Jones walked out.

"I gave her and the kid some pro tips. I think they'll both appreciate me later."

Malik grunted.

The guy was just not particularly chatty.

Gray crossed the threshold of room four.

Malik lingered near the doorway. "That's a lot of blood," he noted.

Yes, it was. "He was shot in the heart. Bled out fast."

"Guess the Night Striker doesn't play."

Uh, right. The Night Striker. Gray had received a text from Cass. One saying that Cass had taken out the attacker who'd...

He fired first. Three times. No choice.

Then...

I left a dead body for you. Cass had given the location of Findaway, Mississippi, and Cass had known that he had to do cleanup.

Except...

He turned on the lights inside the motel room. "Come inside and shut the door," Gray ordered him. Not like he wanted Naomi to come in and get an up-close look at his investigation.

The door closed softly.

Gray whistled. When he'd spoken with the local sheriff earlier that day, Gray had ordered the guy to leave room four exactly as is. Sure, the body could be bagged and tagged, but Gray had wanted his own eyes on the scene. He even had his hand-picked evidence team at the ready. They were currently waiting in a van outside.

He ambled toward the bed.

One shot in the pillowcase.

Two shots in the mattress. Technically, the shots had gone *through* the sheets. He picked them up with a gloved hand. Yep, those two bullets had gone through the sheets and into the mattress.

But...

There was another pillow on the floor. A pillow and a worn, gray blanket. The blanket was stretched out, as if...*as if someone had been sleeping on top of it. On the floor?*

"Guess the perp thought he was going to catch them unaware."

Ah, that was a whole sentence from Malik. Impressive. "It would seem so." What bothered him, though, was the fact that the perp had found Cass and Agnes so quickly.

Did someone sell you out, Cass? Cass had been playing a

dangerous game for years. And Gray had warned him, time and again, that he needed to get out.

But Cass had told him it was too late. The only way out was in a body bag.

Well, someone had been taken from that motel in a body bag. Only it hadn't been Cass.

He let the sheet drop. Gray studied the scene once more.

The pillow on the floor didn't fall there. It's positioned deliberately. So is the blanket.

His stare shifted toward the main door.

The wood was broken. The lock shattered. The perp had kicked it in, going for the element of surprise. He'd kicked open the door and immediately aimed for the bed.

Cass had been on the floor, Gray was sure of it. No way would Cass have let Agnes hunker down on the floor while he took the bed.

But...

She hadn't been hit.

She did the firing.

A good FBI agent would have kept her gun close.

He glanced at the nightstand. She'd probably had it positioned right there.

So, the door had flown open, but Agnes...she hadn't been asleep. She'd leapt off the bed. Maybe even tried to protect Cass because that was what an FBI agent would do. Only the prick in the doorway would not have run after he fired his three rounds. He would have realized he'd missed his target. He would have been preparing to fire again...

Agnes shot him.

Gray was pretty damn sure that when an ME examined the dead body, they'd find a bullet—maybe two—lodged in him that matched up to the weapon assigned to Agnes.

Gray nodded. Of course, Cass could always say that he'd used her weapon to fire but...

You lied to me, Cass. Agnes is the one who took the shot.

He turned around, studied the room yet again. He always liked to make sure he'd considered every possible element in a crime scene.

The silence stretched and stretched.

"What's the plan?" Malik finally asked.

He was still working on his plan. But he did think he understood what had gone down in that room. "A gun was recovered near the fallen man. The friendly sheriff told me that three shots had been fired from that weapon." Three shots that had not found their mark. "Clearly, this is a case of self-defense." His gaze slid to Malik. "You see anything here that makes you doubt that assessment?"

Malik's jaw hardened.

Gray sighed. "Spit it out, Agent Jones."

"I see plenty that makes me think Agnes is a sitting duck. No one is gonna buy that BS scene at The Bottomless Pit."

Ah, he disagreed. Some would buy it. Some wouldn't. Some wouldn't give a shit either way. They would just want her dead. Her and Cass.

Malik took a surging step toward him. "Agnes is alone. She's defenseless. She has no backup. This case is too risky."

Four sentences. Nice. But Malik was wrong. "She has backup."

"Who? The Night Striker?"

"He will protect her." Gray was certain of that fact.

"Will he? Or will he abandon her in an instant to protect himself?"

Clearly, Malik was not a Cass super fan. He got it. "We don't need to be worried about Cass at the moment."

"Uh, yes, yes, I believe we do."

That was because Malik did not fully understand the situation. Or Agnes. "Shit is gonna hit the fan." Because he couldn't really hide a dead body. He could...quiet things, but only for a time. Especially when the ballistics report came back and linked the shooting to her gun.

And certain people—well, they noticed when Agnes wasn't around. People who had been a pain in his ass for a very long time. Ever since he'd agreed to take Agnes onto his team. In spite of their very, very strong protests against the decision.

Those people. Those two individuals were going to be hugely problematic. The question would just be...could he keep things quiet long enough for Cass to complete his mission? Or would this whole thing explode in his face?

The door creaked open.

Immediately, he whirled for it. So did Malik.

From the corner of his eye, Gray saw that Malik had pulled out his gun.

Gray hadn't though because...

What if it was the kid?

Shit. Ever since he'd learned that he was gonna be a father, he'd gotten into uber protective mode where kids were concerned. Something that could be dangerous because the person who'd just opened the broken door was *not* a curious Naomi...

It was a man. Heavy jacket. Shaggy hair. Pissed expression.

Dammit to hell. Talk about someone who'd gotten to the scene fast.

The unwelcome guest filled the doorway. "Where the fuck," he began, voice a dangerous rumble, "is my sister?"

Gray motioned for Malik to stand down. Not like they

needed to have bullets flying unnecessarily. Then he causally positioned himself between Malik and the guy in the doorway. "Your sister?" He scratched his chin. "I'm afraid you are gonna have to be way more specific. I have no clue who you are—"

The man surged toward him. Stopped when they were toe to toe. "Where the fuck," he said again, "is Agnes?"

"Oh, right. Her. Agnes. Your sister."

The unwelcome guest glared.

"Hey, Malik? Do me a favor, would you?" Not really a favor. This was an order. "Tell the evidence team in the van to give me five minutes, and then they can come inside."

Malik stalked out. He closed the broken door behind him.

"You can call, you know," Gray told the man in front of him. "Or text. No need in you rushing out and appearing in person." *How in the hell had he even known to come here?*

"I was told she'd left the FBI. Left you. *Taken up with some asshole MC leader.*"

"Um. And does that surprise you? Does it surprise anyone?"

The man's hands fisted. "You were supposed to watch out for her."

He damn well had been. He'd watched her. Protected her. Freaking interfered in her investigation with the Twins at times in order to protect her. He'd done everything this jackass wanted. "Agnes is a very determined individual."

"And I'm determined to keep her safe. She will never be broken again."

Gray pitied the fool who tried to break her. "She's so much stronger than you understand. She wants justice, and she will not stop." They were alone. Gray could speak freely. So he did. "I think your sister is going after her end

Cynthia Eden

goal. And if we are not careful, if *she* is not careful, Agnes may just tear down the whole world as she gets her vengeance."

The man's eyes—a dark, angry brown—narrowed. "Do you think…" A shake of his head. Not red hair. Black. "That I give a shit about the rest of the world?"

Gray sighed. "Unfortunately, I figured that would be your response." His phone rang. A loud, shrill, and demanding cry. "Hold the thought for one moment, would you?" He put the phone to his ear, but only because the number came from a VIP at the Bureau. "Not the best time…" Gray curtly informed the caller.

"Thought you might like to know that Judas Long is dead. He was just found with sheets wrapped around his neck and hanging from his cell bars."

Shit. "Thanks for the update. Talk real soon." *Fuck.* He shoved the phone back into his pocket. "Your sister is safe," he said.

But the bastard near him shook his head. "Gray, you know I can tell when you lie to me."

Dammit. This prick was one of the select few that knew him that well. Gray prided himself on having very minimal tells. "Okay, how about this…" He exhaled on a long, hard breath. "She's in extreme danger, but she's with a man who would commit murder in a heartbeat if it meant *keeping* her alive. So, is that better?"

A fierce glare and then, "Yeah, that is a bit better."

Well, fan-damn-tastic.

"Now give me his name," Agnes's brother Ryan demanded, "and tell me exactly where to find him."

"Yeah, that's not gonna happen. See, Agnes is undercover. And as far as where she is…I don't exactly know." He sorta knew. "She'll come back home alive, though."

Ryan moved to stand toe to toe with him. "If she doesn't…" The former Marine turned assassin didn't even blink as he said, "I will burn down the FBI around you."

Gray smiled at him. "I love our talks, Ryan. They always make me feel so *warm* on the inside."

"I want to see my sister."

"Good luck with that."

Ryan's eyes narrowed. "Why did I see blood stains outside this room?"

"Um…" He scratched his chin. "Possibly because your sister killed a man."

"Sonofabitch."

"Indeed." *And if you think that's bad, wait until Agnes discovers that the man she's with is one of the Twin Cobras.* Shit. Gray wasn't really sure how she'd missed seeing Cass's tattoo—not if the two of them really had been, uh, fucking all night long. But maybe her eyes had been on other places.

When she did find out the truth, though…

Oh, man, but Cass would be in for a world of trouble.

Agnes had never taken betrayal very well. *And that is why she is going to be so pissed at me, too…*

Chapter Twelve

SHE WASN'T ALONE.

Agnes knew this incredibly important fact even before her eyes opened. She *felt* the big, warm hand that was pressed to her stomach just as she became aware of the soft mattress beneath her body. A mattress—a bed? She was in bed with someone?

What. The. Hell?

Slowly, her eyes opened. Her head turned. *Cassius.* His head was on the pillow beside hers. His eyes were closed, and his dark lashes looked incredibly, impossibly long and thick. His dark hair was tousled, his muscled chest bare. She didn't know if the rest of him was bare or not since Agnes could not quite remember how she'd wound up in bed with him. When she strained, the last thing she recalled was trying exceptionally hard not to topple off the back of his motorcycle as he thundered down an endless stretch of road.

His eyes opened. "It's not polite to stare at someone while they're sleeping."

Fair enough. But he probably should have realized an

important point about her before this moment. "I'm not particularly polite."

His lips hitched into a faint smile. Damn if it wasn't sexy.

Too much about him was sexy.

And...

Dangerous.

Her gaze slid over his chest. Lots of tattoos there. Swirls that she'd seen before during their wild, hot night together. What she could *not* see...that would be the tats on his back. Like the two-headed cobra.

Her heart drummed faster. "You know what else isn't polite? Hauling a woman into your bed without her permission."

He immediately sat up. The covers fell away. She looked down automatically because—again, not polite—and, dang it, she saw jeans. He was wearing his jeans.

She picked up the thick, black comforter and realized that she was still in her pants and shirt, too. Very wrinkled clothing. And she was probably very, very much in need of a shower.

Her growling stomach reminded her that she needed food, too. Stat, please.

And coffee. Coffee would be a blessing.

"I didn't *haul* you in bed." A low rumble from Cass. "For the record, you hauled me in here."

She sat up, too. "I don't recall that." A prim response.

"You were practically falling off the bike, princess."

That part she did recall.

"I even thought about tying you to me because you were scaring me so badly," he admitted gruffly. "But we made it here. Then I *did* carry you inside."

She wondered exactly where...*here* was. Her gaze

Cynthia Eden

darted around the bedroom. Gleaming, wooden walls. High-end furniture. Expensive curtains near the two windows that she spied. Not some no-tell motel this time. Fancy. Pricey.

"I carried you into the bedroom, but when I turned to leave," Cass continued in that rough and sexy voice of his, "you grabbed my hand. *You* told me to stay. You proceeded to fall dead into bed, and I...I just slept next to you. That's it. End of story."

That was it. Check. No hot sexing that she didn't recall, though, seriously, Agnes didn't think that she could sleep *through* hot sex with Cass. "Where are we?"

"A safe house in Texas."

"A safe house," she repeated. Sure. Yes. "Because MCs have those."

"Yeah, they do." He climbed from the bed. "The MCs have all sorts of interesting things that Feds don't know about." The curtains over the window to the right were parted a bit, and light had drifted into the bedroom. That light allowed her to see the tattoos on his back.

The two-headed snake with its fangs bared.

She lunged for the nightstand. Her frantic fingers yanked open the top drawer because it was second nature for her to store her gun either on a nightstand—like she'd done at the Grove Motel—or in the top nightstand drawer. Since the gun wasn't on top, she figured it must be in a drawer. Exhausted or not, she would have followed her routine. Because that routine was about staying alive. Whether she was at home, in a motel, or—

There was no gun inside the top drawer. Or in the second, bottom drawer, either.

"Looking for this, sunshine?"

Her head whipped toward Cass.

He had her gun in his hand.

Her breath seemed to freeze in her chest.

He blinked, then frowned at her. "Why in the hell are you staring at me like that?"

"Oh, I don't know." *And how am I looking at you? Like I'm scared? Like I think you're my enemy?* She tried to school her features. Normally, Agnes had way better control of her expression. This just was not a normal situation. She also had not had coffee, so...yes, not normal. *He has the cobra tattoo. He has my weapon. Has he been playing me all along?* Agnes swallowed. "Maybe I'm a little...off because you're pointing my gun at me—"

"I'm not *pointing* it at you."

"—and because you're the enemy."

His teeth snapped together. He'd been standing about five feet away from her, but at that one word...*enemy*...he immediately stalked back to the bed. Still holding her gun.

Her chin notched up. Fine. So she didn't have a weapon. She could still fight like hell, so if he thought she'd be an easy target, the man was dead wrong.

"What is it that you think I am going to do to you?" Cass demanded. Then he slapped the gun down on top of the nightstand. "I told you before...*I will never hurt you.*"

Her breath heaved out, but she remained tense. She also decided to jump out of the bed because staying there didn't seem like the best idea. Her hand automatically went for her gun.

He made no move to stop her.

The weight of her weapon was reassuring and...

She frowned. Then checked it. "What in the hell?"

"There aren't any bullets in your gun right now. Figured that it might not be the best plan ever to give you a loaded weapon to point at me while you are still pissed." He sucked the inside of his cheek. "And you're clearly pissed at me."

He had no idea how truly *pissed* she currently felt. "You lied to me."

"Sweetheart, I lie to everyone. You're not special."

And that *hurt*. His brutal words slammed right into her heart. They hurt far, far more than they should have.

She backed up. Bumped into the side of the bed.

A frown pulled at his dark eyebrows. "What is it?" His hand lifted, as if he'd touch her.

She dodged his touch. "I need a shower. I need to brush my teeth." Desperately. "And I need coffee. A boatload of it."

"I..." Cass stopped. Pressed his lips together. "I...upset you."

"Give the man a giant cookie. Yes, yes, you did upset me. Hey, pro tip, don't tell the woman you fucked into near blackout bliss that she is not *special*. Think it, sure, whatever." *Jerk.* "But don't say the actual words. Not cool. Total dick move, in fact." She'd spied an open door that led to what she thought-slash-hoped was the bathroom. Fantastic.

"You're the best fuck I've ever had."

She rolled her eyes at the absolute jerk. "Best fuck, not special, check. A body in the dark. Got it. Look, buddy, you are doing yourself zero favors here with me. You should probably stop while you are already fifty paces behind where you need to be."

"*Agnes.*"

"*Cass.*"

His breath heaved out. "I meant..." Gritted. Snapped. "I spend most of my days lying to people. It's who I am. I am a liar. I am a criminal. I am a thief. I am a killer."

"And you have the tats to prove that, don't you?" As if she didn't know all the tats on his body held different meanings. *I am a killer.* She wasn't rolling her eyes any longer. She was staring dead at him. She still gripped the gun. The gun that didn't have any bullets in it.

His square jaw tightened. "The snake tattoo is what makes you so angry."

Was he *serious?* "I was twenty-one years old," she snapped at him. She wasn't pissed. She was so furious that her whole body practically vibrated. And if she had not been so exhausted when they arrived at this—this safe house, then she would have given him hell sooner. But she was awake now, and it was time for that hell to be given in full force. "A bastard who was part of your Twin Cobras— he *stalked* me and my fiancé—"

"Fiancé?"

"Max had just asked me to marry him. We were going to have a beautiful life." She stopped. Huffed out a breath. The pain was just so strong that she huffed out the breath as she tried to *push* the ache from her body. But it was an ache that never left. "We *had* a beautiful life." A careful correction. "Had one. Our time together was beautiful. It was just way too short. I should have been with him forever. I should have loved him forever."

Cass took a step back. His expression had turned into a granite mask. No emotion showed.

"But I didn't have forever with Max. I lost my forever one dark night when a man with a Twin Cobra tattoo on his wrist thought it was fun to terrorize us. Max jumped in front of me, but Max—he didn't know how to fight. Certainly not how to kill." Max hadn't even been on the football team in high school. He'd been in the band. The drum major. She'd gone to every game and cheered wildly for him, though, as if he'd been the star quarterback. "He didn't know about violence. Killing was not in his nature."

"I know how to kill." Dark. As dark as his expression. As dark as his eyes. "That's my specialty."

She barely heard him. "Max was going to be a doctor. He was going to *save* lives. But that bastard took his life. Just attacked Max so that he could get to me." She pressed her left hand to her stomach. "Seven times. I felt every stab. I was on the ground, and Max was beside me, and that monster just—he slit Max's throat in front of me. I knew Max was dying, and there was nothing I could do, and I *prayed* that I would die, too."

"Agnes."

She had never admitted that stark truth to anyone—that she wanted to die. She'd kept the painful secret. She hadn't told her brothers. Not her shrink. "I didn't die. I woke up in the hospital." Without Max. With stitches in her that had turned into scars that were constant reminders of the worst night of her life. "I woke up, and the thing that kept me going after I buried Max was that I knew that I had a purpose."

Cass waited.

Her purpose... "To find him. To kill him."

Cass's gaze searched her face. "And that's when you became an FBI agent."

A mocking laugh. As if it had been that easy. "Not like you flip a switch and get accepted into the Bureau. I finished my degree first. Started self-defense training. Learned everything I could about criminal psychology, crime scenes, evidence collection...." Agnes released a long exhale as she tried to steady herself. "And then I got my ass in the FBI."

"You got on Gray's team."

A negative shake of her head. "Not right away. That took time. I started at the bottom. I learned and I grew. I worked my way through the ranks. I quickly discovered the world was full of monsters. So many more monsters than everyday people realize." And that was why she'd fought so hard to get on Gray's team. Because he understood monsters. "They are the worst kinds of predators, and someone has to stop them."

"You're that someone."

"I might not look overly intimidating." A twisted smile curved her lips. "But it's better for my enemies to underestimate me that way."

His stare did not waver. "I will never underestimate you again."

"But you are my enemy." Something he had not denied. Why not? *Just deny it. Please.*

He stepped closer to her. Still did not touch her. "I do not want to be your enemy."

"I told you about the tattoo, and, in response, you told me that I was trying to get you to kill the *boogeyman.* Like the Twin Cobras weren't real when you were sporting one of their tattoos on your back!" The betrayal gutted Agnes.

His eyes glittered at her. "We were interrupted during that conversation. I seem to recall a jackass breaking into our motel room and *shooting* at us."

"Shooting at me," she corrected. "I was the one in the bed. You were the one on the floor."

"The prick didn't know that, Agnes. He was shooting at *us.*" Cass's hand rose. His fingers skimmed against her cheek. Rough calluses. Power held in check. "I'll do it."

His touch seemed to burn her skin. "You'll do what?"

"I'll kill the boogeyman for you."

"I don't *need* you to kill him." Was he listening at all?

147

"I'll do it." She would make the kill with no hesitation. "I just need you to help me find the bastard! I never saw his face. He kept his stupid visor on when he was near me. I saw the tat on his wrist. He turned away, when he was sure I was gonna bleed out and die next to Max, and the man made a damn phone call. He flipped up the visor as he walked away, and he was bragging about getting a redhead. He attacked me because of the color of my hair!" Tears filled her eyes. She could feel them, and they made her *angrier*. "Is that the shit that your group does? You go out and attack people like it's some kind of game? What in the hell did you have to do in order to get in that freaking club?" She had the gun between them now. She'd lifted it up, and it pressed to his stomach.

Cass glanced down. "This would be why I took out the bullets."

"I'm not *shooting you!* I'm not the monster!" Or, wait, was she? Sometimes, Agnes wasn't so sure. Sometimes, she didn't know who—or what—she'd become. "You lie to everyone," she breathed. "Why? I don't want lies from you. I want the stark truth. I sided with you. I turned my back on the FBI to be here with you—"

"All for show," he cut through her words to say.

A tear leaked down her cheek. "The hell it is for show. I am here because there will be no going back." Gray had guessed at her intention. He'd warned her that, sometimes, you just couldn't go back. Not when you crossed certain lines. "I'm getting my justice." One way or another.

"I will do it for you." He wiped away the tear.

"You're one of them."

And...

Something broke on his face. In his eyes. "The fuck I am!" Cass rasped. His shoulders heaved. "I'm breaking them the hell apart. They are my last mission. The final takedown. You think it was easy getting inside? You think I was gonna play their games? I don't hurt innocents. Not fucking *ever*. So to get their attention, to get in with the bastards who are fucking *serial killers* playing some kind of game as they zig-zag across the US, hell, yes, I had to do bad things. So I took out bad people. I made my own rules. I tracked the SOBs, and I am within range. I am *eliminating them*."

"Serial killers? No." She shook her head. No, he was mistaken. "They are killers, yes, but not serials—"

"It's not all the Twins. Not all the members, I mean. Don't you see that? It's two. Two at the top of the hierarchy of the Twins. *Two sadistic pricks playing a game. Two killers.*"

Her life—Max's life—had not been a game.

"Two heads. Two monsters." Rage rumbled in his voice. "You have to cut them both off to kill the beast. *A pair of killers.* It was hard to notice the patterns because they are spread across the country. I came across one of the matched kills by accident. Local cops were thinking it was a robbery gone wrong. It was *not*. It was deliberate. a matched set of victims over one thousand miles apart."

The drumming of her heartbeat was far too loud. Betrayal burned viciously inside of her. All the time that she'd been chafing, wanting so desperately to find the monster from her past—had Gray been deliberately misleading her? Why? "How many victims?"

"I don't know." His mouth tightened. "But if I'm right, the game has been going on for a very, very long time so...a lot."

Her breath came faster.

"You said the man who attacked you made a call. He

told his partner who he'd targeted, and...I'm betting his partner then killed a woman who looked just like you. Probably a woman and a man since they took out your fiancé."

Max's blood, pooling toward me.

"They hunt in pairs. That's what they always do. Every six months, from what I have been able to piece together. Only their kills are all over the US. It makes it hard for authorities to figure out what the hell is going on and to connect the attacks. They are everywhere because *they are on their motorcycles.* They go wherever the hell they want. They travel, and they hunt. Always twin kills."

"No." Another shake of her head. "They aren't *serials.*" He was wrong on this. Wasn't he? "We hunt serials at the FBI. Gray—That's Gray's specialty. He would have told me. He would have said something to me if he thought the perp was a *serial killer."* They'd built a profile, but Gray had never said anything about the perp being the rare breed of predator that counted as a serial.

He'd also certainly never mentioned that he thought it was a serial killing pair. Talk about the rarest monsters out there.

Cass just stared at her.

She...she squeezed her eyes shut. "Gray would have told me."

"Not if he is protecting you because you aren't just a Fed...you're a victim."

She didn't want to be a victim. "I don't need protecting." She needed for the perp who'd hurt her to be punished. She needed for the crimes to stop.

"And maybe he wouldn't tell you because..." A soft sigh. "He has a man deep inside. Someone who is working the damn case."

Breathing was too hard. Cass was working the case… that was why he had the tattoo. He was taking down the Twins.

"*He didn't tell me about you, Agnes.* I had no idea why this mess was so freaking personal to him. I just knew—hell, I was working my own agenda. I've been doing it for years. The Twins weren't on my radar, not until I came across that first matched set. Then Gray started asking questions that got me to dig even deeper into them. And once I did that digging, I knew I wasn't gonna let those bastards roam free. Not once they made it on my list."

Goosebumps rose onto her arms. "What list?"

"Aw, sweetness, you really think you're the only one with a kill list? That is so precious." His hand fell away from her cheek. "Go take your shower. I'll find some coffee. Then we have to talk about our agenda items."

Item one on her agenda was getting her boss on the phone and potentially ripping him a new one. Betrayal burned through her. Gray had known, he'd *known* how badly she wanted her justice, and he'd misled her. Lied to her.

She felt another teardrop slide down her cheek. Her eyes remained closed.

"Dammit, stop doing that." His fingers were back on her cheek. Brushing away the tear. Catching it? "I don't like it, and I want you to stop right now. Do you hear me? *Now.*"

Her lashes fluttered as her eyes opened. More teardrops fell down her cheeks. "I'm not a faucet. I don't just turn on and off."

He brushed aside—caught—more of her teardrops. And looked increasingly haggard. Which was odd.

"*I don't like them,*" he growled.

Another leaked out. "I don't care. I just found out my

boss has been keeping secrets from me, *lying* to me. He point-blank told me that no agents get undercover with the Twins. That it doesn't happen. That he's tried to get people in, and they vanish. Or else they're found cut up in little pieces. He even told me this tale about the Twins blowing things up. Obliterating people." Her heart ached. She'd trusted Gray. Completely. "But here you are. You're not in pieces."

"Yeah, and hopefully, I won't be." His thumb brushed under her right eye. "But I'm not an agent undercover. I told you before, *I am not undercover.* What you see is what you get."

"Liar." Almost a caress. "You lie to everyone, remember? I'm not special."

He stepped back. Stopped touching her. "Unfortunately, I think you may fucking be."

"Be still my heart," she huffed.

He swung away. Her gaze immediately fell on his broad back. *The two-headed snake.* Her stomach twisted.

With fast, angry steps, Cass advanced toward a heavy, wooden chest of drawers. He yanked open the top drawer and hauled out a black t-shirt. He wrenched it over his head and covered all the tats on his back. His head turned toward her as he glanced back over his shoulder. "Take as long of a shower as you want. There is a bag of clothes in the bathroom—should be stuff in there to fit you."

She blinked. "You have clothes for me?" Since when? And how?

"I made arrangements for some items to be here waiting when we arrived last night. Something else you don't remember." An exhale. "They were on the porch. I grabbed them when I carried you in. Should be the right sizes."

"Who in the world did you get to buy clothes for me?" And how had he known her sizes? Had Gray told him?

"Clothes, shoes, underwear. Makeup, too. Whatever you need is in there."

"How?"

Now he shifted toward her. "Haven't you heard?" Mocking. "I'm the leader of the Night Strikers. When I snap my fingers..." He snapped his fingers. "Shit gets done."

Uh, huh. "Is that supposed to be reassuring or threatening?" Because it definitely seemed to be a bit of both.

His hand dropped. "I'm not threatening you. I told you before, and I'll say it again, *I will never hurt you.*"

"Because you don't hurt innocents." She put the gun down on the bed. She'd been holding the weapon the entire time. As if it would have done her any good without bullets. *As if I could have shot him.* "I'm not innocent."

"Yeah, I know. But you are mine."

His... No, she was *pretending to be his.*

He'd whirled away once more and was heading for the door. He hauled it open.

"*I'm pretending* to be yours," she clarified. Because it seemed like an important clarification to note.

A brief hesitation. Then, "If that's what you have to tell yourself."

What she had to tell herself?

"You're mine, Agnes, and I always guard what belongs to me."

And on that deep, dark, *possessive* note, he left her. The door shut softly behind him.

Chapter Thirteen

"We have a problem," Gray told him.

Cass glared at the coffee pot. Was he doing this crap right? He'd poured in the water and shoved several scoops of coffee into the thing and now the light was red, and something was hissing.

"Are you listening to me?" Gray demanded.

"The phone is shoved against my ear, and I hear your voice annoying the hell out of me, so, yeah, I'm listening." Black liquid had just begun to slowly drip out. A quick smile curled Cass's lips. "I'll be damned."

"Yeah, we both know that, been aware for years and years, but focus on the *current problem,* could you?"

"I have lots of problems. The newest one would be that Agnes wakes up feeling ragey. Definitely not a morning person. No one warned me about that quirk. I open my eyes, and the woman beside me in bed is about to go in for the kill."

Silence. Then, "Beside you in bed..." A rough expulsion of air. "Don't want to know that shit. Don't want to know because it does not help the current problem. *At all.*"

"You didn't tell me you wanted the Twins taken down because of her. You *never* mentioned the name Agnes Quinn to me." That pissed him off. "Not. Once."

"Uh, and so what if I had mentioned her to you?" Gray seemed genuinely confused. "What good would that have done? You didn't know the woman. Your paths had never crossed until you met not too long ago outside my office."

"Her fucking fiancé was killed right in front of her. She *loved* him." The coffee kept dripping and hissing. He'd put in a few different blends because he wasn't sure what Agnes liked. He'd figured if he added them all, then he was bound to wind up with a taste she might enjoy. "The prick slit her fiancé's throat. She watched him bleed out and she wanted to die right there with him."

"She...wanted to die?"

He didn't take his eyes off that stupid, dripping coffee. How long was this gonna take? "She didn't know we were after a serial team." The Twins. That was his target. *Not the whole MC network. Just the two at the top. The ones who got off on killing and their sick, sadistic game.* Two killers. Two monsters. "She works for you. She profiles with you. But you never once told her this shit? Newsflash, the woman is pissed at you."

"I've been trying to protect Agnes. You do not know what's fully involved here."

"Uh, shocking. Because you keep secrets."

"*So the hell do you.* I told you to get out long ago, but you wanted vengeance, so you burned down the world. You went after what you wanted. I've been trying to protect your ass, trying to keep you out of prison, and I can only control so many fires for so long—hell, especially since you keep setting them every time I turn around!"

"What can I say? I like the way the flames dance."

Cynthia Eden

"*This shit isn't funny.* I never thought you and Agnes would collide this way, all right? Never suspected you two would hook up in a one-night stand or whatever the hell you did. I'm a profiler, but I'm not psychic. I could not predict that twist."

He thought that Gray's profiling skills were often so scary that the guy seemed psychic. "Someone needs to take some deep breaths," Cass advised.

"Someone needs to keep his damn jeans zipped! That's you—but, hell, you are already in bed with her, again, aren't you? That's what that whole waking up beside her bit was about. Do you understand how emotionally tangled you are about to get? Do you get how *fucked* you truly are?"

His shoulders tensed. "Agnes tugged me down in the bed with her." She'd been dead tired. And he'd been too worried that some other crazy intruder might burst inside and shoot at the bed. No way would he *ever* leave the woman alone in a bed again. From here on out, they would always be sharing a bed, and he didn't care if that made actual sense or not. He was doing it.

If I'm with her, the bullet will have to go through me before it hits her. Done.

"She *tugged* you, right. And you outweigh her by, like, one hundred pounds. But she tugged, and you could not resist. Got it. Thanks for explaining."

He hadn't wanted to resist her. "There is no emotional entanglement. Zero. I am not emotionally involved with Agnes. Not in any way, shape, or form."

The floor squeaked behind him. Because, of course, it did. He whipped around.

Surprise, surprise, Agnes stood in the kitchen doorway. Agnes, with her hair wet around her shoulders. Wearing

156

jeans that fit her like a second skin. A blue shirt that made her eyes burn brighter.

No shoes.

No shoes. Because if she'd worn shoes, he would have heard her coming. She had not worn shoes. Sneaky Agnes.

She had heard him say that he was not emotionally involved with her. At all.

Dammit.

"You are such a liar," Gray snapped in his ear.

"A situation has sprung up," Cass said. "I'm gonna need to call you back."

"You *lied* about shooting the man at the Grove Motel. Agnes did that, didn't she? When the ME performs the autopsy, the slugs that he pulls out of the vic will match her gun."

"Not a vic, a perp. You need to understand that important distinction. What you have is a dead perp in a morgue. He broke into our motel room. He fired first. She even ordered him to stop, but he was gonna fire again."

"*She* shot—"

"Doesn't matter if it was her gun. My hand was around it." It had been. True story. Because Gray was often too good at spotting little tells that gave away lies. *My hand curled around hers, and we held that gun together.* "Agnes isn't guilty of anything. Make sure that's how the record shows things."

"You are such an asshole." A ragged sigh from Gray. "Listen to me, *listen...*"

Agnes began to tap one foot. Her hands were on her hips. Red fired in her cheeks. Hmmm. Had it been the "not in any way, shape, or form" part of the conversation that infuriated her the most? Quite possibly. "Got to go," Cass rumbled. "Fun talk. As always."

"It was not fun, and we need to talk *more!* Dammit, before you left town, I didn't get to tell Agnes that you were also hunting for the Twins because I was too busy trying to get all the players in place for the scene at The Bottomless Pit. I didn't have time to break down an investigation that has been years in the making."

"Yep. Understood. But I sure am thinking you should have made time for that chit-chat. Or maybe just *told* her about the investigation long ago. The woman does not appreciate being kept in the dark."

"I promised them I would keep her safe. That meant keeping her out of the investigation. Things are screwed now."

Agnes took two steps forward. Her hands remained on her hips.

"Promised who?" Cass zeroed in on that point. Because that part seemed important. Gray didn't just go around making promises to just anyone.

"You're gonna find out." A desolate sigh. "She's there, isn't she? Because your tone changed. Dude, have you lied to everyone else for so long that you're now lying to yourself, too? No emotional involvement, my ass." Another ragged exhale. "By the way, Judas Long is dead. He was hung in his cell."

"How about that." His gaze remained on Agnes. *No one walks up to her with a knife and plans to take her from this world.* Not on his watch.

"Fuck. Did you order the hit?"

Did Gray seriously think he was just gonna confess? In what universe would he be that dumb? "You are right."

"Cass?"

He added, "Agnes *is* here." *Did you think the prick who tried to stab me in the back and who then went off to kill her would get to keep living?* Nah. He'd been a dead man walking. Though he'd died faster than Cass anticipated. "Her coffee is ready."

"Her coffee—"

"Talk soon." He hung up the phone and tossed it on the counter near the coffee pot.

Her gaze went to the phone. Then to the coffee pot. Then to him. "Guessing that phone is untraceable?"

He rolled one shoulder. There were technically ways to trace just about every device, but as far as safe calls went, yeah, his phone was pretty good.

"That was Gray," she added into the silence.

No point in denying what she obviously knew.

"I will be having a talk with him." A firm nod. "*After* coffee."

He motioned toward the pot.

She grabbed a mug after opening three cabinet doors, and then she reached for the pot. "No emotional involvement, huh?"

She'd definitely heard that part.

"It's not like I was expecting you to fall in love with me." She poured the coffee in the mug. Her fingers were shaking, though, and she poured too much. The hot liquid splashed on her hand, right in the curve between her index finger and her thumb.

Even as Agnes hissed out a breath, he was pulling the coffee—the pot and the cup—from her fingers and then hauling her toward the sink. He yanked on the cold water and slid her much smaller hand beneath that spray, holding her in place as he glared at the faint, red marks that he could already see on her skin.

"What in the world are you doing?" Agnes asked.

"Cooling the burn." Uh, obviously.

She tugged her hand. "Stop!"

He did not stop. He also did not let go. "You're supposed to immediately put the burn beneath cool water. Don't even think of moving for ten minutes." His grip tightened on her. He *hated* that she'd been burned.

"Ten minutes? Where are you getting this number?" She tugged again.

Again, he did not let go.

"Cass...*let me go.*"

Fucking never. His head turned. He looked down at her. Their faces were inches apart. "No." *Not ever, sweetness.*

"It's..." She sucked in a breath. "It's not even a real burn. I barely feel anything at all."

"You were upset."

"I was moving too quickly. Should have slowed down. Again, not a big deal. I've had way worse."

Yes, he knew she had. Far worse than a few, faint red marks on her skin. And that *far worse* pissed him off. Cass did not like the idea of anything or anyone hurting her. He was also afraid that *he'd* hurt her. Even though he'd said that he wouldn't...

I think I hurt her when she heard me talking to Gray.

"You're staring at me," Agnes pointed out.

What the hell else did he want to see? The coffee pot? The fridge? No, he'd much rather keep his gaze on her. *I get lost in her eyes.*

"You're also, um, caressing my hand."

He was. Even as he held her hand under the spray of cool water, he was running his fingers lightly along her palm. "Why did you pick me?" He seriously needed to know. "Was it just because you wanted to fuck me so I'd help you get your vengeance?"

"Don't remember asking for any sort of vengeance help before we commenced fucking." She wet her lips.

He would be kissing those lips. Soon. His head began to dip more toward her.

"I don't remember asking for anything from you when we fucked, either. I wasn't using my body as some sort of bartering tool. That's pretty insulting to suggest, Cass."

"I tend to be an insulting guy."

"And one who freaks out over mild coffee burns."

He had to know. "Why did you fuck me?"

Her breath caught. He didn't think she was going to answer him. Fine, probably hadn't been the most tactful question to ever ask but—

"Because I'd been in cold storage since Max died. You were the first person who ever made the ice around me melt." She tugged again. "Happy now?"

He didn't let her go, and he was not happy. In fact, Cass wasn't sure he could remember the last time that he'd actually been happy. But he did feel something, all right. Desire. Need. Lust. *The first person who ever made the ice around me melt.* "You say shit like that...and you expect me not to fuck you here and now?"

Agnes sucked in a breath. "Didn't know that option was on the table."

"I want you on the table." The kitchen table was about three feet away. He would love to have her on it. Or against the wall. Or on the floor. Anywhere he could get her would be great, thanks.

Her gaze slanted toward the table.

Hell, why not just be honest? What did he have to lose? "I want you spread wide open, my dick deep in you, and I want *you*, coming, moaning my name." Because maybe he'd felt like he was in cold storage, too—*already dead, just going*

161

through the motions of living—until a wild redhead had marched up to him in a bar that she should never have entered. When she'd come to him, she'd changed both of their lives.

Agnes cleared her throat. "I, um, came in here for coffee. I didn't realize that sex on the kitchen table was part of the morning routine."

That visual was about to make him insane. His dick pressed hard to the zipper of his jeans. "Thought maybe I'd try giving you some *truths*. You know, seeing as how all I do is lie...but you're my partner now. We're tied together in this nightmare." They were, for better or worse. "Might as well be married," he muttered.

Her eyes widened. "Did you just propose to me?"

Don't think of that. Don't think of a life with her. A future. Close the door on that image. Lock it away because it will never happen. "That life isn't for me." Another truth. "I fucked you endlessly that night, should have gotten my fill." The water kept running onto her hand. "I didn't. I want to fuck you again and again."

She swallowed.

"But that's dangerous. Wanting you so much, so badly, is dangerous. Gray is always preaching about emotional involvements wrecking his cases. People go undercover. Lines blur. And mistakes happen." He couldn't afford to let anything happen to her. "But I can fuck, and I can keep my emotions separate." A deliberate pause. "Can you?"

"I don't..." She shook her head even as she rose on her tiptoes. "Screw it. Just kiss me."

He did. Because her mouth was right there. Because he'd fantasized about her ever since The Bottomless Pit. Because he hadn't immediately fallen asleep the night before. He'd watched over her. Pulled in her sexy scent.

Yearned for her. Wanted her. He'd been a gentleman all night as they'd been in that bed together, and need had nearly wrecked him.

Then, when he'd woken up, he'd still wanted her. Even as she'd felt betrayed by him.

His mouth pressed to hers. Not a hard, demanding kiss, though that was what he wanted. He wanted to drive his tongue past her lips and taste and take until she belonged to him completely. Until they both forgot about the monsters in the world and the only thing that mattered was the wild need that they felt for each other.

Her left hand—not the hand she'd burned—pressed to his chest as she pulled back. "You taste minty." Husky words.

"So do you." He'd used the toothbrush in the spare bathroom. Had he planned to kiss her? Hell, yes. And he'd taken the damn time to use that toothpaste.

"Kiss me again," she whispered. "Even if it means nothing."

He did. But it meant something. It meant far more than he could ever tell her. Far more than she would ever know. Her lips parted even more for him. His tongue swept inside, and he tasted every bit of her goodness. She pressed closer. Her body so warm and tempting. He could pick her up. He could put her on that table. Strip her.

Pound into her. Send them both careening into an avalanche of body-quaking pleasure.

She moaned, and he swallowed the sound. Drank it up so greedily. He loved the sounds that she made for him. Loved the way she responded. Nothing held back. Passion. Desire at one hundred miles an hour. They touched, and they both ignited.

Fire whipped through his blood. He wanted to touch

and taste and claim every single inch of her. He wanted to *own* her. Brand her. Mark her.

Oh, fuck, I forgot about that...

He stiffened.

And she...

She felt it. Because she immediately pulled back, too. "What's wrong?" Then, her eyes widened. "Why am I even asking? Everything is wrong. I—let me go."

He did. Reluctantly. With his jaw locked tight and her taste still on his tongue.

I want her on the table. Against the wall.

I will have her everywhere, and she will scream for me.

"My hand is fine." She turned off the water he'd left on. "I just...I'm not here to fuck you senseless."

"What a crying shame."

Red stained her cheeks. "I'm here because...*you* are working with Gray. I'm working with Gray. You are going to brief me on everything. You're going to tell me all about your undercover mission. You're not going to fuck me in order to get me off track."

Laughter boomed from him. And maybe that was good. If he was laughing, then he wasn't grabbing her and pulling her back against him.

A faint furrow appeared between her brows. "You have a nice laugh."

He hadn't actually laughed in...*Shit, I can't remember when.*

"I like it." Her head tilted to the left. "But I don't like that you're laughing at me."

His laughter died away. "Sorry, princess." He was. Kinda. "But fucking you to get you off track? Nah. Not my plan. I just fuck you purely for the pleasure of the event."

The red in her cheeks deepened. She grabbed a fresh mug. Reached for the coffee pot again.

He was on her in an instant. "Let me." His fingers curled over hers. Need—surging desire—still pulsed through him.

Her head dipped down as she looked at their fingers. His hand swallowed hers.

"You confuse me," she whispered. "The way I feel when I'm with you confuses me, too. I wish you would just be honest with me."

He was trying. Had she missed the whole *truths* part moments before?

"You're working with Gray. You're not a villain. You are not a monster. Just *tell* me. Tell me everything because I can't walk in the dark with you."

Oh, baby, I'm afraid that is exactly what you are doing... walking in the dark with me. And he wasn't sure he could let her out of the darkness.

"In an undercover mission, you have to trust your partner completely. I need to know the real you." Her head lifted. Those incredible eyes locked on his and tried to steal his sanity away.

"You don't want to know the real me." He reached out. Took the pot of coffee and poured the very, very dark and thick liquid in the mug for her. Only three-fourths full. No way did he want her burned again. Then he stepped back. One step, two.

She turned and put her back to the counter as she faced off against him. She brought the mug of coffee to her lips and lightly blew over the steaming liquid. "Try me."

Okay. Fine. "I'm not an undercover Fed. You were right before, though, about the other shit I've done. I've been a criminal since I was a teen. Started in gangs. Underground fighting." A roll of one shoulder. "Definitely did your profiling due diligence on that one. I loved the hell out of fighting. Also realized it was one helluva way to make some cash."

"That's why you were so good at The Bottomless Pit. You've had plenty of fighting experience." She blew on the coffee again.

She had beautiful lips. *I love it when she blows me.* Yeah, fuck, he had problems. Mainly, the lust he felt for her was getting in his way. By getting in his way—*obsessing me. Consuming me.* "I had goals in mind, every step of the way. Gray tried to stop me. Hell, he wanted me to join the Marines like he did back in the day. Wanted me to get the hell out of the world he could see sucking me under." His lips twisted. "Semper Fi," he murmured. "That's Gray. Through and through."

"Always faithful," she whispered as she cradled her coffee.

Yeah, that motto described Gray perfectly. Even when he should have turned his back on Cass, he hadn't.

"That's not you?" she asked. "That's not who you are?"

Hell, no.

She began to lift the coffee to her lips.

"I'm resolute." He was. "Determined." Those were nice ways of describing him. The not-so-nice ways? "Bloodthirsty. Relentless. You were actually right before, when you were telling me how you'd profiled me. That I was an eye-for-an-eye type. I am." She had to understand all of him. "You take from me, then I take from you, only I take *everything.* I entered this madness with my eyes wide open. I knew the risk. I knew the danger. I knew I'd lose every bit of my soul. But I had to do it. There were goals I needed to reach."

"What were those goals?" Her head angled closer to the mug.

Tell her. You can't hold back. Tell her.

"Cass?"

"My goals." He rolled back his shoulder. "Killing my uncle." Flat. "And killing my father. I'm happy to say that both goals have been achieved."

Agnes spat out the coffee that she'd just put in her mouth.

Right. Yeah, he'd figured that might be her response.

"You're staring straight at a monster, sweetheart." He sent her a cold smile. "You fucked one, too."

Chapter Fourteen

"Oh, and by the way," Cass said in that deep and rumbling voice that was both dangerous and sexy, "Judas Long isn't a threat to you. He never will be one again. He was found dead in his jail cell."

She gaped at him. That cold smile that curled his lips. The dark, soulless eyes...

He's wearing a mask right now. And she'd deal with that, along with the BS line of—

You fucked a monster...

—she'd deal with it all in just a moment. She would deal, really. But first...

She flew to the sink. She poured all the coffee in her mug down the drain. She rinsed out the mug and then she poured fresh water into it before she drank greedily in an attempt to get the worst taste in the known universe out of her mouth.

"Uh, Agnes?"

She put the mug on the counter. Her hands grabbed onto the edge of the sink, and she shuddered in remembered revulsion. "Were you trying to kill me?" A question that had to be asked.

A sudden, sharp inhale. "Judas was not working for me. You *can't* think that. I would never send someone after you that way, and I made sure that he would not hurt you again."

Oh, jeez. Did Cass order the man's death? She spun toward him.

"As for my uncle and father...you're lucky you never met them. Believe me on that. They are real monsters. The tricky part with my old man, though, was that he pretended to be good. He wasn't. His smile hid the worst evil in the world. My mother ran away from him a very long time ago. She took me away with her. She protected me for my whole life, but I wasn't going to let him stay out there, hurting other people. I wasn't going to—" He frowned, as if just realizing something. "Why did you spit out the coffee? And, uh, you... you don't seem overly shocked about my family history."

She didn't seem overly shocked because she was *not* overly shocked. "I knew who your father was. I knew what he'd done. I'm not shocked. But...he died in a motorcycle accident." She'd read the report. "You didn't kill him."

"He was running from me. He lost control of the bike."

That was not what she'd read. "Witnesses said he deliberately pulled over into oncoming traffic."

"Because I was behind him. He knew what the hell I would do when I caught him." He looked behind her. "The coffee...?"

"Yeah, I spit that out because it was *horrible*. What in the hell kind of coffee did you put in the pot?"

His gaze jumped back to her. "I...wasn't sure what you liked."

"I like plain black coffee. Basic, boring. It totally works for me."

"I, uh, put scoops from all the coffee in there."

All the coffee? She turned to the left and grabbed for the cabinet door. Inside that cabinet, she found some very, very old coffee canisters. With an assortment of flavors. Caramel. Mocha. French Vanilla. Two different kinds of Roast.

"You...like coffee," he muttered. "So I put a lot of them in there."

"I may be getting over the whole liking coffee bit." She let go of the cabinet door and squinted at him. "You don't make coffee a lot, do you?"

One shoulder lifted and fell in a shrug. "Don't drink it. So, no, I don't make it. If I don't drink it, why ever make it?"

Great question. And Agnes had what she believed to be a great question of her own to toss back at him. "But you tried to make it for me...because you're a soulless monster who goes around killing his own family for shits and giggles?"

His arms crossed over his chest. He looked extra grim and broody.

"Don't buy it." She didn't. "I don't buy the scary image you're trying to present. So let's change things up, shall we?" She stalked toward him. Eliminated the small bit of distance and poked him in the chest with her index finger. "I've read your father's rap sheet. His and your uncle's. They were connected to murders, robberies, drug-running. They were far from what I'd call saintly." More like they'd been tied to the devil.

"The Night Strikers were created by my family. I took them over when I defeated my uncle."

"Defeated doesn't mean *killed*." A very important

170

distinction. "I searched through every database that I could access." And she'd been able to access plenty of them. "There is no record of your uncle's death."

Cass smiled at her. "Sometimes, it's easier when there is no body to find."

Scary. And truthful. It *was* harder to prosecute a murder when there was no body—or, uh, no victim. "What happened?"

He glanced toward the wall on the right.

She followed his gaze. Saw the big clock. "Are we expecting company or something?" She really needed to figure out where the hell they were. Other than in a safe house that belonged to the Night Strikers.

"Or something," he muttered.

"If we're about to have company, then maybe you shouldn't have been offering to fuck me on the table," she snapped. "Because I don't like for strangers to walk in when I'm naked. Future reference note."

His gaze returned to her. Glittered. "No one else will see you naked." A vow.

"Well, good to know. Thanks."

"But you are gonna have to get tatted soon."

Wait, wait...*what?* She laughed.

He did not.

Oh, no, he did *not*. "Cass?" Husky. "Are you teasing me right now?"

"Do I look like I'm teasing?"

He looked like he'd never teased anyone a day in his life. "No."

"Some undercover missions require a lifetime commitment." His head tipped forward. "You're about to commit to me."

Uh, huh. "A tattoo." She wet her lips. "Like the two-headed snake on your back? Was that a lifetime commitment?"

The darkness of his eyes had almost completely swallowed the gold. His jaw hardened.

Extra broody. Damn but that vibe worked for him. She stopped poking him in the chest and let her hand fall to her side. "Did you think I wasn't going to get back to your cobra tattoo? To your membership in the Twins? I wish you'd just lay your cards on the table and tell me everything so that—"

"You're getting tatted today. I'm the leader of the Night Strikers, and my lady has to wear my mark."

"That's...barbaric."

"That's the Night Strikers."

Shit. "For full clarification, you're the leader of the Night Strikers...and you're in the Twins?"

A slight inclination of his head.

Her stomach knotted. "The worst of the worst are pulled to join the Twins."

"Then I guess you're looking at the worst out there. Like I said, you fucked a monster."

"No, I fucked a man, and I had the time of my life doing it."

His lips parted.

"Where, exactly, will I wear this mark?" She'd never gotten a tattoo in her life. The idea of needles going into her skin didn't exactly fill her with never-ending joy. But, she was an FBI agent. She had this. Totally.

"Anywhere I choose."

Double shit. "You get to pick the tat's location?"

"I pick the location and the design."

"This feels like a really crappy game show. Do *not* pick something I'll hate."

He didn't offer up any promises.

Damn the man. "I should mention to you that I don't like pain."

He didn't blink. "I'll hold your hand."

Was he mocking her? And had she just heard the growl of...motorcycles? Faint, in the distance, but...

Getting closer.

"Tell me that you aren't a cold-blooded killer," Agnes demanded.

"Thought you'd profiled me. Is that what your profile said? That I'm a cold-blooded killer? I mean, I *did* just confess to offing my own father and my uncle so..." A shrug. *A shrug.*

They weren't talking about the freaking weather. They were talking about lives. "My profile says that you are highly protective. That you will do anything to protect the ones you believe belong to you."

But...*If he killed his own father, his own uncle...*

The profile on him had to be wrong. Didn't it? Was she completely wrong about him? What could have been real fear sent goosebumps rising on her arms.

His hand rose, and he casually tucked a lock of her hair behind her ear. "Guess what, Agnes?"

What, Cass?

"*You* belong to me."

"Just...just for pretend."

His hand lingered.

"Did you order the killing of Judas Long?" Anger hummed inside of her. And plenty of fear, too. Because... *What if I am wrong about Cass? What if Gray is wrong about him?* Gray could be blinded because they were family. As for her, maybe she was blinded because...

What? Because he was good in bed? Because maybe, just maybe, she'd developed one serious soft spot for a man

173

who was far too dangerous when she should have *known* better—

"Judas was dead the minute he went after you."

Her mouth went dry. She swallowed. Twice. No good. Her mouth remained dry.

"But, no, sweetheart, you can let that terror fade from your eyes."

There had not been any terror in her eyes. She was far too good at controlling herself. Wasn't she?

"I didn't have to order any hit. People know that he came at me in The Bottomless Pit. I have allies everywhere. He made a fatal mistake. The jackass tried to gain glory by shoving a knife at my back."

"So...you *didn't* order the hit?" Relief had her shoulders sagging. *See, he isn't really a monster. I was right about him. I knew it—*

His callused fingertips slid down her cheek. Then her neck. His fingers stopped to rest right over her racing pulse point. "I didn't have to order it. He was dead before I could make the call."

The house seemed to shake as the growling of engines filled the air. Motorcycles were swarming outside.

Cass's head leaned toward her. His breath blew lightly over her cheek. "But, for the record..." His words were almost a caress against her. "I would have ordered the hit on him in a heartbeat. Because no way did he get to keep living after targeting *you*."

Yes, yes, he'd just casually confessed to planning to kill a man.

And, what? You're gonna act all pristine and perfect when you were the one who held a gun to Judas's head as you tried to get info on the Twins?

But...she wouldn't have pulled the trigger.

She would *not* have pulled it.

Even without Malik's interference.

She wasn't that far gone.

Was she?

"Get your game face on, sweetness. It's time to meet the crew." His fingers lingered against her throat. "Remember, you're mine." Possessive. Hard. "You love me more than anything. And in a heartbeat, you'd kill to keep me safe." A half-smile twisted his lips. "Just like I'd kill for you. In. A. Heartbeat."

* * *

GAME FACE. *Game face. Game. Face.* Agnes thought she had it on. She certainly hoped she was wearing the appropriate expression. She'd choked down some of the vilest coffee in existence before heading out because a woman facing a motorcycle gang needed some caffeine churning in her blood, even if the coffee tasted like hell itself. And, for the record, it had.

She'd also paused long enough to slip on the tennis shoes that had been waiting for her. She still didn't know exactly who to thank for the clothes and shoes, and Agnes was basically just grateful to have the new goods.

Cass marched out of the house—what she now realized was a ranch-style house in the middle of pretty much... nowhere. She saw no other homes. No barns. Just some big fields that eventually gave way to thick woods.

And lots and lots of motorcycles. A quick tally had her realizing that twelve very large motorcycles—all equipped with very large riders—waited in front of the ranch house. The engines were still snarling and growling. The men still gripped the handlebars and stared straight at Cass. Cass, not her, even as she peered around him to try and take in the full scene.

Showtime.

It was probably a good thing that there were no neighbors close by. These guys and their motorcycles were loud. The air practically vibrated as she stood on the porch.

Cass lifted his hand. He closed his fingers into a fist.

Silence. All of the engines stopped at once. Kickstands went down. Boots touched the ground.

The riders didn't climb off their bikes. They waited. Um, was she supposed to do something? *Keep that game face on, woman. Act like you belong.*

Cass reached back and caught her hand in his. He pulled her forward, positioning Agnes to stand right beside him. "We've got a new member."

Some of the men wore helmets with face shields. Because of the shields—visors—she couldn't see their faces clearly. Some had flipped up the shields and their faces—the ones she could see—were stone cold. She didn't detect any hint of joy. They were definitely not pleased to have her there.

"She's a Fed," one called out.

"She's mine," Cass snarled back.

That shut the guy up.

She lifted a brow at the man who'd pointed out the fact that she was a Fed. Big, beefy, with thick, dark hair. A jagged scar slid down his right cheek.

"Not a new member," another called out. A man with a lot of silver chains around his neck. Curly, black hair. Dark eyes. Gloves on his fingers. "She might be your lady, but she doesn't ride with us. No initiation. No proving loyalty. You can fuck her—"

"Absolutely, I can, Hugo." Cass squeezed her hand.

"And I will. Thanks. But you will not ever disrespect her again." He stepped off the porch and headed toward the motorcycles. "Now, if you don't accept her, then you don't accept me. Let's cut the shit. I don't have time to waste. Got business to handle. Enemies to eliminate. So if it's coming, bring on the challenge, *now*."

Wait, wait, what...what was happening? What challenge? She darted forward—

"Hi, there."

Her forward dart was instantly stopped by Javion. He was just there. He'd hopped off his bike and lunged straight into her path. He caught her arms. "His fight," Javion told her. "Not yours."

She could feel her jaw dropping. "Why would he be *fighting?*"

"To keep you, of course."

To keep me?

"Not like he just snaps his fingers, and everyone accepts a Fed. He'll have to fight to keep you. If he wins, good news...you can both stay alive."

Whoa. Whoa. *Whoa.* "Back up," she muttered. "If he *wins...?*"

"Um." Javion glanced over his shoulder. The men had climbed off their bikes. At least *four* of them advanced on Cass. "Look at that. Only four challengers so far. Pretty sure he can take down four guys."

At one time? She was pretty sure he could not. The four men included the guy with the scar on his face, and the one Cass had called Hugo.

"Oh, change that. Five. Six," Javion corrected. "Six to one. Looks like those are the final odds."

Six men faced off against Cass. They were ditching their helmets. They were putting down...uh, knives. Guns.

Cynthia Eden

Okay, so at least they weren't using weapons.

"Hand to hand," Javion shouted. "Those are the rules. If you're fighting to take down the leader, you have to do it with your bare hands."

That was something at least. "So they'll come at him, one at a time?" Cass could probably handle that. He'd get tired, but he had told her that he'd been fighting since he was a teen. That had to mean he knew how to take care of himself.

Javion laughed. In her face. "Fuck, no. They'll come at him all at once—"

They jumped Cass. Slammed into him all at once as the others cheered. First thing in the freaking morning, in the middle of nowhere, Texas, they attacked Cass, and she *screamed*.

Chapter Fifteen

S‍HE SCREAMED.

Cass made the mistake of looking back at Agnes when her scream cut through the air, so Axel got in a solid punch to his jaw. Lucky bastard. Cass grunted at the impact, and then he launched his own attack. He managed to give an upper cut to Axel's glass jaw—*I know every one of their weaknesses*—just as Ronnie came at him with a bellowing roar.

Cass kicked hard for the SOB's weak left knee. A hit that turned Ronnie's bellow into a howl as the man collapsed on the ground, holding his knee.

Then Cass was grabbed from behind. No, not grabbed. *Hit.* It felt like a sledgehammer pounded right onto his spine. *Ah. Has to be Bear.* The biggest guy in the MC. When Bear hit you, you knew it. And Cass *almost* hit the ground after that punch. He staggered, he stumbled, and Agnes screamed again.

"Stay up!" Agnes blasted.

Well, what in the hell did she think he was trying to do? Kiss the dirt? He dipped, weaved, and then came around on a quick spin. Bear had his hands raised—his fingers locked together in a hammer fist strike—and Cass just drove his clenched fists toward the guy's gut and ribs. Rapid-fire hits that made Bear stumble back. A swipe of Cass's leg had Bear tripping and slamming down onto the ground.

"*Cass! Three more!*" Agnes yelled.

Uh, yes, he was aware. "Thanks for the tip."

The three other men attacked him all at once. They jumped on him, kicking and punching. One hit connected right under Cass's left eye. Another slammed into his right side, down low, almost a kidney punch. A boot collided with his shin. Fists were flying, and they were working hard to take his ass down to the ground.

Fuck. I'm losing my footing.

He punched the dick of the guy closest to him, and Hugo bellowed out a curse even as he curled over.

"Knife!" Agnes's shout. "That bastard has a knife. I thought there were no weapons! He's breaking the rules, the sonofabitch!"

He had a flash of her red hair. Javion should have been holding her back, but, suddenly, Agnes was there. She jumped on Levi's back. Levi—big, blond, far stronger than her, the Texas cowboy who'd proven he never fought fair time and time again. The prick who did have a knife because the blade glinted beneath the sun.

And he...

Levi sliced that knife back toward Agnes as he tried to shake her off him. "*Bitch!*"

Oh, the fuck, no.

Bodies slammed into Cass again. Men he'd taken down who had gotten back up to come at him *again*. They rushed in, thinking he was going to lose the battle.

An inhuman roar poured from him. Because he'd seen that knife going toward Agnes.

And Agnes...

Red hair hit the ground. He saw her *on the ground.*

A killing fury consumed him. *Everything* around him turned red as a haze of fury utterly devoured Cass. He stopped holding back. Because, yeah, he fucking had been. These were his men, after all. His MC. Not like he'd wanted to kill them.

Until he'd seen the knife go toward Agnes.

And he began to *destroy.* His hands moved in rapid-fire attacks. He used his full strength. The attacks were constant. Brutal. Bone jarring.

Bone breaking.

He was hit, too, but the blows just fired him up all the more. The men fell around him. Axel. Ronnie. Bear went down with a bellow and a crash hard enough to shake the earth. Then it was Hugo. Hugo actually held his hands up and backed away. Light glinted off the chains around his neck.

"Done!" Hugo shouted. Blood dripped from his nose and lips. "Done!"

Mathus swung with his left hand—he was a southpaw with a powerful fist—but Cass caught that fist, and then he slammed his head right into Mathus's.

"Aw, fuck," Mathus breathed. "Enough...*Done.*" His face twisted in pain, making the scar on his face heave and coil.

Cass let the bastard fall. Breath heaving, hands fisted, he whirled for Agnes.

She was still on the ground. But...no, she was *on top of Levi.* Levi was on the ground. Agnes straddled him. Her knees pushed into the dirt on either side of Levi's body, and she had a knife pressed to his throat.

"Pretty sure no knives were supposed to be involved," she snapped. "You must have heard Javion. *I* heard him."

Was that a bruise on her cheek? It sure as fuck looks like a mark. Still red...as if someone had hit her, and the mark would soon become a bruise.

A growl broke from Cass.

She did not glance his way. Instead, her fierce focus remained on Levi and on the blade that she had against his jugular. "I *distinctly* remember Javion saying this was supposed to be a hand-to-hand affair. Hand-to-hand, not knife-to-hand because that's not fair. But you tried to break the rules. Granted, I am new to the lifestyle here, but that sort of thing seems *wrong*—"

An inhuman cry broke from Levi as he grabbed her hips. He surged upward, ignoring the knife that she held against his throat. The bastard probably thought that Agnes would not actually use it on him.

But she did.

Blood flowed over his neck. And even as Levi grabbed her by the hips, Agnes was sending her left elbow careening into his nose.

Crunch.

Bones had to break. A distinct sound.

But Levi didn't stop. Fury twisted his features even as blood seeped down his neck and—

"Let her go or die right here." Lethal. Low. A grim promise from Cass.

The words, though soft, caught everyone's attention. Agnes and Levi both whipped their heads toward him. Levi's eyes widened, and fear flashed on his face. Yes, he needed to be afraid.

As for Agnes, a wide smile curved her lips. "You won!" She bobbed her head toward him. "Not that I doubted you. Not for a second. Well, maybe, for one brief, flashing second when I saw this jerk trying to sneak up with his blade. And you *know* how I don't like knives *and* bastards who sneak up behind you with them, so I had to intervene."

She didn't like knives, but she'd just cut Levi's throat with one. A cut that wasn't too deep, not yet.

"I didn't have a beer bottle to throw this time," she continued in what sure as shit sounded like a *sunny* tone. "So I had to throw my whole body at him."

"She's bloodthirsty." Javion ambled to Cass's side. "I like that about her." Javion had not participated in the challenge. Mostly because, on more than one occasion, he'd let Cass know that running the MC was not in the future for him. Javion craved freedom, not the constraints of having the MC's full responsibility planted on him. Too bad, because he was the one Cass thought would be the best leader of the crew.

Levi's hands had torn away from Agnes's hips. His fingers slammed into the ground.

Agnes continued to straddle him.

A pose that Cass did not like. *I don't want her anywhere near the prick.* "Agnes, up. Now."

She blinked. "Well, someone is bossy. You win one fight against six guys and then you get all—"

"*Agnes.*"

Her mouth hung open for an instant. Whatever she saw on his face had her nodding briskly. She rose to her feet. Bit her lower lip as she darted a glance down at Levi. "I think we're going to be enemies now, aren't we? Unfortunate, but I had to protect Cass. He'll always come first for me."

And she will come first for me.

Wait, hold the hell up. No, no, she would not. This was a ruse. A lie. A trick. A...

She still gripped the knife as she walked toward Cass. Agnes stopped right in front of him. She tipped her head back as she stared at him.

Yes, that is a fucking bruise forming on her cheek. Rage nearly swallowed him whole in that instant. His hand rose, and his fingers brushed lightly over her cheek. "Levi hit you."

"Uh..." She wet her lips. "If I say yes, will you go off the edge and do something terrible?"

Oh, she was fun. His hand slid over a bit so that his fingers sank into the thickness of her hair. "Agnes..." His head lowered toward her. Adrenaline and fury fired his blood. His lips pressed to hers. His tongue dipped inside her mouth to steal her sweetness. "I'm going to do something terrible no matter what you say." A whisper against her mouth. Because Levi had attacked *her.* Because he'd tried to sneak up with a knife and kill Cass. *What is up with sonsofbitches coming at my back?*

Cass's low words made Agnes stumble away. One step in retreat. Her eyes were wide as she shook her head. "No, don't—"

Oh, he definitely *would.* He took the knife from her fingers. "Go inside. I'm the leader of the Strikers. I'm staying the leader."

There were grunts. Mutters of affirmation from the men around him. Men who'd just had their asses kicked. Men who'd *watched* the others get their asses kicked. But it wasn't like these were the only members of the Night Strikers MC. These were just the ones in the top-tier positions. The ones who had earned the right to challenge him.

They'd challenged him. They'd failed. Now they would fall back in line...

Most of them.

One would not be falling back in line because he'd just proven what a traitor he really was. Something Cass had suspected about the prick for a while now...

"Don't kill him." She inched closer to Cass once more. "Do not."

The sexy Fed was giving him orders? So cute. So clueless. "You think he wouldn't have killed me?" Behind her, he saw Levi rush to his feet. Only the guy didn't get far when he tried to run.

Hugo and Bear closed in lightning-fast, even with their injuries. They both slapped their hands on Levi, one on each shoulder.

Levi's neck continued to bleed.

She looked back at Levi. "I don't think I cut you too deeply."

Cass would correct that situation. He would cut the other man very, very deeply. So deep that—

"You should still go to a hospital, though," Agnes added. "Maybe get a stitch or two."

Ronnie burst out laughing.

She frowned at him. "Stitches are not funny."

"You suck up the pain," Javion explained. He'd been watching the scene with his hands shoved into the pockets of his jeans. "You let it make you stronger."

"Uh..." She shifted a bit, moving more to Cass's side instead of standing in front of him. "You get wounds cleaned and stitched up so you don't get infections and *die*."

More laughter—this time from Ronnie and Bear.

"What's the point?" Hugo wanted to know as he rolled back his shoulders. "This bastard is dead already."

Cynthia Eden

There were nods from the others.

Agnes's hand flew up to press against Cass's stomach. He almost hissed out a breath because that was a spot where he'd taken a vicious punch. From Hugo. "Don't kill him," Agnes pleaded with Cass, her voice barely above a breath. "Don't do that. He, uh, Levi isn't armed now." Her hushed words were just for him. "Don't do something you can't take back."

She was trying to be an FBI agent. Getting him to follow the law. Like he didn't know that killing a man in cold blood was wrong. But...

Attacking Agnes? Trying to hurt *her*?

That was fucking wrong. The worst sin that Levi could have committed. "I told you to go inside, Agnes. Either go on your own, or Javion will carry you in."

Her hand pressed a bit harder against him. "You're being the villain." Again, just for him. So low he barely heard her. "Be the hero."

Screw that. Voice deliberately loud, he ordered, "Take your sweet ass inside. I'm dealing with Levi." Each word was guttural. "Then I'm fucking you."

She didn't get that they weren't in her *safe* world any longer. Yes, in her black-and-white world with FBI agents and cops, you didn't kill a man in cold blood.

They were in Cass's world. Not hers. And in his world, you didn't let some sonofabitch try to knife you in the back. And you damn well didn't let him hurt *your* lady. Cass had a rep to protect. But this went so beyond his rep. This was about Agnes. About *no one hurting her. Not ever.* A message had to be sent.

He'd send it. In blood. Levi's blood.

He'd—

Agnes yanked him toward her. Cass's head went down

just because he was ready to take that hot mouth of hers again. She met him with open lips, with her tongue stroking his, with need and desire, and lust burning right back at him. She kissed him frantically, deeply. She didn't act afraid. Not turned off by the violence or terrified of what he might do. No, she acted like—

Her mouth tore from his. "I'm fucking you." Her breath heaved. Agnes raised her voice as she promised, "And I'm gonna fuck you even harder if you don't kill him. Get your pound of flesh. Get your MC justice, but it's better for him to live with the humiliation of knowing that little old me..." She glanced over her shoulder. Glared at Levi. "That I was the one who took him down. Bet it will be helluva hard to let the world know that a woman half your size had you on the ground in two seconds flat."

Then she whipped her head around. Kissed Cass once more. And she was off...striding back toward the house as she tossed a wave at Javion. "I don't need you to carry me! But you might need to haul Levi the hell out of here. Oh, but we should keep his motorcycle, don't you think? Because I could totally use one."

Then she was back in the house. The door slammed behind her.

Silence.

And...

"Can I get one of those? Like, does she have a sister or something? A scary best friend?" Bear rumbled. "I'd like one...similar to her. Similar but bigger. And, damn but yours is really, really good with a knife."

Cass had been staring at the house's closed door. Now, though, he turned to face the current threat.

Levi, you dumb bastard.

Silence.

Everyone seemed to tense as they waited for Cass to act.

He was still holding the knife, a knife wet with Levi's blood. Taking his time, Cass closed in on his prey.

"She..." Levi swallowed. His Adam's apple bobbed. "She said not to kill me. I heard her!"

Cass smiled at him. And he brought up the knife. He let the tip of the blade press into Levi's right side. "Do you think..." The blade pressed hard, cutting past the fabric of Levi's shirt, cutting past skin, and sinking into muscle. He sliced across with the blade. "Do you think I give a flying fuck what she said?" Jaw locked, rage fueling him, Cass yanked the blade down in another slice.

Levi began to whimper.

Agnes had scars on her stomach. Her abdomen. One is nearly in the exact same spot where I just slid this blade. Cass's gaze darted over his prey. Blood poured from the wound he'd just given Levi.

"I'm sorry!" Levi cried out. "S-sorry! She wasn't my target—I fucking *swear!*"

Cass pulled the blade out. He watched as the blood drip-drip-dripped onto the ground.

Agnes was stabbed. Seven times. Left for dead.

His head lifted. The better for him to stare his prey straight in the eyes. "Do you want to die?" Cass asked Levi softly.

"Oh, fuck. Oh, fuck. *No!* Please, please, look, I just—it was the heat of the moment. I was...I wasn't thinking straight! I just went in for the attack. You were fighting Hugo and Bear, and I just—" A heaving breath. "I will do anything you want! Don't kill me! Don't!"

"You *were* thinking straight." He kept staring at Levi. Seeing the fear and desperation twist the other man's face.

"You thought you'd be leader. You thought you'd take away everything I had."

"I'll disappear!" Levi promised, frantic. "You won't ever see me again!"

Cass shook his head. "That's not how it works. You don't just walk away from the MC."

The others remained dead silent.

"I don't see any reason to let you live," Cass told Levi. "I only see about a million reasons to let you die."

"No!" A high-pitched, whining cry. And then—then Levi surged forward, somehow breaking free of both men who had been securing him. He lunged, not at Cass, but around him, trying to just run the hell away.

As if that would happen.

But Levi was hauling ass toward the big field near the ranch house. A sprawling field that had a twisted patch of woods to the far right. The bastard thought he was getting to those woods. He was wrong. Cass tackled the jerk and took him to the ground. Cass flipped him over as Levi begged and pleaded, and Cass brought that knife up, even though holding it made his gut twist.

Someone drove a knife into Agnes seven times. And he was holding a blade. And he was a monster, too. And he shouldn't ever touch her but all he wanted was *her—*

"He's not dead, man!" A rough whisper from Levi. "He told me to get in the gang, told me to get close to you, to watch you, *but he's not dead!"*

The frantic words had Cass pausing. "Who the hell..." Dark. Hard. Grating. "Are you talking about?"

"He wanted me to take you out! It was all him!"

So now you're saying you didn't come at me in the freaking heat of the moment? You were following orders?

189

There sure seemed to be a lot of people trying to kill him lately. "Give me a name."

"Y-you know."

Did he look like he freaking knew? If he knew, why in the hell would he be demanding a name?

"You didn't kill him." A low rasp. "Had to know...*no body*. No body... He's been waiting. Getting stronger...he's coming for you."

Cass hauled Levi to his feet. Held the bastard in front of him. No body? Shit. "You're damn well not talking about my uncle. Winston Striker is dead. I am not going to believe that bullshit—"

Thunder. No, a gunshot blast. He heard it and *felt* it at the same instant because pain tore across the edge of his right shoulder. Even as his shoulder burned with pain, Cass automatically let go of Levi. The bastard staggered back even as Cass dove for cover.

Another gunshot blast.

A hit, right in Levi's chest. Because he'd just been *standing there,* with a dumb smile on his face. But that smile vanished when the bullet hit him.

And all hell broke loose.

Chapter Sixteen

"*Take your sweet ass inside. I'm dealing with him. Then I'm fucking you.*"

Seriously. What in the ever-loving-hell?

Agnes paced inside the house. She'd been taken out of the action, sent away, and just where did Cass get off thinking he could toss around arrogant asshole statements like...

Then I'm fucking you.

Her heart pounded. Her palms were a little sweaty. And maybe her breath panted out too much.

She paced faster. She'd grabbed her gun as soon as she'd gotten inside, and now the gun was tucked at the base of her back as she paced. *Damn the man.*

He'd defeated five men in a fight like it was nothing. Granted, he'd originally been up against six guys, but she'd taken care of number six for him, and had the man even thanked her? Recognized her as the amazing partner that she was to him? Oh, no.

He'd just said he was going to fuck her.

And he'd sent her away.

Cynthia Eden

Yes, yes, the MC had rules. Understood. He was the alpha. They might as well be a pack of wild wolves, but he did *not* get to go around killing—

Boom.

She heard the shot. Was pretty sure that it stopped her heart. For an instant, Agnes completely froze, then she lunged for the door of the house.

Boom.

Another shot. Fear exploded within her. She grabbed for the doorknob with her left hand even as her right yanked out her gun. She rushed outside as fast as her legs would carry her while fear had her heart ready to burst out of her chest.

Terror clawed at her. So did rage. Because if those booming shots had been fired at Cass, if she found him dead...

A body slumped in the dirt. Not moving. Facedown. The body was sprawled in a field about twenty feet from the house. Twenty feet, thirty?

Motorcycle engines roared. The big bikes were spinning and flying from the graveled drive. One, after the other, after the other, and the man in the field wasn't moving. She raced toward him, and it dawned on her that she was staring at blond hair.

Blond. Not the darkness of Cass's hair. That wasn't Cass on the ground.

But she'd already dropped to her knees beside the fallen figure. She had to put her gun down so that she could flip over the body, and when she did...

So much blood.

Not just on his throat where she'd cut him. Cut him with the knife that *he* had intended to use on Cass. But on his stomach. His chest. Blood trickled from his mouth, and his eyes were closed. She stared at him, horrified.

Then training and instinct took over. Her hands flew over his wounds. Maybe she could stop the blood flow.

He gasped. His eyes flew open.

He stared straight at her.

She should say something comforting. Tell him that he was going to be all right. Let him know that everything was going to be all right.

"You...you should have died that night," he rasped.

"What?" All thoughts of saying anything *comforting* fled.

He stared at her and a smile tilted his lips. His bloody lips. Blood covered his teeth, too.

The man is hurt. He's confused. You're an FBI agent. Help him. Comfort him. "Y-you mean when Judas attacked me. When the guy came for me in Atlanta." That must be what Levi meant. "Cass told you about that?" Her gaze dropped back to his injuries. The blood that covered his chest flowed the heaviest and there was a hole in his shirt, near his heart. A big, torn, blood-soaked hole.

"I mean...in Texas."

Ice covered her.

Motorcycles were growling. Snarling. Most seemed to have left, but one's roaring engine grew louder and louder. She should look toward that loud growling. It seemed to be coming straight toward her. But she couldn't look away from the man on the ground.

"Thought you'd die...with the boyfriend."

Her heart stopped. Then she was lunging forward. Grabbing his right arm and yanking it up so that she could see if he had that damn two-headed cobra tattoo leading toward his wrist.

Not there.

She checked the other arm, moving blindly, even though she knew the tattoo of that long ago attacker had been on his right arm, not the left. *Along his right inner wrist.*

But when she shoved up the left arm...

A two-headed cobra. Fangs bared. Scaled body twisting. Not the same tattoo that she'd seen so long ago on the man who'd wrecked her world. This one was different. It circled Levi's wrist, coiled, then came back with those fangs wide open.

The roaring of the motorcycle filled her ears, and it drowned out the scream of fury that burst from her lips.

"You're one of them!" Agnes cried out. "You know what happened! You know—"

He was still smiling, but his eyes had sagged closed.

No, this could not happen. "You're not dying, you bastard! You don't get away that easily!"

Hard arms curled around her and yanked Agnes away from the bloody man and to her feet.

"No!" She struggled blindly, wildly. Kicking back. Clawing at the hands and arms that held her. Elbowing the jerk who'd grabbed her. Her gun was still on the ground. "No!"

But he lifted her up like her struggles didn't matter, and she damn well knew that they did. She wasn't being *gentle.* She was fighting like a tiger, punching, twisting, going for maximum pain, and she was *not* going to stop.

"Agnes!"

Cass dropped her onto the seat of the motorcycle. Because he'd been the jerk to grab her from behind. Like she hadn't recognized his touch.

She immediately tried to spring up.

"The hell *no*," Cass blasted at her. "A shooter is out there! Dammit, why didn't you stay in the house?"

Because Cass might have needed her. Because Cass might have been shot. But she didn't say that. Instead, she lunged up again.

He slammed her right back down. Then he jumped in front of her on the motorcycle. *"Hold on."*

Screw that. She had to get back to the man on the ground. "He *knows*!"

"He's *dead! Levi is dead!*"

No, Levi wasn't dead. He'd been talking to her, taunting her. He'd been there, the night her world had upended.

"Levi is dead!" Cass repeated. And, before she could jump off the bike again, something slapped around her wrist.

What in the world?

Cold. Metal.

A handcuff?

"How in the hell is this supposed to work?" Agnes fumed.

Cass locked the cuff on his left wrist. "Either we stay together, or we fall off the fucking bike."

Fall off and—what? Crash? Die? "You can't drive like this! You don't have full range of motion. You can't—"

He could. He did. Sure, her arm stretched, but she was already holding her arms around him pretty tightly anyway because the man had *taken off.* He hurtled them away from the house and—not toward the road—but through some twisting, tangling trees to the far left even as her head whipped back so that she could stare at Levi.

Levi...still on the ground. With blood around him. With her gun dropped beside him.

Levi...

His head turned. She was sure of it. Was he gazing after her? It sure as hell seemed like he was. "You bastard!" Agnes shouted.

"Yeah, I fucking am," Cass snapped back at her. "But I'm not leaving you behind to get shot, so stop fighting me, hold on, and keep your eyes out for the shooter."

The shooter?

Now she tensed. The motorcycle vibrated between her legs. One of her arms curled around his waist, the other twisted with the cuff and... "You didn't shoot him?"

Because, well, after she'd found the wounded man on the ground, she'd thought...

"No, I didn't. We're under attack, and I'm getting you the hell *away*."

And he did. Branches whipped at them. The motorcycle snarled like a demon coming out of hell, and Agnes and Cass left a bleeding man behind them.

A bleeding man—a dead man? The man who knew about her past. The man who could potentially have given her answers.

And he was either dead...or dying.

Dammit.

* * *

"I LIKE THE JEWELRY," Javion praised as he waved a hand toward her. "It's new, right?"

Oh, fun. A comedian when rage had her shaking behind Cass.

Cass had just braked near Javion's motorcycle. They were at some rundown bar—shocking, she knew—but Cass seemed to have some sort of innate talent for locating hole-in-the-wall places.

They were still in Texas. She'd figured that out thanks to some road signs that she'd finally seen, once they'd gotten out of the woods with the branches that had slapped at her. They had only driven for about an hour. At least, that's what she guessed. They'd driven hard and fast and potentially left a dead body behind. Because... why not? That seemed to be the way they rolled these days.

Her body ached. Her stomach had twisted into about a million knots. And...worst of all, fury still fueled her. She'd been moments away from getting answers. And now...

The dead can't give me answers. But if Cass had just let her stay a few moments longer, she could have forced Levi to tell her the truth.

"Is there a particular reason why the pretty lady is cuffed to you?" Javion asked Cass.

Cass grunted. Typical. The man's conversational skills were killer.

He's a killer.

She truly had thought that he'd been the one to shoot Levi. Before going into the ranch house, she'd tried to convince the man to hold back, to be a hero...

But he'd basically laughed in her face after those particular words.

"She's cuffed so she won't run. The woman didn't want to get on the bike. Had to take the choice out of her hands."

"The *woman*," she snapped right back, "didn't want to leave an injured man behind. And, hey, important little FYI tidbit, my gun is back there next to his body."

Javion whistled. "That could be a problem."

Tell her something she didn't know.

"Our guys are still searching for the shooter," Javion said as he rocked back on his heels and stood beside his motorcycle. "They'll report back when they know something. Until then, this place should be good."

This was a good place? Truly? She squinted at it. The windows were boarded up. A big NO TRESPASSING sign hung near the double doors that had to be the entrance to the place. At first, she'd thought it was a rundown bar, but now, Agnes realized it appeared that the building had been closed down for a very long time. Not just rundown. More like shut down.

"Your security should still be in place from last time," Javion continued.

"Ahem." She cleared her throat. With her non-cuffed hand, Agnes tapped on Cass's shoulder. "Not to be a pessimist, but we've been found by your enemies at our last *two* safe spots. The no-tell motel?" In case he'd somehow forgotten that amazing experience. "And your ranch house. What's to stop us from getting attacked here, too?" And, quite clearly, the man had a large target on his back.

That target is why two different people have tried to stab him in said back.

"I believe Levi was feeding our locations to my enemy." A low, furious rumble. "Dead men can't feed shit to anyone."

"Uh, no, no, they can't feed, ah, shit to people." *Who is your enemy?*

"I scouted around before you arrived." Javion's hands rested on his hips. "It's good."

Was it? Not like she was ready to jump onto the "good" reassurance so quickly. At this point, she didn't think any place was *good* where they were concerned.

"Go help the others with the search," Cass ordered. "I've got her."

Yes, he did. He had her *cuffed* to him.

"If you find the shooter," Cass added when Javion turned to mount his motorcycle, "keep him alive."

She brightened. Awesome, he was not killing—

"Keep him alive long enough for me to beat the bastard to death," Cass finished.

And she stopped brightening.

"Message received," Javion replied. He spun his bike around and roared out.

As for Cass..."Keep holding on," he told her. And he drove right for the big, double doors that led to the old bar. She did keep holding on because it wasn't like she had much choice. When they got right up to those doors, Agnes realized a keypad was attached to the door frame. He leaned forward, punched in the code, and the doors swung open with a click.

Then the man just *drove* his motorcycle inside.

The doors closed.

And...

Lights flashed on. One after the other after the other. And, yes, it was a bar. But not some rundown place. Gleaming, polished wood on the high bar countertop. Four huge pool tables. About fifteen to twenty tables scattered around the place, all with chairs that had been flipped over and placed on top of them.

A jukebox waited in the corner. Old-school. With soft lights and fat buttons in the front.

She turned slowly. Not a full turn, not like she could do that with the cuffs, but as much of a turn as she could make. Her gaze took in everything she saw, including the narrow hallway to the side and the line of monitors that filled the right wall.

Cass strode toward the bar—which meant she had to stride there with him since they were still connected. With his free hand, he reached behind the bar and pulled out what looked like a remote. After clicking a button, the monitors turned on, and she saw images of the bar's exterior. The road out front. What she suspected were the woods out back. "Ah, guessing this is...your gang's hideout, huh?" So much for the Night Strikers just being primarily an East Coast crew.

He put down the remote, turned his head, and locked those glittering, intent eyes on her. "We have a problem."

"We sure as hell do." Her chin jutted up. "That bastard you left bleeding out had answers! Levi had one of the tattoos!" Anger and fear and frustration rolled within. She jerked on the cuff that still held them together. The cuff was loose enough on her wrist that she could twist her hand around, but she could not get *out*. "Did you let me question him? No, you cuffed me and then basically kidnapped me! That crap is not cool! It's not what partners do to each other."

He was...

Moving. Storming away. Dammit, she had to storm, too. "We're connected!" Agnes snapped at him. "At least undo the stupid cuff!"

He whirled toward her. They were right next to one of the pool tables. "That stupid cuff kept you alive."

She glared.

So did he.

"Bullets were flying, Agnes," he gritted out. "And I get that you thought I was the heartless monster who did the shooting, but in this instance—"

"You're the one who keeps saying that you're the monster. I've *never* said—"

"The shooter was still out there. He nicked me. The first bullet was supposed to be for *me*."

200

Her eyes widened. Then her stare was flying all over him and— "Blood! Cass!" She tried to reach for his shoulder. How in the hell had she missed that?

"Nothing. Barely a scratch. The second bullet landed in Levi. Dead in his chest. I was already dodging for cover when the second one flew, but that bastard didn't get down. He stood there, smiling, like the cavalry had come, and the bullet took him out. One look, and I knew there was no way an ambulance would get to him in time, not given where we were."

In the middle of nowhere? "But we didn't even *try* to save him!"

"He tried to kill me. He would have killed you if you hadn't taken the knife from him. Given that, are you so sure he needed saving?"

A brutal statement. Chill bumps rose on her arms. "He had the tattoo," she whispered. "You must have known. You *had* to know that he was part of the Twins, and you didn't say a word to me. I am so sick of being kept in the dark!"

His jaw hardened.

"You're holding back on me," she accused. "Dammit. We are partners! We are—"

"You are a Fed working your own agenda. You want vengeance, and I swear, I'll make sure you get it. I will cut off both cobra heads. You can count on that." His nostrils flared. "And I'm holding back because, no, I don't trust you."

She backed up. As much as she could. The cuff bit into her wrist. "That hurts." It actually did. And she wasn't talking about the sting of the cuff as it cut into her skin. She was talking about the lancing pain his words had just delivered.

"Does it?" Doubting. "Does it really hurt that I don't trust you?"

Yes, it really does freaking hurt.

"Because when I look at you, I see a woman who was willing to use me to get her vengeance. You're in love with a dead man."

If she could have, Agnes would have retreated even more. "Stop." Because he was hurting her. How could he not see that? And hadn't he said that he wouldn't hurt her? Hadn't he made that promise?

"You can't crawl in the ground with him." Hard. No, brutal. "I'm not going to fucking let you do that. So, hell, no, I was not going to let you stay out in the freaking open with Levi. Not while the shooter was still there."

"He had *answers!*" Her words were as ragged—as jagged—as she felt. "He said I should have died that night! Levi wasn't talking about recently—he was talking about that terrible night in Austin. He said I should have died with my boyfriend. He was *not* the one who stabbed me, the tattoo was all wrong. But he was either there or...or maybe he was the one on the phone. He knew what happened. He knew who I was. He remembered me, he—"

"Levi was following orders. His boss told him who you were."

Her heart slammed into her chest. "I thought you were his boss."

"So the hell did I...until he tried to plunge a knife into me, and then he told me that a ghost from my past was still walking."

She could only shake her head. "I have no idea what you're talking about." Anger had her voice going husky. "Because you don't *trust* me."

He jerked on his hand—the hand cuffed to hers—and Agnes stumbled forward, caught off guard. But...

He caught her. Hauled her closer. But their bodies

twisted and heaved, and the stupid cuffs had them all tangled. *"Get the cuffs off!"*

Cursing, he reached into his pocket. His fingers came back up with a key, and he put it in the lock, and he freed his wrist. The *snick* as the cuff opened was far too loud. His cuff, then hers.

She immediately attempted to retreat, but he grabbed her in a flash. She didn't know if he'd dropped the key or what the heck he'd done with it. She just knew that he held her tightly, and his dark gaze seemed to burn as he demanded, "If it came down to it, if it was a choice between me and the Feds you treasure so much, who would you choose?"

She could feel a thick, dark tension swirling between them. He'd gone from the violence of the fight, to the shooting, to the frantic ride that had brought them to this place. Adrenaline, rage, and so many twisting, heaving emotions filled the air.

"You wouldn't choose me, would you? Because I'm a means to an end. The devil you want to use." He nodded. "Done. Use me. I will kill for you. In a heartbeat. I'll eliminate the threats. I'll get you the vengeance that you need, but I won't trust you. I won't let you beneath my guard, I won't—" But he broke off. Just stopped.

And she wanted him to continue. "You won't...what?" The cuff around her wrist was open, and she shook it off. The handcuffs dropped to the floor.

"I won't fucking care," he snapped. "I will not care about you."

She sucked in a breath at the vicious blow. Her eyes widened as she stared at him. And then... "Liar," she called.

That muscle flexed in his jaw again, and the gold buried in the darkness of his eyes glittered all the harder.

"You already do care," she whispered as she realized the truth. *He warned me that he lied all the time. He's lying now. But I can see through the lies. He says he won't care but...he does.* Her hand rose to press to his chest. "You care about me. Otherwise, you would have left me in the field with Levi. You would have left me to get shot. You wouldn't have saved me then, and you wouldn't have rushed to the rescue when Judas was coming to attack me."

"I didn't rescue you," he bit out.

"No, I did that myself, but you were still there to have my back." Agnes knew she was taking a huge risk, but she could not seem to stop herself. "I'm not in love with a dead man."

His lips thinned.

"I will always love Max." Adamant. "Never doubt that. Understand it. Accept it. Deal with it. I will love him until I go into the grave myself—"

"*You're not going into the fucking—*"

"But I am not in love with him, not anymore." Her breath whispered out. "Though I do really fear that I might be falling in love with this arrogant, alpha jerk of an MC leader who makes some truly crappy coffee even as he calls himself a villain—"

His mouth crashed onto hers.

Agnes squeezed her eyes shut. *I'm super afraid that I'm falling in love with you...and there is nothing I can do to stop that fall.*

Chapter Seventeen

SHE IS NOT IN LOVE WITH ME. SHE CAN'T BE IN LOVE WITH me. Agnes does not love me.

She wanted him. He wanted her. He wanted to fuck her endlessly. To mark her. To possess her. He wanted the world to know that she was his and he was hers and he was—

What the hell? I am hers?

But she moaned and her soft body pressed harder against his, and hell, yes, he was hers. He didn't want anyone else. Since he'd had Agnes, she'd consumed his thoughts. He wanted to fuck her endlessly, but fucking was basic. Physical. Addictive, yes. Absolutely. But it *was* just fucking.

Yet with Agnes...

He also wanted to protect her. To take her away from any and every threat in the world. He wanted to make sure that she never felt a moment of pain, that she was safe and happy and— *she cannot be happy in my world.*

A fundamental fact that he had to accept. She would not be happy in the life he currently led.

His mouth tore from hers. "Mistake."

"Yes, falling in love with you is probably a mistake." No hesitation. "I get that you don't love me back."

Falling in love with you. He didn't hear anything past that part. The words pounded into him with the impact of a sledgehammer. He spun around, grabbed her waist, and lifted her onto the pool table.

"Not like you'd love a Fed," she added.

At least, Cass thought she added that part. He barely heard her because he was already leaning in, pulling in her sexy scent, and kissing her frantically again. Plunging his tongue deep into her mouth. Tasting the sweetness that waited. *His* sweetness. She was his. He would keep her. Protect her. Kill for her.

Her legs had parted, and he stepped right between them. He hauled her to the edge of the pool table, and he knew he would be taking her. There. Done.

I did warn her. After the fight at the house, I told her what would happen...

Her right hand went between their bodies. She jerked at his belt. Yanked it open. Unsnapped his jeans.

She wants me. I'm taking her. Now.

His mouth pulled from hers, but he didn't go far. He kissed a path down her neck. Licked. Bit lightly. Maybe left a mark.

Only fair. She's marked me, soul deep. I'll wear her mark until I die.

Her flying fingers went to work on the zipper of his jeans. "The position is making this hard," she gasped out. "I can't reach you enough—"

"Princess, I'm the one who is hard." And he bit her again. Lightly. Sensually.

She shuddered. "Do not joke *now*."

Who was joking? Her stroking fingers had to feel the giant cock that was hungry for her. He never bothered with underwear, so when she'd unzipped his jeans, his dick had surged into her hot hands.

"I'm gonna fuck you right now." He could barely speak. Control was long gone. "Unless you tell me to stop." She needed to tell him—

Her long lashes lifted so that she was staring straight at him. "Fuck me right now," Agnes told him.

He backed away. One step. No more. He yanked off her shoes. Hauled down her jeans and panties, and she was completely bare from the waist down. Her legs parted, showing him the treasure that waited.

His.

He had to taste her. Had to put his mouth on her as she sprawled back on the pool table and opened wider for him. He had to lick her clit. Over and over. Had to drive his tongue inside of her.

"*Cass!* I don't want to come until you're in me!"

His tongue *was* in her. In and out. Lapping her up greedily because her taste obsessed him. He could not get enough. Wasn't sure that he would ever be able to get enough. *More, more, more.*

"*Cass!*" He heard the pleasure break in her cry.

A savage smile curled his lips. He grabbed for his wallet and yanked out the condom inside. Thank fuck for that condom.

He rolled it on, had his jeans around his knees, and he hauled her as close to the edge of the pool table as he could position her. Then Cass *took* her. Drove deep and sank into the tightest, hottest paradise he'd ever reach in this lifetime.

Cynthia Eden

His dick slammed home, he buried himself as far as he could go, filling her and feeling the tight, eager clasp of her body around him.

Her hands flew over the pool table. Balls went flying behind her. They hit. Clinked. He was pretty sure one even went into the corner pocket.

Screw the balls.

He withdrew. Pulled nearly out of her. Then...

In. As deep as he could go. Forcing his cock in, inch by inch, making her take him as she lifted her hips up against him. As she stretched out on the pool table and her legs rose to lock around his hips. He leaned over her. Drove into her. Pounded into her as she twisted and moaned and heaved against him.

Too hard. Too rough. Too fierce. He knew all of these things. He should have given her care. Tenderness. Except there wasn't a whole lot of care or tenderness in his life. He didn't even know *how* to show care. There had been so little that was delicate or precious in his life, not in a very long time.

"Don't hold back with me!" Her demanding cry.

He stared down at her. Her bright gaze met his. So sharp. So stunning.

She thinks that she loves me.

His stare darted over her. A red line circled the wrist he'd cuffed. *I did that to her, dammit. I hurt her.* He hadn't meant to hurt her. He'd just wanted to protect her.

Her much smaller body was beneath his, open, taking him. Ready.

I can't hurt her. Don't want to hurt her.

"Cass!" She shook her head. "Don't. Hold. Back."

He didn't. He let go. Need took over. Control

208

obliterated. Hell, who was he kidding? His control had long been obliterated with her. He never, ever should have taken her the first night. But, now his fate was sealed. So was hers.

He would not let her go. He would not lose her.

Fear for her had nearly swallowed him whole when he'd looked over and seen her out in the open, crouching near that traitorous bastard Levi. Cass had driven straight to her, so desperate to get to her. She'd been his only focus. And, hell, yes, he'd cuffed her to him.

He'd kidnapped her, as she'd claimed. Taking her to safety had been his only goal.

And now...*taking her* was his only thought.

He pounded into her again and again. She arched up to meet him. Her moans urged him on. He plunged into her, and she squeezed him so greedily that Cass knew his mind was long gone. His temples throbbed. His body ached. Yearned. Needed.

The slap of flesh against flesh filled the air. He did not look away from her gaze. He could not. He saw the pleasure take her in the widening of her eyes and heard it in the sharp cry that broke from her lips. Her head tipped back as she gasped and moaned and seemed to go boneless beneath him.

He erupted into her. Hips thrusting, body taking, soul *craving* hers. Again and again, he emptied into her until he swore that there was nothing left of himself.

There was only...*us. Together. Whole.*
Us against the entire freaking world.

* * *

SHE'D HAD sex on a pool table. A first for her. Not the most comfortable position ever, but Agnes wasn't about to complain. Maybe the table hadn't been mattress soft, but the two orgasms she'd just gotten?

Stellar. Ten stars. More.

Her legs were still wrapped around Cass's hips. Her right arm still clinging to him. She let that arm fall onto the table as she heaved out a breath. She should probably lower her legs. Release him. Cover up. Do *something*.

He raised up. Stared down into her eyes.

And an odd wave of uncertainty filled her. She couldn't read his expression. Truth be told, she had a very hard time ever quite getting a read on him, despite all of her talk about profiling him. Sure, she *thought* she understood his motivations, but when it came down to his core, Cassius Striker was truly a secretive SOB.

Fair. She was pretty secretive, too.

Except the secrets that they both carried might just wreck them, if they weren't careful. "I will trust you." There. Done. She'd take the first step. She sort of had to do it, considering that she'd already given the man her body and her heart.

He doesn't want your heart. Try to pull back. He clearly wants your body, and you want his. Take the pleasure he offers. Don't let your emotions get so wrapped up in him.

But...

Too late. Too late for that warning. Maybe it had been too late from the moment their paths had crossed that very first time. Fascination and curiosity had come first and then, the more she'd learned about him, the more she'd wanted to explore the darkness that clung to him.

"You *will* trust me? Or you already do?" A deep rumble as he remained inside of her.

"I already do." True statement. Despite everything, despite all the reasons she should not. "If I didn't trust you, then I wouldn't have walked into the house after the big fight scene. You know, when you were telling everyone how you were going to fuck me? Remember that? I wouldn't have just casually strolled inside."

And, surprising her to her absolute core—the core that still had fun little aftershocks of pleasure zipping through her—Cass smiled. A real smile. A slow one that stretched his lips and made the gold in his eyes gleam. "It was my turn."

She could not look away from that smile. And maybe it had made her brain processing speed slow down because she could not understand what he meant. "Excuse me?" His turn for what?

"You strode that sexy ass into *my* bar and announced that you were going to fuck me. Figured it was my turn to do the announcing. We're even."

Even? She snorted.

His grin actually *stretched.*

And her heart seemed to melt.

What is happening here? Actually, she knew what was happening. She'd just discovered that Cass had a lethal, secret weapon. His killer smile. After sucking in a couple of breaths, she was able to say, "I believe..." Her voice came out prim. *Prim* when he was still balls deep in her. "I believe I walked in the bar and simply asked what I had to do to, ah, get fucked by you. And I was just saying that for our audience."

He leaned over her.

He was getting *bigger* in her again.

Uh, oh. They were gonna need a new condom.

He braced one hand on the pool table. His face lowered over hers. He was intimidating. Dominant. Sexy as hell.

Her inner muscles tightened around him.

He growled. No more sexy smile. His face had gone hard and serious. "I *wasn't* just saying that for the audience. I was saying it because I fully intended to fuck you at the first opportunity."

She wet her lips. "Goal achieved."

His impossibly dark and long lashes flickered. "What in the hell am I supposed to do with you? Other than, of course, kill for you."

"Keep me," she whispered. But what she meant was... *Love me.* Good thing she managed to hold that part back.

"You don't belong in my world."

"You don't belong in the world you're in, either. You think I don't see that?" And she held her breath.

His jaw hardened. He began to withdraw.

"Trust has to start somewhere," she murmured.

He stilled.

"I could believe that you've been deliberating misleading me from the word go. That you are part of the Twin Cobras, and you knew who I was all along. That you're involved in whatever sick game the leaders play. You carry their tat. One of your MC members carried it. Violence surrounds you. Maybe you're fucking me as twisted part of their savage game. You'll fuck me, and you'll kill me."

"*Never.*"

She swallowed. "See, I happen to trust that to be the case. That you *won't* kill me. That you won't use me. That you won't betray me. I think...I think something very bad happened to you a long time ago. I also think that, deep down, you're just like me. We both want justice."

"*Vengeance.* That's what you want. You want to make them pay for what they did to you. If you just wanted justice, you'd still be sitting at the FBI with Gray." And he withdrew completely. Only he didn't go far.

He stood near the edge of the pool table. Cass yanked up his jeans. He had his clothes in place quickly, and she sat up, her legs dangling over the edge of the pool table. Agnes tugged her shirt down, covering herself as much as she could. Her jeans and underwear had been tossed about ten feet away.

He glowered at her. "It's about my profile, isn't it? You think you know so much about me because of it."

"I think..." And this was not a conversation she wanted to have while half-naked. "I think bad things happened to us both. I think someone you loved was hurt, and you went out to get payback."

He shook his head and turned away. "I am the bad thing that happens to people, sweetness."

"Not to me."

He swung back toward her instantly. His hands flew out and curled around her waist. He lifted her off the table. Held her in front of him for just a moment.

"Talk to me," she said, and the words were a plea. "Let me in." *In your life. In your world. In your heart.*

But something started to beep in the bar. An alarm? Her head turned toward the bank of monitors. She could see a motorcycle heading toward the bar.

"Javion is coming back." Cass had also looked that way. "You need to get dressed. If he sees you like this, then I'll have to kill him, too."

A joke. Not a funny one. "He's your friend." Agnes slanted a glance Cass's way. "You would not kill him." Certainty.

But he smiled. Not the grin that had disarmed her

213

before. Something altogether different. Harder. Colder. With more than a hint of cruelty. "Sweetness, I told you before. I killed my own father. That was the dead truth. So believe me when I say, I sure as hell would not hesitate to kill a friend."

And her jaw nearly hit the floor.

Chapter Eighteen

"Oh, come on. Thought we were being honest with each other, *trusting* each other." His voice held a cruel edge. What was he doing? What did he want? *For her to run away?* "I'm wicked to the core, sweetheart. You had to suspect the truth. You're the one who did all the digging on me. That's when you knew I was your perfect assassin."

Javion was getting closer. Cass had picked a really piss-poor time for the confession, but it was too late to change things now. *She doesn't love me. She should fear me. I need her to understand that truth. Now. Before...*

Before he allowed himself to hope for something that just would not, *could* not, happen.

"Your father...he was the former leader of the Night Strikers." She'd dressed. Fast. Good. Because if she'd been naked when Javion came in, he would have needed to fight the guy.

Sweetness, I wasn't kidding. No one gets to see what is mine. When it came to her, he wasn't quite rational. Then again, maybe he was never overly rational. As to the statement that Agnes had just made...

215

Fun point. "Actually, my uncle was the leader of the Strikers. My dad was his second-in-command. Most people didn't get that, though, because my uncle liked to stay in the shadows. He was all about pulling the strings from behind the scenes. He let my father be the public face. Let his enemies focus on my old man. And all the while, though, the biggest threat was standing in the dark." *Is the sonofabitch still in the dark?* Because Cass had truly thought that he'd eliminated Winston Striker. Only Levi had sure as hell made him second guess that belief...

Levi had to be lying, right? But...a few details nagged at Cass. Made him doubt. Worry. He didn't like to worry.

The biggest point of concern? Winston's body had never been recovered. Still, Cass had watched that bastard go off the edge of that cliff.

He'd personally forced him off the edge, after all. But no body had ever been discovered.

"Cass..." A careful exhale as she sighed his name. "I read the report. We talked about this before. Your father drove into oncoming traffic. And I *don't* believe that you would kill Javion. He's your friend."

"In this game, friendships come and go." They were also often as fake as everything else in his current life. "As for blood bonds? Those don't really matter. My father and my uncle were my enemies. Every twisted order that my uncle gave..." And Winston had certainly relished those sadistic dictates. "My father carried out with zero hesitation. No matter who he hurt in the process."

And he had a flash of those last moments with his father. Those fucking last moments that were lodged into his brain. He'd been chasing his father down that long, slick road. Night had surrounded him. The flash of lights from other vehicles blinded him every few moments as his motorcycle ate up the distance between him and his old man.

He'd been so close to the bastard, after tracking him for so long. His father had glanced back. Then gunned his motorcycle faster. His father had shifted lanes into oncoming traffic even though the damn big rig had been *right there.* Cass had shouted out a warning.

Why did I do that? Why did I tell him to stop?

But there had been no stopping. The collision had been brutal. The sounds burned into his memory. The crunch. The thud. The shattering of glass and metal. The way his father had cried out even as his body slammed into the pavement. Such a twisted mess.

Cass had braked his bike. Ran to him. Somehow, his dad had still been alive. Nearly every bone broken. Some shattered. Blood everywhere, but the tough sonofabitch had still been breathing. Still...talking. Heaving breaths. Rasping voice. *"You...think I don't r-regret what I did?"* His father's face had twisted with rage and grief and pain. A face that had looked so very much like Cass's own—just older, with more lines. More pain. The same fury. *"You th-think I don't...w-wish I could have chosen your m-mother? Chosen y-you?"*

But he hadn't chosen them. He hadn't protected them. His mother had been gentle and kind. She'd been everything sweet and good in the world. And she'd nearly been broken by the Strikers. His father had claimed to love her, but she'd fled into the night, taking Cass with her.

And...

His father had never followed.

The truck driver had jumped from his rig. He'd been yelling and calling for help. Cass had put his hands on his father's blood-soaked chest. A long hunk of metal—probably a piece of his smashed motorcycle—had pierced his dad's chest.

"St-staying away was the...b-best thing I could...d-do..."

Cold, brittle words. Like abandoning a child was some sort of good deed. Give the man a freaking medal. As if...

As if you weren't responsible for my mother's pain. As if I didn't know the truth.

Then his father hadn't said another word. His eyes had closed. He'd died right there, with Cass's hands on him. With the shriek of sirens in the distance. Cass had stared at him as pain and bitterness raged through him, and he'd thought...*One down. One to go.*

"Cass?"

He blinked. Focused on Agnes.

"It's okay." Her fingers squeezed his. Cass looked down in shock to realize that he was holding her hand. When the hell had he done that? When had he grabbed her hand to hold?

She squeezed his fingers again. Tighter, harder this time. "It's okay. You're not alone. I'm not going to run from you. We're partners."

"I *killed* him," he said again.

"I saw his rap sheet. I know the things that your father did. The drugs, the weapons. The hits."

Yeah, because his bastard of a father had been one cold-blooded killer. His uncle's favorite weapon. *Aim and shoot. Let him do all the dirty work for you while you stay in the shadows. Give him the orders, and he'll do anything you want. He can take all the blame.*

And in the end...

He came after my mother. "He let her go for years. My mother. Let her go. He let us both go. Acted like we didn't matter. That we weren't good enough for him to be bothered with us. I was two years old when she took me away. Ran away in the night. She started a new life. Just me and her at first." He had flashes of that life, every now and then. The little Christmas tree in the studio apartment. The train he'd found waiting on Christmas morning. The birthday cake she'd baked and the dinosaurs she'd painted on white poster boards for him. "Eventually, Gray and his mom joined us. They had their own...issues." He wasn't gonna tell her about Gray's father. Not an MC member. A monster who'd worn the skin of a hero instead. Pretending to be the perfect guy in society, but he'd been just as twisted as Cass's own father and uncle. Gray's story wasn't his to tell, though, and, shit, it was hard enough to share his own past.

Cass swallowed. "My mom lost her hearing in an accident when she was a kid. She taught me sign language, taught me how to read lips—she was a pro at that." He could remember when they'd gone to restaurants and she'd been able to tell him what people far across the room had been saying, just by watching their mouths move. "I used to think she had superpowers." He'd loved his mother so damn much. "No one else could pick up a conversation from the other side of a room. No one else could watch strangers in a mall and tell you exactly why they were arguing without ever hearing a sound from them. No one else could..." Cass stopped.

Agnes sent him a soft smile. "She sounds incredible."

Her hand still held his. No, correction, his hand held hers. But he made himself let her go. "She would have liked you."

Worry came and went on her face. "You sure about that? Sometimes, I'm not overly likable."

"What the hell? Damn straight, you are likable." Why

Cynthia Eden

would she think anything different? Who had she been hanging with? Who had told the woman she was not likable?

She shook her head. "I'm pretty sure I can be a pain in the ass."

"You're my pain in the ass," he groused. "And I like you plenty."

She smiled at him.

Javion was heading for the main entrance. Cass couldn't keep walking down memory lane. He needed to cut to the damn chase. "He let my mother go for years, and then one day...he sent a killer after her. I came home, and she was gone." Cass *hated* this memory. They'd been happy for so long. His mom, him, Gray, Gray's mother—hell, she'd escaped her own pain. They'd all been together. A family. Things had been good, dammit.

Until they'd been a nightmare. "I knew it was a professional hit when I came in. One shot to the head."

"Oh, God, Cass." She threw her arms around him. Held tight.

Had that part not been in the files she'd read on him? His profile? Huh. Maybe Gray had covered that up.

"Everything changed then." Fast. Because he had to get the words out. "My world went to shit. Gray and I—well, I guess you could say our paths diverged. I turned to the streets. Gangs. Fighting. I knew I had to go into the darkness in order to find the bastards who hurt her." A pause. "My father. My uncle. I had to get into their world and hunt them down. As for Gray, my cousin was meant to protect the world. He became a Marine. I became a killer."

"Your father *drove into oncoming traffic.* How many times do I have to remind you of that fact?"

He drove into traffic to get away from me. "I cornered

220

my uncle on a long, desolate stretch of road in Arizona. He was between me and my gun and a cliff that would send him to hell. There was no way out. He spun away after telling me that *he'd* ordered the hit on my mother because he'd learned that my dad was watching my mom again, that he was still clinging to the same old *weakness.*" His mother had never been a weakness. Nothing about her had been weak. *My mom had superpowers.* He swallowed. And maybe his hands closed around Agnes and he hugged her. "My uncle...Winston drove that motorcycle of his right off the cliff even as I fired my weapon. I hit him, I know I did, and his bike crashed. I stood at the edge of the cliff, and I looked below, and I saw the wreckage. I *know* my shot found its mark. I shot him in the back..."

Wait. Fuck.

"Cass?"

He pulled away from her. "I shot him in the back," he repeated. "And all of these sonsofbitches are coming at *my* back. Fitting, huh? Or maybe they're just following orders. I'm not the only one in the family who was—is—an eye-for-an-eye type."

"Orders?" Her brow crinkled as she peered up at him.

"His orders. Because if Levi Addams is to be believed...I didn't kill the bastard. Somehow, despite getting shot and flying off a freaking cliff, Winston Striker is still alive—and he's after me." He rolled one shoulder. "Guess that means that, this time, I will just have to carve out his heart in order to make sure he's dead."

Javion was pounding on the double entrance doors. No more waiting. No more time.

Cass swung away from her so that he could go meet the guy.

But her hand flew out to curl around his left arm. "Why

221

didn't you tell me that Levi had the tattoo? You must have known about it."

"Yeah, I knew."

"*Why* didn't you tell me? And do any other members of your crew also carry it? If so, I want to see their arms. I have to see the tats. That tat is the only way I can truly identify the man who tried to kill me."

"What if more than one person has the exact tat? You think of that?"

"Of course, I thought of that." Her eyes narrowed. "I remember his height. I remember his walk. I remember the sound of his voice. I remember the exact way the tat looked against his skin. If I see the SOB, I will know him."

He believed she would. He also believed that Javion was pounding harder out there.

"It was a very specific tat, Cass. The scales were the most detailed I've ever seen. A real Rembrandt of a tattoo artist made the design."

Yeah...about that...

The tattoo is the key, and I can give her the key. But they just didn't have *time.* Not for a full explanation. Not with Javion coming in. "Don't say anything about the tat in front of Javion. We'll talk when we're alone." Hard to get her alone, though, with his whole crew now about to swarm in protective mode. *An attempted hit was made. They will be out for blood.* Fair enough, he was out for blood, too.

"You don't trust Javion?" She truly seemed surprised. Cute.

"At this point, I only trust you."

Her lips parted. She let him go. "I think that might be the nicest thing you've said to me."

Really? Then he should probably step up his game. He

ambled for the door. "You've got incredible eyes. Each time I look into them, I feel like I lose a piece of my soul."

"What?"

"Your mouth makes me want to sin. And your ass— you've got the best damn ass I've seen. Curved and hot. I want to grab it and hold on for the ride."

"Cass."

He reached for the door. Stopped. "And you're not unlikable. Don't know who told you that shit. You're tough. You're fierce. You're determined. You're also bloodthirsty, which is fucking sexy to me."

"You...you're saying nice things to me."

"Yeah, I am." When he never said nice things to anyone. But with her, he wanted to give compliments. Actually, he wanted to give her the world. Just to see those amazing eyes of hers light up more.

But he didn't have the world to give her.

Though I am working on giving her the vengeance she craves. Because she wasn't in love with a dead man...*she's in love with me.*

He yanked open the door. Stood toe to toe with Javion. "That was fast."

"Problem." A muscle flexed along Javion's jaw.

Why was everyone telling him about problems? Just once, couldn't someone come to him with an actual solution? Was that too much to ask? "I am aware," Cass returned with roll of his shoulders. "Pretty sure we left a dead man in a field."

"The shooter took out Hugo."

"What?" Shock rolled through him. Hugo was dead?

"And Axel swears he got a look at the rider with the gun. That he was on a bike belonging to the Western

Mavericks. Not just any bike, though. *The leader's ride.* That the shooter was *Bayne Hendrix.*"

Behind Cass, Agnes cleared her throat. "That name is familiar."

Cass grunted. Damn straight it was familiar. "He was in Atlanta. He's the prick who told me that Judas was coming after you."

"That would be why it seemed familiar," she murmured. "I thought you'd taken care of him already?"

By "taken care of"...did she mean beat hell out of him? Because he'd damn well used force in order to get the guy to cooperate with him before. He'd also ordered Bayne to get the hell away from the East Coast. "Apparently, the man is determined to keep being a problem. One I will need to permanently eliminate."

Javion's dark gaze held Cass's. "Don't worry, boss. I've got a ghost on him right now."

Her feet padded closer. "A ghost?"

Javion's stare cut to her. "It's a name for an MC member who won't be seen. He's tailing the rider. He'll report back and we can swarm on him when we have a final location." He grunted as his stare focused on Cass once again. "Obviously, Bayne is trying for a power play. He wants you eliminated. Must have been working with Levi. Maybe he decided to fire at Levi before the guy could out him to you. And dumbass Levi just stood there because he never thought his partner would turn on him."

Cass didn't move. "Yeah, you just can't trust anyone these days."

Javion gave him a little salute. "Good thing you got me covering your back, huh?"

"Absolutely," Cass told him. "But..." He reached out for

Agnes. His fingers twined with hers. "It's even better that I have *her*."

Javion's brows climbed.

Cass brought her hand to his lips. "My ride or die, aren't you, sweetheart?"

"Um, how about me being your ride or kill? That's better, isn't it? Because we keep living that way and our enemies die?"

Yes, that was better.

"You staying here?" Javion wanted to know. "Keeping low until we eliminate this prick?"

"Do I look like a coward to you?" Cass asked, voice silky.

Javion backed up a step. "No, I never meant—"

"It's good that you have a ghost on him, but I think that I know where Bayne is heading. I suspect we're all going to the same place, actually." They'd eventually, wind up there, anyway.

Agnes cleared her throat again. "Sorry, but where is that? Exactly? Like...is it hell? Are we all heading to hell?"

He kissed her hand again. "Pretty close."

"I was joking," she muttered.

"I wasn't," he returned without looking away from Javion. "You know I had a meeting scheduled in Arizona." It was the whole reason he'd been traveling across the country. A meeting with the leaders of the biggest MCs in the US.

Javion glanced over at Agnes. "You're really taking her? There?"

She sidled ever closer. "He missed the ride or kill part of our relationship."

"She's getting tatted," Cass said. "I fought for her. I took the challenge. She's in the MC, and where I go, she goes, too."

"She's a Fed." Javion's eyes narrowed. "You're gonna start a war with her at your side."

"Kinda think I already have started one." He grinned. The grin slowly faded, though, as Javion shook his head. "She's not a Fed," Cass rumbled.

"No?" Javion was clearly doubtful. "Former Fed? Like that makes anything better?"

"She's mine," Cass returned. "Anyone who has a problem with that can go through me."

Javion nodded. "Pretty sure that's why bullets are flying at you. Because Bayne has a massive problem with you—and her."

"Then I'll just kill him and eliminate the problem." Done.

Agnes elbowed him.

He kept holding her hand. "I have a meeting in Arizona. I won't be late. She will be there. We'll walk into hell together." Finally, his head turned toward Agnes. "Ride or kill, huh?"

She bit her lower lip. He loved that lower lip.

Slowly, she let it go. And nodded. "Ride or kill," she whispered.

He leaned down and kissed her.

Javion swore. "You're both fucking insane." He whirled and stomped out.

Cass's head slowly lifted. As he gazed at her, Agnes's thick lashes rose so that she was staring straight at him. Trying to steal his soul again.

No need to steal it, princess. Pretty sure all that I am—hell, everything belongs to you. He swallowed. "You meant that bit about trust, didn't you?"

"Yes."

"You trust me, completely?" He could hear more motorcycles arriving. They would have to get moving. But before he made the big meeting in Arizona, he had one important pitstop to make. A pitstop that he was making for her. He'd come to this area of Texas to help Agnes achieve her goal. Getting vengeance.

A Rembrandt tattoo artist, huh? One exceptionally good with scales.

"I do trust you," she assured him.

"Good." His lips pressed to hers once more. A tender kiss. Because he could do tender, sometimes. At least, he could do it with her. "Remember that, will you?"

"Cass, what are you going to do?"

"I'm gonna take you to see a very bad man...about a very bad tat."

Chapter Nineteen

ANOTHER DAY, ANOTHER DEAD BODY LEFT BY CASS AND Agnes. They were truly monumental pains in his ass. Individually, they were problematic. But put them together? *Monumental pains in my ass.*

"So...you're with the FBI, huh?" The deputy pulled off his hat and clenched it in his hands. "You flew in on your own plane? That happen a lot, the Feds just zipping around on private planes?

No, it did not, in fact, happen a lot. Gray crouched near the body. Malik had come with him on this not-so-fun excursion, and the other Fed watched silently from about five feet away. "I'm not your typical Fed," Gray responded. "My job comes with perks."

"Like...a private plane? Because I heard talk about it landing at the strip near town."

He was staring at Levi Addams. A Levi with a cut throat, a stab wound in his lower right side. And a bullet wound in his chest. "The cut to the neck wasn't deep enough to kill him." Just a slice. "Neither was the one in his side. But that bullet to the heart..." Yeah, it would have done the trick. His head turned as he tried to figure out just where the shooter must have been. "Where were you when you fired?" he murmured.

"Uh, sir?" The deputy again. Deputy Jaxon McClint. His badge was all shiny and new. "Sir, we recovered the gun right next to the body."

Yes, he'd heard about that discovery. "You think it was an up-close shot?"

"Well, yes, sir, the gun was right here—"

"There is a lot of blood splatter at this scene." He'd seen blood drops all over the place. "And the bruising on the vic tells me that there was one hell of a fight that went down here." He did not like this, at all. He turned again. Surveyed the woods not too far from him. A whole lot of woods out there. After a moment, Gray pointed to one particular area. "I think the shooter was there."

Jaxon scratched his chin. "There, sir?"

Malik did not speak.

"Blood splatter tells a story. Haven't you ever watched *Dexter?*"

Jaxon shook his head. "Who is he?"

Who is...*hell*. "I think the bullet that tore through Levi's chest was fired from a rifle. Probably one with a scope. Killer got him in his sights, he took the shot, and bam, Levi was eliminated."

Jaxon pointed to the ground. "But the gun was found right there."

"Yes, I am aware." He was also aware, based on the description of the weapon that he'd been given, that the gun near the vic had probably belonged to Agnes. Her gun, her prints. And...shit, total clusterfuck of a situation.

The radio on Jaxon's hip crackled. He pulled it out and almost dropped it on the dead body. Luckily, he caught it just in time. "S-sorry." A flush stained his cheeks. He hustled back, fingers fumbling with the radio.

Gray glanced over at Malik.

Malik simply raised an eyebrow.

"*Another* body?" Jaxon demanded as he clutched the radio. "Where? Shot, too? And you say a rifle was found near him?"

Yeah, sometimes, it almost hurt to be right all the time.

"We got another body," Jaxon loudly exclaimed. "Male, about six-foot-two, with about a dozen silver chains around his neck and a discarded rifle at the scene."

The description of the vic sounded like Hugo Lorens. The guy was in Cass's crew and always sported his silver.

Jaxon turned away and kept talking into his radio.

Malik closed in on Gray. "What's going on?"

"A war, from the sound of things." He pointed down at the body. Levi had been covered up before they arrived. Not moved, per his instructions. The scene had been secured and blocked, and he'd hauled ass on his private plane to get there. But it wasn't like they could just leave the body outside much longer. Decomposition and all sorts of screw-them issues would be occurring.

He eyed the ranch house. It had already been searched. Nothing important had turned up. Nothing overly useful.

"They can't be that far away," Malik murmured. "We were here damn fast."

Yes, they had been. Because he'd gotten a text right after the shooting and had been on the way instantly. A text that had not come from Cass.

Are you holding out on me, cuz? He didn't like that Cass hadn't told him about the shooting. Not the best sign.

"Do you know where they are headed?" Malik asked.

Oh, he had a pretty good idea. The finale had been in the works for a very long time. But the players in the finale had shifted a bit. Agnes shouldn't have been involved. She was, though. And maybe...maybe that was a good thing.

Especially if Cass's own crew couldn't be trusted.

Or maybe Agnes being involved is bad. Bad as in, the worst mistake I've ever made. Because he could have stopped things. He could have planned an alternative that didn't involve her riding off with Cass. But when he'd plotted, and, yes, *profiled,* having Agnes at Cass's side had seemed like the best option.

Because I trust Agnes completely. She might doubt herself, but I don't doubt her. And I know that she will protect Cass's back. Cass. His family. His cousin, yes, but more. His brother by choice.

But Cass wasn't aware of the other players also closing in. One particular player was pissed that Agnes was riding straight into danger with Cass. Ryan Quinn was a dangerous bastard on his good days. On his bad days? The man was hell on earth. He usually worked covert ops for Uncle Sam, but this time, he was going off script. And making new problems for Gray.

As if Gray wanted more problems in his life.

Why couldn't Ryan have been tied up with a case in Spain or Russia or somewhere else across the Atlantic right now? Instead, Ryan was screwing up Gray's plans.

I'm staring at a dead body. The second one since Agnes and Cass paired up. That couple is lethal. And as to why the guy on the ground was dead...

"He betrayed Cass," Gray said as his gaze flickered back to the dead man.

"How do you know?" Malik asked.

Cynthia Eden

He crouched beside the body once more. With his gloved hand, he lifted the edge of Levi's shirt. "When you betray your MC leader, you don't walk away clean." In fact, you rarely walked away. He pushed up the bloody material to reveal the slash in Levi's side.

"Shit." An exclamation of surprise from Malik. "Is that a 'T' carved into his skin?"

Yes, it was. "T for Traitor," Gray murmured.

"Damn." Then. "Damn...what in the hell has Agnes gotten herself into?"

I told you already, a war. One that has been a long time coming.

"You swore to me Cass would watch her back." Now Malik was angry. Fair enough. The guy liked and respected his partner. A week after Malik had joined Gray's team at the Bureau, Agnes had shoved him down two seconds before a bullet would have blown his brains out. She'd spotted the shooter hanging out in the alley. Malik hadn't. She'd saved his ass.

He'd been watching hers since then. And Malik didn't always think others could protect the woman as well as he could. But in this instance, Gray was sure that Cass wouldn't let anyone hurt Agnes. *I better not be wrong.* "He *will* watch her back."

"Until what...the others find out she's working undercover? Then is she gonna get a T carved into her skin, too? And what the hell will happen to Cass? If the others find out the truth..."

Gray rose to his full height. "Cass has always understood what will happen to him. As for Agnes, I don't think Cass will let anyone carve up her skin."

"You don't *think*? Or you know he wouldn't?" Malik's strained expression showed his worry.

"He wouldn't." Gray hoped that he sounded confident. Usually, people couldn't see past his lies. And they never saw when he was uncertain. *I am very, very uncertain right now.* "He won't let anyone even so much as put a mark on her."

* * *

Agnes eyed the needle. She bit her lower lip. She squinted and eyed the needle *harder*. "So..." A long, drawn out *Soooooooo*. "Where will you be putting the tat?"

The tattoo artist sighed as he shifted in his chair. A big, burly guy with a body full of swirling and actually quite stunning tats. He'd admitted to drawing the tats himself. The hulking man seemed truly talented.

They were in his shop. Apparently, a must-stop visit in the middle of their current madness. The wall to the right was filled with tattoo sketches. Lots and lots of snakes. Some dragons. A medusa with a gorgeous, heaving snake body.

Someone is really into snakes.

Cass came up behind her. A Cass who had stripped off his shirt and slapped a bandage over the wound on his right shoulder. She was sitting in the black lounge chair for customers, and he leaned over her, locking a powerful hand on the armrest to her right.

"You're looking a little green sunshine," he purred.

They'd driven for three hours to get to this place. Her whole body ached, she was hungry, she wanted more answers, and she did *not* relish getting jabbed with a needle again and again.

"I think the tattoo should go..." His left hand feathered over her body. Darted down between her breasts.

She hissed out a breath. Her hand flew up to grab his.

But he...he caught her hand. Brought it to his lips. And pressed a kiss right along her racing pulse, on her inner wrist. "Right here," he said, as his gaze met hers above the hand he held.

The tattoo artist grunted. "And what am I inking her with? The Striker emblem?"

They had an emblem? And what did that look like?

"She doesn't belong to the Strikers." Cass's mild response. "She belongs to me."

A little shiver went down her spine.

Cass's head turned toward the tattoo artist. "You gave me the newest tat I carry—you marked me with it not too long ago. You did a good job on it."

Again, the guy grunted. Clearly, he was not a conversational kind of fellow.

"It was the two-headed cobra," Cass added.

And another shiver had her shifting in the chair even as her gaze sharpened on the artist. As if she hadn't already figured out—based on all the snake tats on the wall—that this man had given Cass that very specific tattoo. Her attention shifted from the artist to the wall of sketches. So many sketches.

Her gaze lingered on one of the dragons. Goosebumps rose on her skin. *The man is talented. Definitely talented. His art is unique.* Her attention tracked back to him.

The tattoo artist licked his lips. Eight gold hoops climbed up his right ear lobe. "I ain't putting a two-headed cobra on her."

"Of course, not," Cass murmured. "Because she's not a member of that select group. But...you know who the members are, don't you? Because I was referred to you. To you, specifically. You're the one who does the best snake work."

"It's all in the scales." His forehead began to sweat. His gaze darted to the doorway.

Javion had just entered the tattoo parlor.

"Scales. Yeah. Right. You also tatted one of my crew, Levi Addams."

A curt nod from the artist. "Levi's cool," he muttered. "Had some drinks with him and—"

"He's dead. I fucking carved a T into the traitor's body and left him to bleed out."

He'd carved a *what?* She snapped her mouth closed to hide her shock. Agnes had not been aware of the *carving* portion of the event.

The tattoo artist leapt to his feet. "I thought you were tatting her."

"Um. Change of plans." Cass smiled. "I've decided I like her just the way she is. I'll put a ring on her finger if the others need to see proof of my claim, but no one is touching her. Not with hands. Damn well not with needles."

This would be why he'd asked her to trust him. The whole scene was a setup. She'd rather suspected it might be.

Cass inclined his head toward the artist. "I need information from you, Raz."

Raz?

"I am looking for a very specific tattoo. I want to know who is wearing that tattoo. I strongly suspect, see, that you are the designer who placed the tattoo on the individual's body. After all, you do the best snakes. All in the scales, right?"

She sucked in a breath. Cass had high-tailed it to this place so that he could get a name, for her? *So freaking sweet.*

She'd tried searching for the tattoo and the tattoo artist before, but that had been like searching for a needle in a haystack.

Cass had just found the, uh, needle for her. The tattoo needle, that was. Excitement quivered through her. They'd been surrounded by his crew during the drive, so they hadn't been able to talk freely. When they'd been on the motorcycle, Cass had been flying, and the roar of the motorcycle had been so loud. If she'd wanted to talk to him, she would have needed to scream. Not like she wanted her screams overheard by the others.

It's all about trust. Cass was proving that she was right to trust him completely. She jumped out of the chair and grabbed a piece of paper. Raz had plenty of pens around, so she sketched out the image fast. Easy to do because her drawing skills weren't rusty, and her memory of that particular snake burned hot and bright in her mind. "This is it." She slapped the paper against Raz's chest.

He looked down. Eased the paper back so he could stare at it. As soon as she saw the flare of his eyes, she knew he'd recognized the tat.

"Who did you mark with that design?" Cass asked, voice as cool as a summer breeze.

Javion closed in, moving to stand right next to Raz.

The bell over the tattoo shop's door jingled. Another member of Cass's crew had just walked in. The one called Bear filled the doorway. *Filled* it.

"Does your memory need jogging?" Cass asked. Then, when there was no immediate response from Raz, he drawled, "Hey, Bear, come do me a solid and jog this guy's memory with your fist—"

"He'll kill me." Sweat dotted Raz's temples.

"Bear?" A roll of Cass's broad shoulders. The powerful muscles of his chest flexed. "Nah, he'll just shake you up a bit."

A frantic widening of Raz's eyes. "No. The man with that tat. If I tell, I'm dead."

Cass closed in on the tattoo artist. "If you don't tell me, you're dead." He eyed the array of needles next to Raz. "FYI, that death will be very painful. See, I'm not a professional when it comes to the art of tattooing. Don't know how to use all the equipment. And when I try to use these needles on you—and I will have to try, if you don't cooperate with me—it will hurt. A lot."

Her body practically vibrated. This man...Raz *knew* the tattoo she'd drawn. It was his tattoo, after all. He'd been the designer.

Raz's gaze cut to her. "Actually...I-I used that same design twice. Two people have that tat."

Her heart thudded hard in her chest. Cass had said that he believed two men were killing, two leaders in the Twins. Two *serial killers*.

"I'm a dead man," Raz rasped.

"You will be," Bear swore from the doorway. His hands had fisted.

Raz's gaze jumped from Bear to Cass. Then lingered on Cass. "G-gave it to your uncle, Cass. Gave it to Winston Striker when he first came up with the idea of the Twins." He grabbed a tattoo gun. Gripped it tightly in his hand. "That was years ago. When I first opened my business. Wanted to make him something badass. So I worked hard. Went through about a dozen sketches before I created one that he approved."

Cass's uncle had come up with the Twins? She slanted a quick glance at Cass.

He showed no surprise.

"The other bastard...he came to me about eight years ago, wanting the exact design."

Cynthia Eden

Eight years ago. That was right around the time her whole life had changed.

"Tell me his name," Cass demanded.

Instead of saying the name, Raz lunged forward, swiping out with the tattoo gun—

Cass planted an upper cut in his face. Agnes was pretty sure one of Raz's teeth went flying as the man staggered back. The tattoo gun went flying, too. It banged into the wall of sketches.

"His name," Cass repeated, tone patient.

Raz lifted a hand to cover his bloody mouth. "Bayne! Bayne Hendrix!"

That name again. Bayne had been the one who murdered Hugo. The one who'd taken a shot at Cass and killed Levi.

"Put it on his right wrist." Raz had blood dripping on his chin. "Bastard wanted it to match the one I gave Winston, but Winston wore his on his back, just like you! Now I told you what I know." A swipe of his fingers over the blood. His green eyes darted around the parlor. "You're all fucking twisted bastards, and I want you out of here! *Out! I want you—*"

Javion stepped forward and punched him. Raz went down hard. Out cold.

Javion sighed. "He was getting loud. I hate it when they get loud." His lips pursed. "You get what you came for?"

Cass nodded. "Bayne Hendrix is a dead man."

Bayne Hendrix. Bayne Hendrix. The name replayed in her mind again and again. Finally, she had her target. After all of this time.

"But he's a Twin," Javion muttered. "And the leader of the Western Mavericks. Won't that be a problem for you?"

His head turned. His gaze held Agnes's. "I'll make sure he's not a problem *for anyone* again." His fingers curled around hers. "Come on. Let's get the hell out of here."

But when he tugged her, she didn't move.

"Agnes?"

"I kinda wanted a tat."

"What?"

"Yours look really good. All tough and badass. I had worked up my nerve, and I was ready for one." But the tattoo artist was still out cold. Not like she'd trust him to come at her with a needle now, either, so...

"Rain check," Cass told her. "We'll get matching ones."

She quirked a brow. "Now you're just teasing. You're literally being a tattoo tease."

"You're stalling." He tugged again. This time, he pulled her closer to him. "Why?"

Because when she'd glanced at the wall of tats, she'd recognized one. One of the dragons with the detailed scales, and she knew that they might have another problem. "He's really good at scales," she whispered.

Cass frowned.

Before she could speak again, they heard the roar of a motorcycle. Just another one of Cass's gang closing in, right? But...

Her goosebumps were getting worse. *If I'm right about that particular dragon tattoo, then that new rider might not belong to Cass's crew. And...I think I might know who our visitor is.* Someone who'd been doing some hunting of his own. Hunting that had led to Raz's tattoo shop.

He'd been hunting and he kept this from me...typical. Very, very typical of her overprotective...brother. *If I'm right...If I'm right...*

239

Bear ducked out of the parlor, then bobbed right back inside. "He's not one of ours."

This was going to be bad. She could feel it inside.

"Hendrix?" Cass instantly demanded. "Part of his crew?"

"Don't know. The SOB is coming right at the shop," Bear fired out.

Cass's jaw locked. He gently pushed Agnes toward Javion. "Keep her inside."

"No," Agnes said immediately.

"Princess, you keep that sweet ass of yours inside this place. I don't know what I'm facing."

She ran to the window in the front of the small parlor. She peered through the blinds. Saw the man on the massive motorcycle. Saw the black jacket. The black helmet. Saw him stand up, take off the helmet. And the light hit his dark hair. Then his face as he turned toward them.

Her breath caught. "You can't fight him."

"If he's part of Hendrix's crew, hell, yes, I can." Cass stalked for the door.

She jumped in front of him. "No, no, you aren't listening to me. You *can't fight him.*" Her feverish gaze searched his. She'd trusted him with the scene at the tattoo shop. She needed him to trust her now because she could not just spill all right then, not with both Bear and Javion watching and with Raz groaning and his eyelids flickering as he started to wake up on the floor.

She grabbed Cass and hauled him close. Agnes shot onto her tiptoes. His hands flew to her waist as she planted a desperate kiss on his mouth, hard and fast, and then her mouth darted toward his ear. *"Trust me,"* she breathed. Pleaded. Demanded.

His grip tightened on her waist.

Trust. That was what it came down to with them. He had to trust her. Or else everything was about to blow up in their faces.

Cass carefully shifted her to the side. "Bear, there's a storage room in the back. Drag Raz in there and secure him."

Bear immediately stepped forward.

"Javion, keep her in here. If she gets anywhere near danger, I am holding you personally responsible."

"Shit." From Javion.

"She does *not* walk out that front door," Cass emphasized.

"Understood."

Uh, no, nothing was *understood.* "I'm the one who saved your ass last time! You don't bench a good player when the game gets intense!"

Cass sent her a hard frown. "You protect your most valuable asset. Always. Now stay the fuck in here." He slipped around her and reached for the door.

"You don't even have a shirt on!" Agnes snapped.

Axel popped into the doorway. Yes, she'd finally gotten good at attaching the names to all the crew members. Or at least, she'd learned the ones who'd challenged Cass in that fierce fight scene. "We've got unwelcome company," Axel announced.

Uh, yes, Bear had told them already.

"Not someone I recognize." He tossed a black t-shirt at Cass. A t-shirt and a gun.

Instead of putting on the t-shirt, Cass wrapped it around the gun. The better to hide his weapon.

No, no, no. "Cass..."

He looked back at her.

Then he winked.

241

And he walked away.

Agnes immediately lunged after him.

"Nope." Javion locked his hands around her waist and hauled her back. "Can we take a moment and deeply analyze what he meant when he said I would be held 'personally responsible' should you rush out there?"

Chapter Twenty

It took a lot of balls for someone to stand off against the Night Strikers. But the prick who'd just rolled in, parked his beast of a Harley, and was now sauntering toward Cass with his black helmet tucked under the curve of his left arm...this guy showed not a hint of fear at all. In fact, as he drew closer, the only emotion that he did show...

That would be rage.

Rage glittered in his brown eyes. The sun was still up, still hanging in the sky, though definitely dipping lower now, and Cass could clearly see the man's hard features. His black hair. The slight crook in his nose that had probably come from a fight.

Tattoos swirled on the man's fingers. Dipping beneath the sleeves of his black coat. The guy was close to Cass's build. Same height. Shoulders about as wide. They seemed to probably be the same age.

The stranger stopped about five feet away from Cass. Cass was aware that his crew was watching. He'd given them the sign to stand down as soon as he walked out.

Agnes knew this prick, he got that. So Cass figured he

must be staring at some undercover Fed. The dumbass should have known better than to come in for a confrontation. Had Gray sent the dude? Was this about Levi's dead body? Or, hell, maybe they'd found Hugo. *Sonofabitch.*

The stranger swept his gaze over Cass, seemed to take in his measure, and then the guy's jaw hardened even more before he gritted, "You're in my way."

"Am I?" Cass let his brows climb. "You here for a tat?" They were in a semi-busy area. An old strip mall with a few shops left in it. The tattoo parlor. A barber shop. A liquor store. So there were civilians around who might notice if Cass just beat the hell out of a stranger. And then those civilians might do something problematic like call the cops.

If this guy was a Fed, then Cass should probably not beat the hell out of him. Plus, he didn't want Agnes mad.

Trust me. She'd trusted him in the tattoo parlor. Now he was supposed to show the same faith to her.

"Not here for a tat," the man rumbled right back. "I'm here for *her.*"

Cass blinked. "I think you're gonna want to repeat that line." Hard. Intimidating.

The man stepped forward with zero fear. "I'm here," he said, very clearly, "for *her.* I know Agnes is inside. There is no way she'd be far away from you. I tracked you two, I saw the bodies you left, and I am not fucking leaving here without her."

Oh, but this prick was making things hard. "I'm *trying* not to beat the ever-loving-hell out of you," Cass told him, meaning the words. He gripped the t-shirt Axel had given him in his right hand. The t-shirt and the gun. Axel had clearly expected for this scene to go sideways, and he'd wanted Cass to be prepared. "But you are making things difficult."

"Agnes," the man snapped.

"Who the fuck are you?" Cass snapped right back. "And why do you want to see *my* lady?"

"Because I've got unfinished business with her." Angry.

And Cass realized that maybe he wasn't looking at a Fed. Maybe he was looking at someone the Feds had targeted. Agnes had told him a bit about some of her cases, enough for him to know that dangerous people were pissed at her. If this prick had been tracking her...hell, their public scene in Atlanta would have attracted a lot of attention. Maybe an old enemy of hers had come out of the woodwork.

"Consider your business finished," Cass informed him flatly. *You will see her over my cold, dead body.* "Get on your bike. Drive the hell out of here while you still can." He was attempting to give the man helpful life advice. As in, advice to help the jerk keep living his life.

The man's muddy brown gaze dipped to the bandage on Cass's shoulder. "What the hell were you doing? Stopping for a fresh tat?"

Nah. He'd been bandaging a bullet wound and getting answers. It had taken Cass far too long to work his way in with the Twins. In fact, Levi had been his *in.* Cass had never liked the prick, but he'd seen the two-headed tat on the guy, and he'd known that he could use Levi. So he'd poached the man from a different MC. Brought him in the Strikers and then used Levi and his connections to work his way into the Twins for initiation.

The initiation? *Fucking brutal.*

But he wasn't thinking about that shit now. He couldn't.

He had to deal with the SOB in front of him who was

245

not getting to Agnes. Javion had better do his job and keep the woman inside until the scene was clear. "I do like my ink," Cass allowed in response to the stranger's question about getting a fresh tat. But, no, he hadn't come to the shop for ink. He'd come for answers.

He'd thought the tattoos might be the key. Yes, there were other artists that would ink the members of the Twins, but Raz was the best damn tattoo artist out there. A freaking Rembrandt, as Agnes had described, compared to the others. And if they were looking for the two sadistic pricks at the top of the food chain, then Cass had figured those guys would only get their snakes designed by the very best.

And now he had names.

My own damn uncle. A man who should have rotted to just bones in a ravine. Except Levi had tried to say the SOB was still out there, still alive.

And the second name belonged to Bayne Hendrix. A prick who kept popping up in the wrong places. Cass had never seen Bayne without his leather coat. Never had a chance to look at the man's arms to see if he was tatted with a two-headed snake.

But I will be facing off with him very soon.

After he was finished with his current problem.

"So what did you get this time?" The stranger kept his helmet tucked under his arm. "Let me guess..." He nodded when Cass remained silent. "By any chance, would it have been a two-headed snake? A cobra?"

Then the arm that held the helmet shifted. He grabbed the helmet with his opposite hand, and when the sleeve of his coat rode up a bit, Cass caught sight of black ink. Scales.

Claws?

Not a snake, but something big with a whole lot of

scales and razor-sharp claws. *Had that been a freaking dragon?*

And there had been some dragon tats pinned to the wall of Raz's shop.

The stranger's tat was hidden nearly as quickly as it was revealed.

Cass knew he had to tread carefully so... "Maybe," Cass allowed. "Do you happen to sport one of those yourself? You got a two-headed snake twined on your body?"

"No." Brittle. "Because I'm not a murdering bastard. This is your last warning. Get out of my way. I'm getting to Agnes."

"I *am* a murdering bastard." It was what the world saw. *Not Agnes, though. She keeps telling me that I'm not the villain because she is absolutely adorable like that.* "You'll find out that truth if you don't back your ass up and get the hell out of here in the next five seconds."

"This isn't Night Striker territory. You belong on the East Coast."

"I belong anywhere I want." *Five, four, three...*It was Cass's turn to shift his stance a bit, too. Or rather, his turn to move his arm and pull back the t-shirt that Axel had given to him so that Cass could reveal the weapon he held. *Two and one...*

His new enemy glared down at the gun. "Gonna shoot me right here? With witnesses around?"

"Not if you follow directions. Your time is up, though, and my finger is itching."

"I'm not armed. Didn't come out here with a weapon." The man put his helmet on the ground and slowly lifted both of his hands. Except, he didn't raise them with his palms out, the way perps usually showed cops that they weren't a threat. His hands lifted. Both hands. Each hand quickly formed an L shape. The guy's right hand rose toward his chin. His thumb brushed across the faint cleft there, only for the right hand to dip in a fall and tap on top of his still L-shaped left hand. He did the move only once, before both of his hands dropped back to his sides.

Sonofabitch.

Cass's heart raced faster. No way had he just seen the sign that he *thought* he'd seen. But, then again, he knew his sign language. His mother had made sure of that. He'd been signing before he'd ever spoken. And this prick before him— the guy knew enough about Cass to realize that he could communicate with him this way.

"She won't appreciate you shooting me," the man said, his voice low and rough and carrying only to Cass. "In fact, I'm pretty sure that's an unforgivable sin in her eyes. You pull that trigger, and you may as well be the one who is dead to her."

* * *

"Javion, I want us to be friends, I really do." Agnes peered through the window blinds and tried to figure out what in the heck was happening outside. Currently, a lot of bikers were watching the standoff between the two big men about twenty feet from the front of the tattoo parlor. "But if you don't get away from that door and let me out, we are going to have a problem."

"Personally. Responsible." His retort. Basically, the same retort he'd given her before. After that retort, she'd elbowed her way out of his grip, and he'd taken up a guard position near the front door. "That means Cass will personally rip out my spine and shove it down my throat if you get out this door. I don't want my spine ripped out, so

I'm following orders. And we are not friends. We met like four days ago."

"Some friendships happen really fast. Thought that was what we had going on." Her eyes narrowed. Cass and Ryan were having a stand-off. She could see Ryan's lips moving, but she had zero idea what he was saying.

How in the world is my brother here? But he was. As soon as he'd taken off that helmet, and she'd seen his beloved, crooked nose—uh, her fault, by the way. An accident when she'd fallen out of a treehouse as a kid and he'd caught her and her flying foot.

As soon as she'd seen his face in that parking lot, she'd felt like she'd just gotten walloped in the stomach. Her brother should not be there. He should not be riding around on a motorcycle. And he should not be facing off with Cass while her lover held a gun.

Lover.

Her brother and her lover were about to kill each other. Talk about a nightmare situation.

"I need to read lips. Stat." Agnes wished that she possessed his mom's superpower. But she didn't know how to read lips. Not at all. She'd just focused on learning sign language once she'd realized that she needed to team up with Cass. And she'd only learned basics. Not like she knew how to have a whole long conversation in sign language or anything.

Ryan lifted his hands.

"No weapons," she whispered. "So don't shoot him, Cass." *Trust me.*

"That fucker has weapons on him. He might not have them in his hands, but he has weapons." Certainty from Javion. He was peeking out the open front door. A very *slightly* open front door. One he'd cracked open a few inches, the better for him to keep tabs on the scene outside.

It was a door she needed to exit.

Not like there is just one door in this place, Agnes. There has to be a back door, too. Bear had gone toward the rear of the parlor, with Raz. Bear hadn't come back yet.

Her eyes narrowed as she watched Ryan bring his thumb to his chin. Her breath shuddered out. *Sister. He's signing to Cass that I'm his sister.* Not like she could have blurted out that the biker closing in on the shop was her big brother. She just didn't trust Javion and Bear and certainly not Raz with that kind of information.

Ryan...her brother worked deep cover ops. But usually, those deep cover jobs were overseas. They involved cases with the CIA. No way should he have been posing as a— well, what was he? An MC wannabe?

Cass didn't lower his weapon after her brother signed, and that was bad. He *should* have lowered the gun. Cass was supposed to trust her.

She and Cass—they needed more time alone. Time to talk. To really clear the air and share every secret that they had. It was just that, when they actually were alone, they were either, uh, fucking...or being attacked. Their locations kept being leaked.

And how in the heck did Ryan find me?

Which gave her a really, really bad feeling in her gut. Because if Ryan was there, then her other brother could not be far behind. Those two were often a package deal.

Uh, oh. "I need to get outside," she snapped to Javion.

"Cass wants you *in* here."

"Yes, but Cass doesn't understand the full threats that he could be facing." She only saw Ryan. Where in the heck was Nash?

Had Gray ratted her out to her brothers? He must have. She knew Gray and Ryan had served together in the Marines. She'd wondered on more than one occasion if Ryan had pushed Gray to bring her on the team. It would just be like his interfering, overprotective self. But, since she happened to like working with Gray, she'd let the matter slide.

She would not be letting anything slide again. *And did Ryan have anything to do with Gray keeping quiet about the Twins being a serial killing pair?* Her instincts said yes. Especially with Ryan being outside, clearly on the hunt himself.

There was a loud crash from the back of the shop. Her head turned toward the sound. Javion didn't react to it at all. "Uh, shouldn't you run and check that out?" *And leave the front door open and unguarded for me?*

He remained focused on the scene out front. "My job is to make sure you don't get out this door. Bear can handle himself." Then, *"Shit, Cass has his gun pressed to the idiot's chest."*

What? To her brother's chest? After Ryan had signed that she was his sister? No, no, no. Agnes backed away from the window, moving with silent steps. Javion had now opened the front door wider, and the man was clearly thinking about rushing out to help Cass. Though, from the sound of things, Cass didn't need help.

Her brother did.

Agnes pivoted on her heel and went creeping down the hallway. She reached the storage room and—

The shop's back door hung open.

Her gaze darted around the storage room. Raz wasn't there. No sign of the tattoo artist. And Bear had his back to her as he braced his big hands on a nearby counter.

251

So, she could just slip right on out that open door, except... *"Where is Raz?"*

"I let him go." Low.

What?

"Seeing as how he covered for me and kept my secrets, his job was done."

Covered for me and kept my secrets. Shit. Shit.

"Well, not quite done. He *is* getting the van ready for transport." He glanced over his shoulder. "So I guess he hasn't really gone that far yet."

Her darting gaze looked for a weapon even as she opened her mouth to scream.

But Bear was on her in an instant. For someone so big, he sure could move incredibly fast. One massive hand clamped down over her mouth and her nose, and the bastard *cut off her air.* Enraged, desperate, she kicked at him. She punched. She clawed.

"I outweigh you by an easy one fifty, FBI Agent. And, unlike Cass, I'm not fucking you, so I don't particularly care if I hurt you."

Newsflash, she didn't particularly care if she hurt him, either. So her frantic fingers stopped punching and clawing at him, and she grabbed for the hammer she'd just spotted hanging on the wall near his head. She could almost reach it...almost...

"You're gonna say night, night," he told her.

Night, night? What was she? Two?

"And when you wake up..."

Oh, wait, she got to wake up? She'd figured he was just intending to kill her then and there.

I need air. I need to breathe. She'd almost reached the handle of that hammer. Almost...

"You're gonna be in hell. He's gonna stab you again and

again. He'll finish the job he started. Wants to do it personally because you have really pissed him off."

She touched the hammer even as black dots swirled before her eyes.

"And then Cass will come and find your bloody body. Think he'll lose his mind?"

She swung the hammer and brought it careening toward his head. *I'll make you lose your mind.*

"You fucking bitch!"

His grip loosened. She fell to the floor on boneless legs and sucked in air, but she couldn't suck in air and scream at the same time. He plowed his big boot into her stomach, making her wretch and choke as she tried to breathe. She swung out the hammer that she still clasped. It hit him in the knee, and he almost went down. Hell, yes. Now she just had to—

"Night, night, bitch," he snarled. His big hands came at her again. Slapping over her mouth and nose. No air. No freedom.

Darkness.

She didn't even feel it when the hammer fell from her grasp.

Chapter Twenty-One

CASS PRESSED THE MUZZLE OF HIS GUN INTO THE stranger's chest. A stranger who'd just signed that Agnes was his sister. Cass was pretty sure the bastard had signed just to prove how much he knew about Cass. *Proving you know all my secrets, you bastard?* "You don't look a damn thing like her."

"Um. Aren't genetics fun that way?"

Was this jerk truly her brother?

"This is how the scene will work," the man told him. No accent touched his words. "You're going to take me inside. You're going to let me see her. You're going to let me take her away."

"No." Just that. To all three orders. As if this jerk would order him around. "You're not the one in charge here." But it was fun that the guy had confidence. Sort of the same wild confidence that Agnes so often possessed.

But while Cass loved a confident Agnes, this guy just annoyed the hell out of him.

You're going to let me take her away. Nope. Not happening. No one was taking her away.

"Your enemies are gonna kill her." Flat. "They don't buy that she's turned away from the Feds. Or maybe they don't care. She stays with you, and she is dead. Do you hear me? *Dead.*"

A black van hurtled away from the shopping center, with its tires screeching. What in the hell?

His eyes narrowed.

"Cass!" Javion's shout. "Cass, she's gone!"

"He better not be talking about Agnes," his new enemy snarled.

Cass whirled toward Javion.

"*Gone!*" Javion bellowed as he launched out of the tattoo parlor. "She snuck to the back of the shop, and I— shit..." He rushed to Cass, breathing hard. Blood dripped from his cracked lip. "*Bear took her.* She wasn't moving, man."

"You're dead," the man claiming to be Agnes's brother fired at Cass. "Dead." He shoved past Cass and ran toward the tattoo shop.

Cass still gripped his gun with his right hand. With his left, he grabbed Javion's shirtfront and hauled him forward.

"She's not in there!" Javion spoke quickly. "He was hauling her out back, toward a van. I tried to stop Bear, but he punched me—you know how damn hard he hits. I blacked out a second, and when I got up, shit...he was hauling ass and...*she wasn't moving.* I'm sorry, I'm fucking sorry. I'm personally responsible and—"

Cass's bellow of rage cut through Javion's words. All of his crew members surged toward him. "The van!" he roared at them. "Track it. Find it. Stop it. *Now.*"

Men leapt onto their cycles. Engines growled and howled, and Cass jerked on the t-shirt he still held. He gripped the gun and jumped on his own motorcycle.

The stranger with the dark hair flew out of the tattoo shop. He raced toward Cass even as Cass throttled his motorcycle. The prick launched into his path.

Cass nearly mowed the dumbass down right then and there.

"Blood is on a hammer!" The man's eyes were wild. *"What did you do? What did you do to Agnes?"*

What had he done? Failed to protect her. Let her fall into dangerous hands. Served her right up to the monsters from his past because it sure as hell seemed that Raz and Bear were working together.

I am so sick of this two-headed cobra shit. Traitors, everywhere he turned. "I'm cutting off the head of the freaking snake. And I don't care if it's a dead man's head or not."

The guy gaped at him. "Are you crazy?"

Maybe. "Move or get run over."

He moved. He also whipped out a phone. "Tell me you have eyes on the black van that just left," he blasted into the phone. "Tell me, tell me..."

Cass tensed. His feet slammed into the ground. His whole body vibrated.

"Yeah, I think she's inside the van." The man's gaze flickered to Cass. "But I don't know if she's alive or dead."

That was the moment when rage completely took over. Cass didn't know who the guy was talking to on the other end of the line. Maybe a Fed. Maybe someone connected to Gray or Agnes. What he did know...

Alive. She has to be alive. Because if she wasn't, if Bear or Raz had killed her...

I will slaughter them. They will beg for mercy.

"Stay on them. Give us directions. I'm getting the Strikers, and we're coming after them," the man said into his phone. But then he glared at Cass. "Are there any actual *Strikers* we can trust? Because I damn well know that Bear jackass the other guy was yelling about—I know Bear was one of yours."

This guy knew far too much about him. And his crew.

"And he took Agnes?" Rage twisted the man's features. "He *took* her?"

Yeah, according to Javion, Bear had. Cass's fury threatened to burn away his very flesh.

"I got eyes on the van," the man said. "Let's go get her the hell back." He leapt onto his motorcycle. They roared away together.

Bear is a dead man. But Agnes, she has to be alive. She has to be.

Because she was the only good thing he had in his world. The one bit of brightness that had come to him. She'd said that she was falling in love with him.

He'd said nothing in return. But the truth was...

If I could love, I would love her.

But monsters didn't love. They just destroyed. He was ready to destroy for her.

Hard fingers squeezed her jaw. "You're not dead."

Agnes cracked open her eyes. Her body jumped, bumped, and hit the rough metal beneath her. *Because I'm in a freaking van.* She could see the metal outline above the hulking figure of Bear as he crouched over her. Light poured from the front of the vehicle. Probably coming from the front windshield. The one window she could see in the back was tinted.

"I was worried I'd stopped your breaths for too long.

Thought you might be dead." His head tilted. "You're not dead."

No, she was not. She was very pissed off. Her hands lifted. Duct taped. Really? The tape bit tightly into her skin, threatening to cut off her circulation.

The van swerved. Hit a pothole. Her body bumped again.

"We got a motorcycle behind us!" A shout from the front of the van. From Raz. She recognized his voice. "He's been tailing me ever since I pulled out of the lot! *Sonofabitch!*"

"Fuck," Bear bit out. "I told your fool-ass to leave *softly*. Softly does not mean hauling ass with tires squealing, you moron! They would never have known if you had just left *softly*."

"You're the one who attacked Javion. What the hell did you think that jerk was gonna do? Not go running straight to Cass?"

She was trying to assess the situation. What she'd figured out...Her hands were duct taped. So were her ankles. She'd somehow lost her shoes, and she had no idea where those were. Also...zero weapons. She had zero weapons. Oh, what she would not give for a hammer or for a gun.

"The motorcycle is getting closer! That bastard is right on my ass!" Raz yelled. "Do something! He's—oh, shit, he has a gun! He has a gun! He's gonna come up beside us and —*he has a gun!*"

"Don't go anywhere, would you?" Bear growled at her. Then he laughed.

His joke had not been funny.

He maneuvered to the back of the van, and he threw the doors open. Cold air whipped inside the van, and she twisted and rolled so that she could look back. She saw a motorcycle rider. One who was aiming a gun at the van, at Bear.

"He's not a Striker." Fury coated Bear's words. "Who the hell is this guy?"

Bam.

He was a man who'd just shot at Bear. Missed him by inches.

"Do something about him!" Raz screeched.

Bear fired back. He'd yanked a gun from his waistband, and he fired once, twice. The man on the motorcycle swerved and darted, and she was pretty sure both shots from Bear had missed the rider. About seventy-percent sure, anyway.

In the next instant, one of Bear's giant hands grabbed for her, he yanked her up and hauled her in front of him.

Fantastic. Now she was a human shield.

"You shoot at me, you'll hit her!" Bear roared. "Cass will *kill* you for hitting his woman!"

"Yeah," she snapped as she twisted her hands in the stupid tape. She could barely feel her fingertips. "What do you think Cass is going to do to *you,* Bear?"

But the man on the motorcycle had fallen back, and he'd lowered his gun. He was clearly afraid of hitting her. And too much distance was now getting between the van and the rider. She could hear other motorcycles growling, but they were too far away for her to see them clearly. Raz was flooring the van. It was bumping and shaking, and she was only upright because of Bear's grip on her. One wrong move, and she'd be falling out of the van.

Or he will be.

"Cass won't do anything to me. He'll be too out of his mind when he finds your body." Bear fired his gun again.

The blast was sent from right near her ear, and she screamed because Agnes was pretty sure the sonofabitch had just busted her ear drum.

And then...he laughed.

She could barely hear him over the loud ringing in her head and that just infuriated her all the more. "Enough," she snapped. She couldn't maneuver her feet behind him to trip him. Her ankles were bound and she was basically just dangling in front of him. But she wasn't just going to be a good little kidnap victim and let him haul her away to some brutal kill scene. "You don't go to secondary sites." That was like, FBI 101. "Victims taken to secondary sites have over a ninety percent chance of getting murdered."

"You have a one hundred percent chance of getting murdered!"

At least, that was what she *thought* he said. And since the bastard was planning to kill her anyway... "I'll choose my own exit, thanks." Hers, and his. And maybe his massive bulk would cushion her, and she'd somehow make it out of this mess.

The motorcycle driver suddenly revved forward. He flipped up his visor. *"Agnes!"*

Her heart froze in her chest. She could see his face. A face she knew and loved. Of course, her brother Nash would not be far away from Ryan. Her brothers were always close. Had been the best of friends from the day that Nash had walked into their house as a scared and far too thin thirteen-year-old. And was she really surprised that Nash had found her? Her brothers were always looking out for her. It was what good, big brothers would do.

"I'm shooting that sonofabitch," Bear vowed.

No, he wasn't. No one hurt her brother. She launched her body forward, out of the van, heaving with all of her strength. And because he was holding onto her with one arm, he had one ham fist tight around her even as he gripped the gun in his right hand, Bear was whipped forward, too.

Her bound hands flew toward the side, toward the open van door with its handle that she could see. She was leaping for that door, hoping that, somehow, she could grab the handle and hold on, and even if she didn't, then maybe Bear would cushion her fall.

Or, worst case, he'd die...and her brother would be safe.

Bear will die...and I might just die, too.

She grabbed for the handle, a desperate lunge. She actually managed to catch the handle, and her sweaty fingers tightened around it desperately, but Bear...he would not let her go. His grip tightened. That powerful grip yanked her away from the handle. They were both falling, tumbling down, slamming out of the van, and flying toward the pavement.

Agnes didn't have a chance to brace for impact.

He hit the ground first.

She dropped on top of him.

"Agnes!"

Her brother Nash's scream.

Cass saw her fly out the back of the van. The back of the *moving van*. The doors opened. Cass was racing after the van as fast as he could. Her brother—the guy had said his name was Ryan—had been given directions by whoever had eyes on the vehicle. Another motorcycle rider.

He and Ryan had chased after the van, and just when Cass got it in his sights...

The van's rear doors flew open. Bear fired his gun at the rider Ryan had sent to tail the van. And then, as Cass pushed his motorcycle desperately forward and strained to see, Bear grabbed Agnes. He dangled her in front of his body. Cass could barely make out her form as he forced his bike to go faster and faster and faster and...

She jumped. Hurtled forward. Agnes seemed to grab and hold onto the open, right door for one, stark moment.

He roared her name even as someone else screamed it.

And Bear dragged her down because when she'd leapt forward, he'd lost his balance. Bear was falling, too, and Bear hauled her down with him. Bear slammed into the pavement. She crashed on top of him. They both fucking bounced, their bodies careening. The van's tires squealed as it sped away.

Cass almost lost control of his bike as he stared at Agnes in horror. Agnes, now partially sprawled on Bear. Not moving.

Agnes...dead?

Chapter Twenty-Two

OH, SHE HURT. HURT SO INCREDIBLY BADLY. HER LEFT shoulder. Her left forearm. Her left knee. That whole side of her body *hurt*. She was also pretty sure that she—and the cushion for her that had been Bear—had bounced after hitting the pavement. Had they bounced once? Maybe twice? Agnes hadn't even realized that a human body could bounce that way, not when it slammed into the unforgiving pavement.

"Agnes!"

There were lots of yells going on. Lots of squealing tires. She could smell burnt rubber. And she really, really hurt. But that was a good thing, wasn't it? If she hurt, then she was alive. Also, bonus, the ringing in her ears had stopped. So that meant no busted ear drum. Maybe?

"No, dammit, Ryan!" Another shout that she clearly heard. Nash's shout. "Don't stop! Stay on your bike! I've got her!" Hands fluttered around her. "Get after that van and the driver! Now, *now!*"

More roaring of a motorcycle.

Her eyes cracked open. She tried to push up. Only to

have immediate, excruciating pain fly through her left shoulder and down her arm. A moan slipped from her.

She stared down and saw Bear's neck. Bear's face. His closed eyes. Was he breathing? As she focused, she realized there was a whole lot of blood spreading beneath his head.

"I've got you, baby," a familiar voice promised as strong, but gentle fingers slid over her shoulder. The same voice that had yelled for Ryan to keep going. Her other brother, Nash.

Nash was talking. So Nash was okay. That was good. She loved Nash. He was a great brother.

But his touch was *hurting* her. "St-stop..."

"*Agnes!*" A roar. And...a crash. She wanted to turn her head toward both sounds, but she was currently trying to breathe through some pain.

"Tell him I'm okay," she whispered to Nash. Because she knew the roar belonged to Cass. She really hoped that crash hadn't been the sound of his motorcycle hitting the pavement.

"I'm not gonna lie to your biker boyfriend," her brother groused back at her. "You are *not* okay. Your shoulder is dislocated, your left arm is a bloody mess..."

Yep, she was pretty sure a hunk of skin might have been torn away. And leave it to Nash to document her injuries. The man had completed two years of med school before disappearing into the web of the CIA, but he still loved to throw out a diagnosis about everything like he'd gotten his MD—

"And I can see the blood soaking your leg. Also, I'm about ninety percent sure that you're on top of a dead man."

"Gross," she breathed. She was about ninety percent sure of the same thing.

"I need to check you for other injuries. Just hold still

and stay on top of the dead man a bit longer." His hands slid over her, particularly careful near her neck and spine.

"Agnes." Cass dropped to his knees beside her. "Baby, you're okay?"

"On...dead man." That was not okay.

"Who is this fucker touching you?" Cass swatted away Nash's hands.

"I'm her brother."

"What?"

"He's...almost a doctor," she muttered. "Let him finish the exam. Nash will not be happy until he finishes."

"Damn right, I won't be," Nash agreed. His hands went back to work on her.

Bear groaned.

"Oh, good." She perked up. "He's not dead."

"I'm gonna *kill* him," Cass swore.

Nash lifted her up and off Bear. Thankfully. Finally. He carried her a bit and eased her onto the ground that was *off the road*. A good thing to do so that no other drivers might, oh, run over her. When he moved her, she saw the other motorcycles that had just braked about ten feet away. Javion waited near them. "Shouldn't they be chasing the van?" she muttered.

Cass ripped away the duct tape from her wrists, and he freed her ankles. "Javion, get the others and go the hell after the van!" Cass thundered as he tossed away the tape. "I've got her!"

They left. Fast. Which was good because she hadn't wanted an audience. Nash was still examining her, and Cass was hovering. Cass's dark eyes were wild. Agnes could feel his fear. Her right hand rose—the hand and arm that didn't feel as if every bit of skin had been scraped off it. "Snuck up on you, didn't it?"

265

"What?" Cass caught her hand and pressed a kiss to her palm. "Sweetness, I want you to just rest. I'm getting an ambulance for you. Just called while your brother was carrying you. You're going to a hospital, and I am going to *destroy* the threats to you."

She shook her head. "Just...need someone to pop my shoulder back in place." She didn't need an ambulance.

Nash swore. "Agnes is going to be difficult."

Cass's head turned toward him. Slowly. "Who the hell are you again?"

The others were gone, so they could speak freely. For the moment, anyway. Though someone should probably check on Bear. "He's my brother."

Cass eyed Nash. Big, tawny skinned, pitch-black hair, and two very distinct, multi-colored eyes. One blue. One brown. "You two don't look a damn thing alike," Cass rasped. "Let me guess...genetics? Like the other brother told me?"

"No, dumbass," Nash returned without missing a beat. "Adoption. Like blood is the only thing that makes a family."

She smiled. "I missed you, Nash."

"You should not be *here,* Agnes. Gray was supposed to have you working in Atlanta! You are not supposed to be with this asshole...and do you know the things he's done? Do you know what he is?"

Yes, absolutely. She turned her weak smile on Cass. "He's mine."

"Hell." From Nash.

Cass frowned at her. "Sweetheart, I don't think you should be smiling after what just happened. That fucker kidnapped you. You almost died when you jumped out of the van—and why in the world did you do that?"

266

To protect Nash. But, before she said that, more of an explanation might be required. "Ryan..." She had to lick her lips. The throbbing in her shoulder was driving her crazy. "Ryan was at the tattoo shop."

Cass kept frowning. Had he and Cass exchanged first names? For some reason, she doubted it. Ryan didn't tend to be the chatty one. Then again, Nash wasn't chatty either. "My brother, Ryan. He signed that I was his sister. I saw him." She sucked in a breath. "I knew he didn't come alone. Where Ryan is, Nash is close by."

"Someone has to watch his fool back," Nash returned. "His and yours, Agnes."

They'd been watching her back forever. "When I saw the motorcycle behind the van...saw the rider—I knew it was Nash." She'd suspected it was him even before he'd flipped up his visor. "Couldn't let anyone hurt my brother."

"So you flew out of a van?" Cass shook his head.

"Not like I had a ton of options." She wet her lips.

Nash cleared his throat. "Just so you know, that shoulder of yours is *definitely* dislocated."

She was aware. "Push it back, would you? I have work to do."

Cass shook his head. "You have a hospital to get to!"

Nope. "I don't want to be benched. Please, don't bench me." She felt Nash's fingers curl around her shoulder.

"This is gonna hurt," her brother warned her.

"Can't hurt worse than it already does."

Bear groaned again.

About him... "He can use that ambulance you called for, Cass." And speaking of calls... "We should call Gray." Her stare flickered over Cass. "Snuck up on you," she said again.

A line cut between his brows. "What did?"

"Me. The way you feel about me. I can see it. You love
—*ah!*" A scream of absolute agony tore through her because
Nash had just shoved her dislocated shoulder back into
place. Dry heaves broke from her.

Cass immediately threw Nash into the air. *"Don't ever
hurt her!"*

He hadn't been hurting her, well, okay he *had* hurt her,
but the shoulder had needed to go back in place. The pain
was ebbing, and it was more of a dull throb now. Plus, she
could actually move her arm a bit, so, win.

But before she could share the winning news, Cass
scooped her up into his arms. He began rushing away with
her, and she was pretty sure he was rushing blindly. "Cass...
I'm okay." Mostly. Maybe she needed a few stitches.
Hopefully not, though.

"Hospital." Just one, snarled word from Cass.

"Cass, we are so close to our goal." They could not stop
now. "Raz and Bear were taking me to the bastard who did
all of this. He wanted to kill me himself and leave my body
for you to find." Because he was a twisted SOB, obviously.

Cass's face hardened. His eyes spat dark fire as he
looked down at her. Rage burned and promised hell in his
gaze.

"Let's give him what he wanted," she said. "We can do
this. We *can*."

"I am not giving you to anyone. You are mine, Agnes.
Mine. I screwed up protecting you today, but I will never,
ever do that again. Do you hear me? You matter. You. I don't
give a shit about anything else. You could have died right in
front of me. When you came out of that van and hit the
pavement I thought you *had* died." A hard, negative shake
of his head.

She didn't point out that—technically—she hadn't hit

the pavement. She'd hit Bear's big body. At least, she hadn't *initially* hit the pavement. Bear had softened her fall, but then she'd slammed into the pavement after she bounced off him. That slam had been centered all on her left side.

"You're going far away," he vowed. "Far away from this nightmare. I will get Gray on the phone. And then Gray is gonna take you away. You are gonna be safe. You will never face this kind of threat again."

"Stop being adorable. I'm an FBI agent. I face threats each day. It's part of the deal I signed up for."

"We've got a vehicle approaching," Nash said as he moved to stand beside them. He had drawn his weapon. "Coming fast. Unmarked SUV."

Her heart slammed in her chest.

"No one is taking her," Cass growled.

"Agreed."

Cass gently lowered her back onto the ground away from the road. The two men took up protective positions near her. Not just near her, but in front of her.

The SUV came forward faster. Faster. It screeched to a stop.

Cass and Nash were both armed. She could use a weapon, too. Her right arm was still good. It was just the left one that was currently weak. Time for her to get off the ground and show them that she was okay. And she would get up, as soon as the nausea eased and the world stopped spinning. She hadn't mentioned the spinning to Nash and Cass yet. No need for them to worry.

Car doors opened. Slammed closed. "Stand down!" A hard order. Her head turned as she strained to see who'd given that order. She peeked through and around the legs of Cass and Nash.

Her eyes locked on the man who'd shouted. *Yep, thought that was him.*

Her boss from the FBI, Gray Stone, stood near to the driver's side of the SUV. And her partner Malik was on the passenger side. Both men had their weapons drawn.

Why were so many people pointing guns? They were all on the same side. "Wasting time," she gasped out. "Bad guy is *waiting* for me to be delivered to him...so..." Her eyes closed as she took just one moment to rest on the side of the road. Just one wee moment. "Could someone please deliver me?"

"Over my dead body," Cass swore.

With her eyes closed, she smiled at him again. Or at least, toward him. She didn't even know if he was looking her way. "You love me so much." A mumble that came out like *Youlovemesomuch.*

"Yeah, I damn well do."

Had that been an actual confession from him? Or was she delirious with pain and she'd just imagined those words? Her smile faded as she cracked open one eye to peer at him. "Say that again." Not a demand. A plea.

"I damn well do."

Those weren't quite the words she'd wanted to hear. She swallowed. Opened both eyes.

"I. Love. You." Cass stared straight at her.

Those words were way better than his previous ones, even if they had been gritted out between Cass's clenched teeth. Before she could respond, he added, "And I am going to destroy the Twins for you."

Her breath sighed out. "You say the sweetest things."

"*Ahem.*"

She'd know that annoyed throat clearing anywhere. Gray, trying to get their attention. "He's gonna need to leave, fast," she murmured to Cass. "Because your crew will be back and they cannot see us hanging with Feds in the middle of the street." Good thing it wasn't a busy street. More like an old, country road that just had them on it.

"You *are* a Fed, sunshine," Cass reminded her.

"Nah. I'm yours. Everyone knows that." Her eyes closed again. Just for a moment. Long enough for her to regroup. "Just like you're mine." Her eyes opened. *No more weakness, Agnes. Get this show on the road.* "Let's go end this."

He made no move to end anything. "I want you in a hospital."

"You love me, so you won't sideline me. Not now." She'd wanted this for too long. And it was just a dislocated shoulder. She'd had way worse in her life. "End it... together?"

"Fuck." His shoulders sagged.

Fantastic. "I'll take that as a yes..."

* * *

"She should be in a hospital." Rage had his hands shaking, so Cass fisted them. "*A hospital.* Bear's betraying ass is in the back of an ambulance, and you put *my woman* in the back of—"

"A van?" Agnes called out. And she waved to him. From the back of the van. The same van that she'd flown out of not an hour before. "Time is tick, ticking, Cass. Let's get this show on the road."

She'd been bandaged up by EMTs. Checked out. By some kind of miracle, her worst injury was the dislocated shoulder. A shoulder that her brother Nash had put back into place for her. Now the shoulder was in a sling, she had

Cynthia Eden

bandages on her left forearm and wrapped around her left leg, but she was all right.

She is all right. Something he'd repeated to himself at least a hundred times so far.

Agnes had two brothers. Two brothers that he'd met so far. Ryan and Nash. *Jeez, are there more?* Cass was a bit afraid there might be. More brothers who were pissed that their precious sister had hooked up with an MC leader.

About to be a former MC leader. Because the game was ending. Secrets were coming out. The tightrope he'd walked would be snapping.

Ryan had been the one in the parking lot at the tattoo shop. Nash had been in the background, and he'd hauled ass after the van when it left. As Cass and Ryan had raced to catch up with the van, Nash had been feeding them directions about the van's location.

Nash was currently glaring at Agnes because he didn't like this new plan, either. As for Ryan...he'd brought the van back. He and Javion had come riding back with the van, accompanied by the other Night Strikers, and with a scared-as-hell Raz tied up in the back of the big, black vehicle.

Gray had vanished before they all arrived, thankfully. As had the Fed who'd been with him. Not like Cass had wanted to BS his way through an explanation about why Feds were on the scene to his crew.

Now, though, it was time to act. Time to get the van moving because, yes, Bayne was expecting a delivery.

You're sure as shit about to get one. Only it would not be the delivery that Bayne expected. *You're getting me, you sonofabitch.*

"*I* didn't put her anywhere," Ryan rumbled at him. "She put herself in the van. And she's right. Time is ticking. Let's go get this bastard. Now."

The members of his MC had drifted to the edges of the periphery. They were looking for other threats, ready to follow Cass's orders.

They didn't trust Ryan and Nash. He didn't blame the MC for that. He didn't exactly trust them completely, either. *But I do trust Agnes.*

Javion jogged toward him, with a phone gripped in his hand. "Our ghost still has eyes on Bayne, boss."

Ah, yes. The rider who'd been tailing Bayne since the bastard had killed Hugo. Cass had thought Bayne would keep driving to Arizona, to the big MC powerhouse meeting that waited. Clearly, though, Bayne had other plans.

He never intends for me to make that meeting. He's trying to take me out.

Cass didn't give a shit about the big meeting. His target was Bayne. *And Winston Striker—if that sonofabitch escaped the grave…*And it sure seemed that he might have.

"Our rider says that Bayne is holed up in a warehouse one town over." Javion rattled off the address. "That matches with the destination Raz gave us."

The destination they'd forced from the guy.

It was an address that meant nothing to Cass. He was sure it was some hole-in-the-wall place, but probably one that Bayne had secured. Cameras, alarms, far too many of Bayne's thugs. Not like Cass could just go roaring right up to the place on his motorcycle. The doors wouldn't be opened to extend him a warm welcome.

Well, the doors wouldn't be opened if he drove up on his Harley. But if he arrived in another vehicle…*like a black van that is expected,* then those doors would open. He could ride straight up to his prey. Thus, the current plan. Though he would have preferred for Agnes to be safely in a hospital

Cynthia Eden

bed while he handled the violence that was to come. And, oh, yes, there would be violence.

You thought to take her from me? To hurt her?

"Cass?" Agnes's worried voice. "Why do you look like you're getting ready to murder someone?"

Because he was. He slowly unclenched his fists. "Javion, I want you to secure Raz. He doesn't get away, understand? You hold him, and you make sure he contacts no one." A pause. "He does get to keep breathing, though. For the moment. So don't kill him...yet." Sooner or later, he'd probably have to turn Raz over to Gray.

Later would be better.

"What are you gonna do?" Javion wanted to know.

"I'm going to drive a van." He and Agnes would be going to this final battle together.

"Uh, *I'll* drive," Nash offered. His eyes were kinda eerie when they locked on you. Not because of the color, but because the guy's gaze was so stone-cold. Neither Nash nor Ryan had shown a hint of fear since Cass had met them, not even when the other bikers had come back and circled around them.

Under other circumstances, he might have liked them.

He doubted they would ever have liked him. They probably wanted to kick his ass because he'd fucked their sister. *And I intend to fuck her again, at the earliest opportunity.*

Provided he could give her what she'd always wanted—vengeance.

"I'll drive," Nash said again. "You can stay in the back with Agnes. That way, you can keep watch over her. Plus, not like you want to be recognized on sight when the van pulls up. If you're in the back, it will allow us to get closer to the target."

274

Yeah, it would.

"Besides," Nash was not done, "you need someone you can trust with you."

"What the hell am I?" Javion instantly demanded. "The enemy?"

Cass lifted his hand and put his fingers against Javion's chest when the man started to lunge for Nash. "Easy."

"That prick just insulted me! Easy, my ass!"

"I need you to secure Raz."

Javion glared at him. "It's because I lost her, isn't it? You hold me personally responsible." His head turned toward the back of the van. "Agnes, I told you this would happen!"

"Javion, my *friend*..."

Cass did not know why she'd just emphasized the word *friend*, but she had. He also did not know when she and Javion had become friends, but, whatever.

"My friend," she repeated, "Cass is trusting you with an important job. He's not shoving your spine down your throat. This is a win."

Javion didn't appear convinced.

But Cass needed the man to stay with Raz. "I'm counting on you," he told Javion.

Javion nodded. Reluctantly. But then his chin jutted up. "And I'm counting on you to keep your ass alive." He leaned toward Cass. "Don't care what kind of cons you've been running. You *are* my friend. Come back alive." Then he turned on his heel and stalked toward the other men who waited on their motorcycles.

Javion had never wanted to be the leader of the MC. But, as before, Cass had the thought of...*But I know he'd be damn good at the job.*

Ryan stood near the open, rear doors of the van. His arms were crossed over his chest as he peered inside at

Agnes. "You got that knife I gave you tucked into the sling?"

"Yes."

"And the mace?"

"Yes."

"And you have a gun?"

"Got it." She inclined her head toward him. "And later, you're gonna give me answers about how you wound up here."

"Oh, I can tell you that right now. Got here the usual way. Stalked you. Pissed off Gray. Followed the dead bodies you left." His head cocked. "Want me in this van with you?"

Cass jumped into the back of the van. "I have her."

"Do you." Not a question.

"I do." A definite answer. Cass glowered at her brother. "I vouched for you with the crew. You and Nash. Told them that our paths had crossed before. That you'd proved I could count on you."

"You *can* count on us," Ryan affirmed.

"Good. But I really only need you to do one thing. Well, two things, actually." He was making up plans as he went along.

Ryan waited.

"Tail the van, but stay out of sight." The first order.

"Done."

He'd figured that would be Ryan's response. "Second, make sure that whatever happens to me, Agnes walks away."

Her right hand fluttered across his arm. "Nothing is going to happen to you. You and I are going to win."

"Your optimism is always a plus," he said, but Cass kept his eyes on Ryan, waiting for the other man's response.

"I will make sure Agnes walks away," Ryan vowed.

Good. Some of the tension slid from Cass's shoulders. Nash had already gone to the front of the van. Cass heard the engine crank up.

Ryan slammed one rear door. "You got plenty of weapons on you, Striker?"

He was more than locked and loaded. "I made your sister a promise, and I intend to keep it."

"What promise was that?"

"She gets the vengeance she always wanted."

Ryan didn't slam the second door. His gaze did shift to Agnes. "She's a Fed. She gets justice, not vengeance. Feds lock up the bastards who break the law and hurt others. Feds make them spend the rest of their miserable lives behind bars."

"Right. Understood." Cass sucked in his right cheek. "Agnes, your brother is a killjoy, huh?"

"*Feds lock them up,*" Ryan repeated.

"Sure. Sure. Heard you the first time. Now, if you don't mind, I have a date with a sonofabitch who thought he was going to murder Agnes and leave her broken body for me to find." *You really think I'll just let him get locked up?*

Ryan hesitated. But Nash had the van cranked up and ready to roll. Time, as both Ryan and Agnes had pointed out, was ticking.

Ryan slammed the door closed.

Chapter Twenty-Three

AGNES SAT ON THE FLOOR OF THE VAN, HER LEGS stretched out in front of her. There were no seats in the rear of that van. Just a discarded roll of duct tape. Just seeing that duct tape had rage burning through him. If Bear survived his injuries, Cass would make sure the bastard *wished* that he had died.

"He said Raz covered for him," Agnes announced. Her back was to the wall on the left.

Cass lowered next to her. Very, very carefully, he took her hand. Her right hand. It was so much smaller than his own hand. Far more delicate.

This delicate hand had been bound with duct tape as she lunged out and tried to grab the back door of a moving van. He brought her hand to his lips. Kissed her knuckles softly.

"You were questioning Raz," she pushed. "While I was being checked out by the EMTs."

Questioning him. Driving his fist into the guy's ribs. Yes, he'd done both things.

"What all did you learn?" Agnes wanted to know.

"I learned that when Bayne came to get his snake tat, Bear was with him. Because Bear was his lieutenant."

She whistled. "That's an interesting point to pick up. And, you, uh, weren't aware of that fun fact before?"

"It was eight years ago. And, no, I wasn't aware. MCs are tricky bastards. Allegiances are buried deep. And eight years ago..." He exhaled. "Back then, I was filled with so much fury and hate that I could barely see past my own need for revenge. Those were the days when I was hunting my uncle. I'd buried my father and..." He stopped. Focused on what mattered. *Her.* "Eight years ago...

"That was around the time when I was attacked."

"I wish I could go back." The words were the truth. He'd tried to never regret anything he'd done. Tried not to look at the past because what good did that do? But... "If I could go back, I'd say screw the others. Screw everything else. I would come straight to you. I'd find you in Austin, Texas, and I'd make sure no one hurt you. I'd take it all away, and you wouldn't have this life." She wouldn't be in the back of a crappy van with a dislocated shoulder and with the skin ripped from her arm and leg. He swallowed. "You'd be safe. You'd be painting somewhere." Hell, he'd seen the quick sketch she'd done in the tattoo shop. Her fingers had flown over that paper, and she'd clearly been talented. The snake had leapt off the paper. "You'd be an artist. You wouldn't have ever needed to pretend to be a prostitute for three months, you wouldn't have been nearly drugged by some sadistic asshole," he said, remembering the stories she'd told him about her time with the FBI. "You wouldn't have gone into a prison and been locked away with twisted guards who wanted to—"

"Cass." Just that. His name. Soft. Husky.

He kissed her hand once more, and his head turned

toward her so that he could look into her incredible eyes. The eyes that saw straight into his soul.

She shook her head. "You think you could go back, wave some magic wand, and take away all the pain I've ever felt?"

If he could, he damn well would. "You should not be in the back of a shitty van with a dislocated shoulder and blood staining your clothes." Gruff. "You should never have needed to jump from the van, almost killing yourself, because one of *my* men was a traitorous bastard." All along, he'd thought that he'd infiltrated the Twins. That he'd been on target to take them all down. Now, though, he saw the truth.

It was my group that was infiltrated. People were watching me. I was the target. There had been plenty of attacks on him over the years. That was the nature of the beast. But he'd survived. He'd thrived. Come back harder.

Looking back, though, he wondered how many of those attacks had been due to inside jobs. *Levi and Bear.* Two of those in his inner circle. Working to rip him apart.

Yeah, was it any wonder he had trust issues?

One thing he knew with certainty—she did not belong in his world. "I would change it all," he spoke with complete conviction, "and give you back the boy you loved."

"I'm staring at the man I love."

His heart ached when she said those soft words. "You shouldn't love me."

"Why? Because you're so big and bad? Tell that to someone who hasn't seen you make the worst cup of coffee in the world."

He frowned.

Light spilled from the front of the van, and he saw her lips dip down before Agnes told him, "I don't want to change who I am. Or what I've done. Want to know what my favorite movie is?"

"Yes." He wanted to know every single thing about her, but he was very much afraid he wouldn't. They were running out of time.

"My favorite movie is *It's A Wonderful Life*. Bet you've seen it, everyone has."

He remembered watching the old black and white with his mom, with Gray... "My mom actually lost her hearing when she and her sister fell into an ice-covered pond when they were kids." It had taken too long to get his mother out of the frigid water. She'd gotten an infection, been in the hospital for weeks, and... "She would watch that movie and cry and sign that even bad things could happen for a reason."

"I really wish I could have met your mother."

He did, too. *She would have loved you.*

Her lips trembled. "I miss Max. He was a good person who lit up the world by being in it."

I will never be good. I will never be someone who lights up the world. He was far too comfortable in the darkness. Most days, Cass felt like he was the darkness.

"I will always miss him, just as I will miss the girl I used to be. But I would not change who I am now. Because this woman? The one who probably currently looks like hell?"

"You look beautiful," he assured her.

A weak laugh slipped from her. "Stop being a dirty liar."

"You look beautiful," he said again. "You always look beautiful to me."

"And you call yourself the bad guy."

Like bad guys couldn't see beauty?

She shifted her body a bit against the side of the van. "If

I hadn't gone undercover as a prostitute, more women would have died. If I hadn't gone into that prison, more women would have been hurt, brutalized. I stopped that. I made a difference." She sent him a half-smile with her trembling lips. *"It's A Wonderful Life.* We all make small changes. We all help others, even if we don't always realize it's happening. We *change* others."

She'd changed him. In such a short time, she'd changed him so much.

"We're going to stop Bayne," she told him. "And he won't ever play his sick game again. He won't hunt people in the night. Won't kill them. Won't leave families grieving." A soft exhale. "We both know Gray is tailing us."

Absolutely, he understood that. He understood that Gray would have a team ready to swarm. He got the whole deal.

"He and Ryan served together," she revealed.

The van bounced again.

"They're close," she added as her head leaned near his. "I'd bet my life that Ryan has been texting Gray updates and staying in contact with him ever since he began tracking me. Ryan probably realized what I was doing with our shoot-out scene in Atlanta or maybe he figured out things when we left the body at the Grove Motel. Ryan is a very good tracker."

He thought both of her brothers were very tough bastards.

"I'm sure..." She wet her lower lip. "I'm sure he was at the scene with Levi. Watching from the shadows. When the bullets started flying, he would have reached out to Gray immediately. I figure that's how Gray got here so quickly to catch us with Bear. Ryan was in contact with him. Those two have probably been scheming together all along. I suspect Ryan is one of the reasons Gray held back with me about the Twins."

Cass hadn't been given the chance to contact Gray. He'd been too focused on Agnes. *But I'm not a bit surprised that Gray had other eyes on us.* That was just the way Gray operated. Contingency after contingency.

"We don't have to kill anyone today," she whispered. Her voice had been low the whole time. He wondered how much of their conversation her brother had heard as he drove up front. "We can lock away the bad guys. You and I can both walk away."

You think someone who wants you dead gets to walk away?

"Maybe I'm the one who never should have entered your life," she said, voice a bit sad as he remained silent. "Maybe I never should have gone into that bar."

Screw that. He leaned forward. His lips pressed lightly to hers. "I wish you'd walked into my life sooner. So much sooner." Another kiss. One that lingered.

Then his head lifted.

A teardrop tracked down her cheek.

"Agnes?" Horrified, he caught that teardrop. "You're in pain. You need to be in a hospital. You need meds, you need to be checked out thoroughly!"

She shook her head. "I need you. I need you to stay with me, when this is over. I need to see if, together, we can have a wonderful life. Because I really, truly think that we could. If we just had a chance."

"A Fed and a criminal?"

"We both know you're more than that."

And they both understood that a new life would not be easy. "Danger will follow me." He would always have to be on guard, no matter where he went.

283

"I don't care."

She was tempting him. Making him think that more might just be possible. "I can't be the same person, you know that. I'll have to change everything."

"Surface. The surface can always change." Her hand drifted to press over his chest. "It's what's in here that stays the same. *Will* this stay the same?"

Was she asking if he would always love her? Because the answer would be yes. There was no life—or world—in which he did not love her.

But the van was slowing. Turning.

"Almost there," Nash called back to them.

"We can have a chance." Agnes did not look away from Cass. "Just say you want to take that risk."

"I'd take any risk with you." Done.

"Get your game faces on, people," Nash barked. "Because I'm already seeing the guards on the outskirts. Men on motorcycles. Barbed wire around the fencing at the warehouse. But they recognize the van, and they are just waving me forward. Our lucky freaking day."

"That's just poor security." Agnes sniffed. "They should at least stop to *see* the driver's face."

"Yeah, let's not question their poor judgment," Cass told her. "That just lets us get killing close."

Worry flickered over her face. "You talked to Raz."

Talked, threatened, hurt...

"Did he give you anymore intel about your uncle? Is he dead? Or will you walk into that place and see a real ghost from your past?"

"He didn't have much to stay about Winston Striker." Raz hadn't provided him with much more intel on his uncle, but Cass was ready for whatever or whoever waited in the warehouse. "I'm not afraid of ghosts."

"Neither am I."

The van ambled forward. Cass pressed one more kiss to her lips.

She positioned her gun in the crook of her sling.

Cass had his own weapon at the ready. The van advanced. Slowly.

Turned.

He heard the grinding of a door—a garage door?

"Going through the side entrance of the warehouse," Nash informed them. "Lots of unfriendly faces. When we go in, they may shoot first."

"Nah." Cass was aware of the slight weight of his gun. "We will."

The van stopped.

Silence.

"I love you," Agnes told him.

I'm ready to kill for you.

One of the van's back doors was hauled open.

A booming voice announced, "I want to see the bitch!" A voice belonging to Bayne Hendrix. "Let's see if she begs before I finish carving her up and leaving her body for Cass to find..." His smiling visage appeared as he ducked his head into the back of the van.

But that smile froze when he saw the gun pointed dead center at his forehead.

"Hi, Bayne," Cass told him. "Long time, no see. Also... *Gonna need you to fucking apologize for calling my lady a bitch—and for kidnapping her.*"

Chapter Twenty-Four

Bayne Hendrix gripped a knife in his right hand. He gaped at Cass. Bayne's shoulders heaved in his battered jacket before he tried to back away.

Cass surged forward. He grabbed Bayne by the neck and hauled him close, with the gun against Bayne's forehead. "You aren't getting away. You ordered my lady to be kidnapped. You were ready to *carve her up*." Cass remained in the van, with Bayne's body now jerked half-way inside the vehicle.

There were shouts from behind Bayne. His men, coming to help him?

Agnes scuttled forward. Not like there was a ton of room to maneuver in the van, so she scuttled. "Your men have to stay the hell back!" she yelled. "Stay back!" Agnes ordered them. "Or we blow his brains out here and now!" She thought that sounded suitably intense.

She also thought that the words weren't an idle threat. Cass was looking way too eager with that trigger finger of his.

And in response to her big, bad words...

Laughter.

A cold, mocking laughter that seemed to echo in the warehouse.

Cass swore. Low and viciously. She'd heard some pretty inventive cursing from him before, but this took things to a whole new level...

"Sonofafuckingghostwhorebastardwhowillbe-buriedinthefuckinggroundwithhisspineinhisthroat..."

Well, okay, then.

A loud voice blasted, "Everyone, out!"

Agnes assumed the blasting voice belonged to the sonofa—well, the ghost bastard. Cass's uncle?

Footsteps pounded as men seemingly rushed to obey that blasting voice.

Cass kept his gun pressed to Bayne's forehead. "Gonna need you to follow my instructions," Cass commanded him. "Gonna need you to drop the knife in your hand. Right the hell now."

A knife that she knew Bayne had intended to use on her.

He dropped it. The knife clattered to the floor.

"Good," Cass praised. "Now shove up the sleeves of your coat, would you? Nice and slowly."

Bayne shoved up the left sleeve of his leather coat.

Tattoos. Knives. A skull. Thorns.

Bayne's eyes drifted to Agnes as she pressed to Cass's side. Her fingers were around the gun that she still concealed in the sling on her arm. "Looks like you got hurt, pretty lady," he murmured.

"Nothing I can't handle."

He winked at her. "We'll see about that."

Her breath came faster. "Push up the sleeve on your right arm."

"Why? Because you want definite proof that I'm the monster who ripped your world apart?" Bayne demanded.

Yes.

But...

Footsteps. Slow. And...a tapping. Slow, dragging steps and then a tap...

The second door on the back of the van was opened.

A man stood there, one hand gripping a black cane. Tall, but with his shoulders hunched forward just a bit. A hard face. Handsome but brutally cold. A face that looked far too much like an older version of Cass's face.

Gray streaks drifted through the man's dark hair. Lines darted from the corners of his eyes. And cold, hard fury showed on his face. "I'm that monster, sweetheart," the man told her. "*I'm* the one who gave the orders for the attack that night. Bayne wanted to play my game. Had to, after my other partner was eliminated."

Cass sucked in a breath. "You should be dead."

"Yes, well, for a while, felt like I was. Had to teach myself how to *walk* again after that shit you pulled. Shooting a man in the back...that's a real coward move."

"You were riding away. You were going over the edge of that cliff. *You should be dead.*"

The man—*Winston Striker*—smiled. "And yet, here we are." One hand gripped the edge of his cane. The other reached inside his coat and pulled out a gun. He pointed the weapon straight at Agnes. "I'm assuming the driver is one of yours? When I saw him on the security feed, I knew he didn't look like my talented tattoo artist."

"*You assume correctly,*" Nash snarled. He wasn't in the driver's seat any longer. He was about two feet away, with *his* weapon pointed right at Winston. "Lower the gun," Nash ordered. "You are not killing my sister."

"Of course, I am. She's been on my kill list for years. Bayne should have eliminated her that night in Texas. I'd killed my redhead, and it was his turn. He wanted in the game, wanted to take my brother's place after Cass eliminated his own father."

Wait, wait, *wait*. He was saying that Cass's father had been in on the killings? And that Bayne had come after Agnes because Winston had already murdered a redhead before Bayne had targeted her? Agnes slanted a quick, worried glance at Cass. The only emotion showing on his face was fury. Blazing fury.

"How many times do I have to say..." Bayne rasped. "I thought *she was going to die?*"

"The game isn't about what you think will happen," Winston fired right back. "It's about getting the job done."

What a sick, twisted bastard. "You're seriously saying this was all just a game to you? You picked different people, then got matches for them—"

"They're called twins, FBI Agent Quinn. Our victims needed to be perfect matches. Fit with the theme, you know." Winston's lips thinned.

"Your theme. Right. The stupid two-headed cobra." Bayne hadn't showed her his right arm. Not yet. Her heart drummed in her chest. *"Lift up your sleeve!"*

Bayne shoved up his right sleeve.

And it was there. Right there. The tattoo that had haunted her nightmares for years. The exact same mark. The exact same design. The swirling snake that had come for her and destroyed so much on that one brutal night.

"Your boyfriend bled out much faster than I thought he would," Bayne admitted with zero remorse. "He was purely for bonus points, you get that. You were the main goal. A redhead. Any redhead would have worked that night. But then I saw you. A redhead with blue eyes. A rare combination. Kinda like finding a four-leaf clover."

Fuck yourself and your four-leaf clover. "You just picked people because of how they looked? Their hair color? Their eyes? Their—"

"No, FBI Agent Quinn," Winston cut in. "We *killed* people because of how they looked. It's called having a target. Succeeding in your mission."

"You didn't succeed with me." She was worried because Cass had gone so eerily silent. Silent, but she could feel his rage thickening in the air around them.

"I'm about to succeed," Bayne promised. "This has been a very long time coming."

"Why?" Agnes snapped. "Why has it been so long? Why didn't you come for me sooner? If you wanted me dead, I was there all along." She'd wanted the bastard to come for her so that she could destroy him. Her fingers were so tight around the gun she had hidden in her sling.

Bayne laughed. "Not like you're the only one I had to kill. You had to wait your turn."

Sick bastard—

"And *he* had to follow orders," Winston snapped. "Bayne kills when I say its time. He's not in charge. I am."

Bayne's jaw tensed. "You were gone," he muttered to Winston.

"I'm not gone any longer. And you're not in charge. *I am.* I am the one who directed the kills. I'm the one who pulled the strings," Winston's voice thundered back at them all. "I am the one who—"

"Just made a full confession that was caught on an FBI microphone because you're an idiot?" Nash cut in to say. "Yes, thanks very much for all of that. Now, I believe my sister will officially tell you that you're under arrest."

FBI microphone. For a moment, there was absolute silence. She wasn't wearing a wire. She knew Cass wasn't, either. But...leave it to Nash.

He and Ryan and Gray...always scheming.

"You really think I'm going to let three assholes in a van take me down?" Winston laughed. "My men didn't go far..."

"*My* men," Bayne groused.

"I have watchers here." Winston's eyes gleamed. "They have guns on you all. Bayne isn't the only one who can use a scope on his weapon. Though, your shot was pure shit, Bayne."

"*I hit Levi. He's the one I targeted. You said that you wanted Cass to live.*" Bayne's breath huffed out. "And I had to leave my favorite gun behind. You think it's easy hauling around a rifle like that on my bike when I've got pricks chasing me down?"

"You killed Hugo," Cass charged, finally breaking his silence.

"He was trying to kill *me.*" A fast return.

Sweat trickled down Agnes's back. She and Cass were still in the van, with Bayne and Winston positioned in front of the open, rear doors. She and Cass had pretty good cover. But Nash was out in the open.

He's too easy of a target.

"Your mother taught me some sign language, Cass," Winston suddenly announced. "I quite liked her, actually. I think I might have liked her...too much. That's the reason your father told her to leave."

Wait, Cass's father had *told* his mother to leave?

"Because he knew I would be taking what I wanted. Sooner or later, I always do." A smug smile pulled at Winston's lips. "Let's see if I remember this right..." He let go of the cane. It hit the floor. He made a quick "A"

Cynthia Eden

sign with his hand only to almost immediately drop his hand.

She blinked, not understanding. The only sign she knew that kinda looked like that one with the drop was a two-handed gesture and it meant—

It meant *now*. Oh, no. "Nash!" Her brother needed cover!

Gunfire erupted. Fast, continuous bullets went flying. Driving into the side of the van, shooting wildly.

She yelled even as Cass shifted his gun to fire at a threat he saw—men swarming from the shadows. Cass fired his weapon. Once. Two times. Three.

With Cass's gun no longer pointed right at him, Bayne leapt forward, surging up into the van.

"Stop!" Agnes yelled. "Freeze!"

He didn't. He'd just pulled out a second knife, one that had been strapped to his waist. "I'm finishing you." Spittle flew from his mouth.

Cass—a bullet hit Cass and sent him surging back. But in a blink, he was raising his weapon again, taking aim at Bayne.

Unnecessary. She had this covered. When Bayne's knife came at her, Agnes fired. Right through her sling. Dead into his chest.

He toppled out of the van.

"I think I'm finishing you," she said.

Chaos erupted.

The sound of shattering glass and banging doors rose to a crescendo. Lots of "FBI!" shouts filled the air. Men and women in bullet-proof vests raced through the warehouse. More gunfire. Lots of bikers running.

Bodies falling.

And...

"That sonofabitch isn't getting away!" Cass leapt out of the back of the van.

"Cass!"

He was lunging forward. Pushing through the madness. She jumped out of the van, too, but immediately crouched beside Bayne. A Bayne who had a very large pool of blood beneath his body. She'd hit him right in his cold heart. Hard not to do at nearly point-blank range.

His eyes were open. On her.

Just as Max's eyes had been open and on her. But, with Max, part of her had been glad that she was the last thing he'd seen. She'd tried to smile for him. Tried to even say, "I love you" in those last moments.

She smiled for Bayne, too. "Enjoy where you're going."

"*Agnes!*" Nash's shout.

Still crouching, she whirled away from Bayne. Nash was near the left, rear van tire. Her brother was *bleeding*. "Get covered!" he barked at her.

She was doing that. She was also going to help her brother. She rushed toward him and immediately pressed her hand to the bleeding wound on his side.

"I'm all right." But Nash hissed in pain.

"You have a bullet in you. That is not *all right*." So many FBI agents. She'd just caught sight of Malik. "Working behind my back with Gray the whole time, were you?" she accused Nash.

"Watching your back the whole time, yeah, that's what brothers do."

It was. Just as it was a sister's job to protect her brother. A man wearing a black leather vest and sporting piercings in his nose rushed toward them with his gun raised. He was aiming for Nash.

She fired. So did Nash.

The perp sank to his knees.

"FBI!" Agnes yelled. "Guns down! Guns *down!*"

The bad guys weren't listening. *There had been plenty of FBI shouts.* The perps were outnumbered. The Feds were taking over, and now that she could actually look fully around the warehouse, she realized why. This wasn't just about her and the man who'd hurt her so long ago. *Drugs. Weapons. Way too many fancy cars.* Agnes would wager that plenty of stolen property filled the warehouse.

But as her gaze darted around, she was looking for one person in particular.

"Cass went through the door on the right," Nash told her. "Went chasing the leader."

He'd gone after his uncle. The real ghost from his past.

Ryan appeared, dropping to his knees beside Nash. "Dammit, Nash, what did you do to yourself?"

"To...myself?" Nash choked out. "You are shitting me. You think I *shot myself?*"

Nash would be okay. Ryan was there. "Guard him," she ordered.

"I don't need *guarding*," Nash rasped back.

She ignored him. Her focus was on the door to the right.

"Agnes..." A warning note from Ryan. "You're a Fed. Do your job."

"I am." Her job—it was watching Cass's back. "Love you both." Then she was darting through the fighters and the Feds and heading for the door that waited. No way would Cass face his nightmare without her.

They were a team. Partners. And your partner always had your back.

Chapter Twenty-Five

"Freeze!" Cass shouted.

The man before him—a man who'd run damn fast for someone who'd used a cane moments before—stilled just steps away. They'd both barreled down a narrow hallway before Winston had kicked open a door and slipped into the growing darkness. The faintest hint of gold still filled the sky, giving Cass just enough light to see his uncle.

Most of the Feds were inside. *Like I didn't know Gray would swarm.* His cousin could be so predictable. A good thing.

A few Feds were probably watching the periphery of the building, but there were too many exits for everything to be thoroughly covered. And Winston had just found his escape hatch. Or, the man *thought* that he had.

This time, though, Cass would make sure his uncle did not get away.

Winston had a gun in his hand, Cass could see it. His uncle had ditched this cane, though. Cass couldn't help but wonder how much the use of the cane might have been for show. *Always trying to throw off potential enemies, aren't you? Making them think you are weaker than you really are.*

"Why yell for me to freeze?" Winston asked, voice curious. "Why not just shoot me in the back like you did before?"

"Turn around," he gritted out.

"I'm afraid I can't do that," Winston said with no hesitation. "You see, I really need to keep going. You would be wise to keep going, too."

Unease pricked at Cass's nape. "What in the hell are you talking about?"

Winston looked back at him. A glance over his shoulder. "You think I couldn't predict that you would be here? Either you would come running *after* that woman was dead, after Bayne had finished carving her up, or you would figure out that you'd been betrayed by Bear and you'd make an appearance *with* her. One way or another, though, I knew you would be in this warehouse. And I'll be honest, I was actually betting that you would come *with* her. Otherwise, I would have been disappointed in you. I hate being disappointed. Your father disappointed me, you know."

"Like I give a shit about your disappointment." But the unease that Cass felt was getting worse. Stronger. Sharper. He'd left Agnes back in the warehouse.

"Your FBI friends came with you to the scene. They rushed to the rescue as soon as my men starting firing. I counted on that happening, you see. I suspect Gray was in there somewhere. You and Gray were always so close as children." He still didn't fully face Cass. "Your father wasn't the only one who liked to keep tabs on you. I know all about your cousin, how close you were. You *are*. Close with the man who became such a powerhouse at the FBI while you sank into the shadows." A brief smile teased Winston's lips. "I never bought that you were fully in the dark. You had too many connections to the light. I blame that on your mother."

"My dad had her killed!" Rage cracked through his control, and the hand holding the gun shook.

"No, *I* did that. She was one of the few people that I could never get your father to hurt. You and your mother. He had a soft spot for you both. Weaknesses. The wrong woman can truly make a man weak. You learned that with your pretty little Fed, didn't you? She's gotten too close and made you weak when you needed to be at your strongest."

"She doesn't make me weak." Quite the opposite.

"Sure, she does. When she explodes into a million pieces—along with Gray and the rest of the Feds in there, and the poor, unfortunate idiots who swore allegiance to Bayne and to me—well, when they are all dead, you'll shatter apart, too. That's when the real weakness begins." That smile again. So very cold. "You see, my vengeance doesn't come from me killing you. Death is entirely too easy. My vengeance comes when you have to live in a world without the person you love most. When you have to suffer through every excruciating day."

When she explodes into a million pieces. His heart had stopped at those words.

"Is the bomb I left on a timer?" Winston asked. "Or do I have the trigger on me? What do you think?"

"Turn the fuck around." *A bomb. A bomb. A bomb.*

"I'll keep running, thanks. The better not to be hit by the blast. And you should run, too. *Away* from the warehouse if you want to stay alive. Or *to it* if you want Agnes Quinn to live."

No, fucking, *no.* "You're bluffing. You've never blown up a damn building in your life."

"People change. We evolve. I had to pick up some new tricks in the last few years. Oh, come on, don't be shocked, you had to suspect the truth. The Feds were working extra hard to bring down the Twins—"

"Because you and Bayne have been *murdering* people!"

"That's just a side hobby. We've been making bombs. Watching the world burn. You like to do that, too, don't you? You like—"

Bam.

Cass had fired. He'd gotten tired of the BS, and he did not have time to waste. Not if Agnes's life might be on the line.

Winston screamed when the bullet hit him in the back of the leg. He fell to the ground, then twisted his body, bringing his gun up and aiming it at Cass.

But Cass was already on him. He'd lunged forward in an instant. He pointed his weapon at Winston's chest even as Winston aimed his gun at Cass.

"If you have a trigger to some bomb on you, throw it to the side, now," Cass barked.

Winston smiled. "No."

"Right. Because there is no trigger. There is no bomb. You are *bluffing.*"

"You have about two minutes. I started the bomb the minute I watched the van pull into the warehouse. The driver *wasn't* Raz, I saw his face. I knew you'd come to the party at that moment, so I set the timer. I knew the way things would end even before Bayne opened the van doors."

Bullshit. Wasn't it?

Winston laughed as he ignored the blood that soaked his jeans. "How many lives can you save in two minutes? Or

298

do you even give a shit about that? Do you care about saving anyone but yourself?" A smug grin. "Maybe you don't even care about saving *her*. Maybe I was wrong about you. Maybe she's not a weakness because you just don't care about her at all. Maybe she means nothing to you."

The door flew open behind him—he heard the hinges screech. "Cass!" Agnes called.

He held his gun in position.

Winston maintained his grip on his weapon. "Am I bluffing?" Winston asked him.

Dammit. "Agnes, we have to get everyone out of that warehouse, *now*."

"What? Why?"

"Because there's a bomb inside."

Winston began to laugh.

Really? The dumb sonofabitch was gonna laugh?

"My brothers are in there!" she cried.

More laughter from Winston. Even as blood pooled beneath his right leg. Then his gaze darted toward Agnes. Cass knew exactly what the bastard was planning. Winston's gun wavered, shifting position slightly—

The boom blasted through the growing darkness. The bullet also blasted a hole right in Winston's upper arm. Winston's gun fell from his nerveless fingers.

"Bas—" Winston began.

Cass fired another shot at him. This time, his left leg.

Winston howled.

Then Cass shot Winston's left arm. Just so things would match up. *And so your ass will not be able to fight back. Bullets in both arms and both legs.*

"You're not gonna be able to run away," Cass told him. "You're gonna die right here with everyone else. Was that in your plans, you dick?"

Horror filled Winston's eyes. Horror and what could very well have been fear.

"You always did have one hell of a survival instinct, Uncle Winston." Cass was betting on that survival instinct to kick in.

He heard Agnes's feet rushing away. He knew she was going to tell the others to get out of the warehouse. That she was going to save her brothers. *She'd better get that sweet ass of hers outside, too.*

Cass sucked in a breath. "Tell me how to disarm it. Tell me where it is. Tell me—"

"We've got less than two minutes!" Winston screamed at him. "Get me the hell out of here! There is no stopping it! There is no disarming. It's in the office on the second floor, hidden in the desk there. *Get me the hell out of here! We have to go!"*

Cass leaned over him. He snatched up the fallen gun. "I'm getting everyone else *out.*"

Winston clawed at his arm. "No, no, you're not a hero. Don't save them! You're just like me, you're just like— "

Cass broke free, leaving him bleeding and screaming.

"You're just like me!" Winston yelled.

"The hell I am." He grabbed for the door.

And nearly ran straight into Gray.

"What's happening?" Gray demanded.

"Bomb inside, second floor office, in the desk. We have to get everyone out." He jerked a thumb over his shoulder. "Someone will need to carry his ass away, but that's the leader of the Twins and he has—"

Screams erupted from inside. Cass stopped talking. He ran in. Rushed through the hallway.

"Bomb! We have to get out! There's a bomb!"

Agnes's yell, rising above the others. The Feds were

scrambling. The members of Bayne and Winston's crew were fighting to get to the exits. Utter hell reigned.

Agnes rushed to her brothers. She and Ryan yanked Nash to his feet. Ryan slung Nash over his shoulder and hauled ass. Everyone was scrambling. Everyone was running for the doors.

But Agnes...she turned and ran back to Cass. *What. The. Hell?*

Her hand reached out to him. "Let's go, Cass!"

His gaze flew around. Then up. The second floor. The office up there. In the desk. "Winston said the bomb is up there. Maybe I can disarm it—"

"How the hell are you gonna do that? You're not the bomb squad!" She launched at him. Grabbed him. "It's a trap. You can't disarm it. Let's get the hell out of here. The bomb squad can come in. *They* can disarm it. We are getting out of here, now. You made my brother promise I'd walk away, remember? Well, here's *my* promise. *We're* walking away, together, right now, and—*Cass!*"

Screw walking. He was running with her. Because she was right. It probably was a trap. Winston might not have given them two full minutes. It would be just like the twisted fucker to say they had more time than they actually did.

He tossed Agnes over his shoulder. He was rushing out, with the Feds in front of him. Everyone was scattering. Almost out. They were all almost—

And then he heard the eruption. Heard it. Felt it. Even glanced over his shoulder and up. He saw the rolling waves of flame coming out of the second floor office.

But he was at one of the open doors. He had almost made it to safety.

Screw almost. I am making it. He launched forward,

holding onto Agnes, and even as the bomb detonated, he was still holding tightly to her.

He would *always* hold tightly to her.

We are both going to walk away, sweetheart...both going to walk away from this darkness and finally, into the light.

Chapter Twenty Six

"Do you remember me?" FBI Agent Gray Stone stood in front of the prisoner. The man was secured in the hospital. By secured—he was cuffed. With guards on either side of him.

Winston Striker squinted up at him.

"Grayson Stone," he said. Just in case he needed an introduction, but Gray suspected that the prisoner definitely remembered him.

Disgust twisted Winston's face.

"You're under arrest," Gray informed him. He'd actually told the guy this before, but he had to make sure that Winston was actually *aware* of the words this time. So he rattled off the man's rights. Made sure Winston knew he could get an attorney. The whole spiel.

"What in the hell am I being charged with?" Winston glared at him.

Oh? Had Winston missed that part? "The FBI has connected you to four bombings that occurred across the US within the last few years. There is also the drug running, the illegal weapons trade, and the murders. We have you and Bayne Hendrix on record confessing to those crimes."

"Bayne..." A low growl.

"He's dead." Gray inclined his head as he delivered that bit of news. "Pretty sure he was dead before the blast. But, yeah, dead. Two other men in your crew were also killed."

Winston's eyes narrowed. "And Cass?"

"What do you think happened to him?"

Gruff, hoarse laughter. "I think that prick believed me when I said he had two minutes. I think he went to hell— and I think that bitch FBI agent went with him."

Gray's jaw locked. "There are lots of definitions when it comes to hell."

"What? What are you talking about?"

"I'm talking about hell." Another nod. "You're about to visit your own hell. With the charges that we have against you, with the evidence, with the recorded confession, you aren't going to walk. You will be locked away for the rest of your life."

More of that hoarse laughter. "Like I'm scared of prison."

"People died in those bombs that you set across the US. Additionally, with that sick-ass killing game that you were playing, you murdered people in half a dozen states. States with the death penalty. You have more than cold prison bars to fear." His head tilted to the side. "You're not going to have any power in prison."

"I have power *everywhere*."

"So does Cass." Low.

Some of the smug cockiness faded from Winston's eyes. "He died."

Gray didn't speak.

"If he didn't die in that blast, *he will be dead*. He can't turn evidence over to the Feds and expect the Strikers and the other crews to just let him walk. *You don't walk away from the MCs!"*

Actually, sometimes, you did.

You just had to know the right people.

People...*like me.*

Chapter Twenty-Seven

THREE MONTHS LATER...

AGNES QUINN STOPPED in front of the bar. It was a small place, in a tiny town in south Alabama. One nestled on the quiet shores of Mobile Bay. She could feel a light breeze blowing against her cheeks, and when she looked toward the old, massive oaks, she could see the Spanish moss swaying lightly.

Sunset had turned the sky a burnished gold. The bar was open, with a few locals inside. She shouldn't be afraid to cross the threshold and walk in and yet...she was.

What if he's changed? Changed his mind...changed his heart.

What if he doesn't want me any longer?

Something that terrified her.

And yet, she hadn't been able to stay away. Not even a day longer.

Her shoulders squared. She strode inside with her chin up and her heart racing. Agnes barely noticed the interior.

Barely heard the soft, jazz music from the performer on the small stage. Her gaze was drawn to the wooden bar counter on the right and to the man who stood behind the bar.

Tall, with broad shoulders, his back was to her. His dark hair had been cut shorter, and when he turned slowly to talk to a customer at the counter, she saw his profile.

Clean shaven. Handsome.

Her lips pressed together.

No leather jacket. Just a faded, gray shirt. He nodded to the customer, and then his head angled a bit more. Shifted to the right.

His dark, dark eyes landed on her.

Longing. Need.

Her breath caught. Then she wasn't just standing inside the doorway any longer. She was rushing across that bar.

He stood there, shaking his head, and then—then he just jumped right over the bar. He caught her in three steps. His hands wrapped tightly around her. "*What are you doing here?*"

"Coming to you." He'd gotten a new life, courtesy of Gray. Gray and all his strings. No more badass MC leader. Now Cass was a bar owner in a small town. A quiet life. Peace.

And she missed him so much.

"*You shouldn't be here.*"

There was no other place that she'd rather be. "What does a woman have to do," she asked, as her hand rose to press against his cheek, "in order to be *loved* by you?"

His mouth crashed onto hers. Not softly. Not carefully. But with a wild, voracious hunger that she eagerly met because this was her Cass. Her partner. Her lover.

Hers.

He kissed her like he'd been starving, and she kissed

him back the exact same way. As if she'd been desperate for him. As if every single day had ripped out her heart, and she'd been walking around empty on the inside because she did not have him.

I have him now. I will not let go.

But his mouth tore from hers. His eyes glittered as he looked down at her and then...

Then he was taking her hand. Marching her through the narrow hallways of the bar and out the back door. He threw open that door and rushed them into the night.

Surprise, surprise, a motorcycle waited not too far away.

You could take the biker out of the crew, but you could not take the bike from the man.

"I didn't want you giving up anything for me, Agnes."

Precious words. He stood with his hands fisted now because he'd let her go. She didn't want his hands fisted. She wanted them on her. "Can we go for a ride?" She'd missed riding on the motorcycle with him. *I missed him. Everything about him.*

"You need to leave."

"Is that what you really want?"

A shake of his head.

"Then what do you want?" she asked.

"You. Here. With me. Always. Because I am a selfish bastard like that."

"It's funny. I guess I'm selfish like that, too. Because I want you, here, with me. Always."

"Agnes—"

"Your uncle is dead. He was murdered in his cell. His throat was slit. Ear to ear."

Cass didn't even blink. "Did you come to ask me if I ordered the hit?"

"No." She hadn't. Cass had pulled out of the MC

world, but...he was gone, not forgotten. The intel picked up by the FBI indicated that Cass still held plenty of power. Javion had taken over the Strikers, and, at the big, bad meeting for leaders in Arizona—a meeting that she and Cass had never quite made it to—Javion had flatly announced that Cass would always belong to his crew, that he would be protected, no matter what.

Rumors were swirling about Cass, though. The man was even more of a myth, a legend these days.

Some people insisted Cass was dead, killed in the blast at the warehouse. They didn't get why Javion would protect a dead man.

Others believed that Cass was in the wind, riding hard as he looked for new trouble. New danger.

And she knew that he'd started a new life, one on quiet shores. Would he still raise hell? Oh, absolutely, because Gray had tipped her off that Cass didn't intend to go easily into retirement. He'd still be working with Gray every now and then.

Maybe he'd even be pulling some backup work for her brothers when the need arose. Did that mean Cass could be going international with his bad self? *Probably.*

He wasn't the type to fade into the darkness. She'd tried to tell him before. Cass just hadn't been made for the dark. Agnes gathered her nerve and her courage and said, "I came to let you know Winston was dead. And to tell you that I don't want to live without you."

"Agnes." A lunging step toward her. *"I can't let you go again."*

"I didn't ask to be let go the first time." She had not. "You were the one trying to pull the martyr card on me."

"You love working at the FBI. You love your job."

She did. She loved protecting and defending and

helping the victims because she knew what it was like to be one of them. "Funny thing. I hear they are looking for a new sheriff in this area. I sort of think that I might make a kick-ass sheriff. I'll even get one of those really cool hats to wear."

"*Agnes.*"

"Did I ever tell you that I love the way you say my name? I used to hate my name. Until you said it the first time. It feels sexy and strong when you say it."

"You are sexy and strong." His hands unclenched, just to immediately fist again. "Sheriff, huh? You gonna be happy with that life?"

"You gonna be happy with me and the kids we'll have?"

Longing burned all the brighter in his eyes.

"You gonna be happy with the life that we will build, together?" Agnes held her breath.

His eyes closed. "You have no idea how badly I want that life."

Good. Great. Fantastic. Her breath shuddered out. "Then take it." *Take me.*

His eyes opened. "You're not a dream."

"No."

"You're really here."

"Yes." Standing in front of him, bold as day.

"And you still love me?" Careful. So very careful.

"I will love you until I die."

He was on her. Kissing her. Hugging her. Pulling her close, and she was finally, *finally* happy because the last few months had been hell. She'd had to close the cases she worked. Had to get the charges set against the criminal bastards who'd been in the Twins. Had to finish her job. Had to miss Cass every single day and night.

But no more. *No more.* She'd told Gray that her choice

had been made long ago. It had been made the first night she spent with Cass. For her, he was it.

She'd do whatever it took to be with him.

A new city, a new job, a new life? She was all in. Whatever it took, she would do it. They would be together, and they would be happy.

He eased back, just a bit. "Your brothers are gonna want to kick my ass."

"They already do want that." But, more... "They want me happy. I'll be happy with you." She smiled at him. "Now, about that motorcycle ride..."

His hands curled around her waist. Cass lifted her up. A few steps had them at the bike. He put her on the seat. Slid in front of her. Her arms curled around him. She hugged him tightly because she'd missed him so, so much. "Hey, Cass?"

He revved the engine.

"Is someone inside to watch your bar?" The bar belonged to him. Part of his new life. *Their* new life.

"Yeah, I've got an assistant."

Good. "Then guess what we get to do?" She inhaled his scent. She pulled in his warmth. Her Cass. *Hers.*

"What, princess?"

Her head turned. She could see the edge of the bay beyond the trees. The sun was dipping into the water. Such a beautiful gold. Kind of like the gold that hid in the darkness of his eyes. "We get to ride off into the sunset." She swallowed. Twice. "And we get to be happy."

It hadn't been easy. Hadn't been pretty. It had been violent and scary and their time together had completely changed them both. But...

He slowly drove toward the sunset and the road that eased along the bay.

They would get to be happy. She'd spend the rest of her days with Cass. She'd watch his back. He'd guard hers. They would be partners. Friends. Lovers.

A family.

"It's a beautiful sunset," she told him.

"It's gonna be a beautiful life," he told her.

Yes, it would be. They would make certain of it.

THE END

Looking for another romantic suspense from Cynthia Eden? If you're in the mood for a dark and twisty read, don't miss COMPULSION.

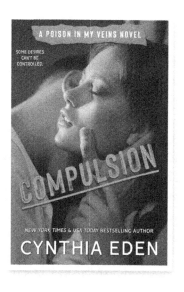

They wake up hand-cuffed together in a serial killer's lair...hardly the cute-meet of her dreams. But then again, her dreams *are* usually nightmares so...

Lily Gallo knows killers. She should, after all, because serial killers are her specialty. She's the daughter of a notorious serial killer, and she's made it her life's work to study the brutal predators. And, recently, she's been researching the offspring of serials. She's looking for others who are just like she is. Her research has brought her into the life of reclusive billionaire Atlas Bennett. He'd refused her repeated requests for a meeting. She'd suspected he might be following in his father's brutal footsteps. But now...

They're both trapped, and they have to rely on each other for survival.

Atlas can't believe it when he wakes up handcuffed to the beautiful and infuriating Lily. The woman thinks he's as savage as his twisted father, but she has no clue what dark secrets he really holds. For the moment, though, escape is their priority. But once they get out of that hell, Lily will be his. He'd warned her to stay away. Now, it's too late. Her fate is sealed.

A killer is after them both. To survive, they have to trust each other. They also have to stay very, very close to one another...

Atlas knows that his reaction to Lily isn't normal. The lust he feels is too strong, too consuming, but she calls to the primitive darkness within Atlas that he's tried to hide from the rest of the world. He's going to need that darkness because a killer is hunting him...and Lily. A predator who is intent on taking out the children of serial killers. Innocence and guilt doesn't matter. Only survival does. The killer has uncovered Lily's research, and he's using it to track his prey. As each day passes, he's also growing increasingly obsessed with Lily.

Being prey wasn't on her agenda.

Lily's mother is the most infamous female serial killer of modern times, and her mother passed on more than a few of her dangerous traits to Lily. Lily has no intention of being some helpless victim, but she will trap the killer who is on her trail. She'll also stick close to Atlas because she knows he holds plenty of secrets. Fair enough. She's got secrets, too. Atlas stirs a part of her that she has tried to fight her entire life. Wild, forbidden, and dangerous, he is a lover she can't resist. He may just be the perfect partner for her... unless, of course, she turns out to be dead wrong about him.

Because some people carry darkness, some people carry sins...and there are some monsters that you never see coming, not until it's far too late.

Author's Note

Thank you so very much for reading WHEN HE GUARDS. I've had the best time writing the "Protector and Defender Romance" series, and I so hope that you've enjoyed the books. I love writing about strong, determined heroes—and pairing them up with equally strong and determined heroines! Agnes was definitely a fierce heroine. She'd been through darkness, and it was time for both her and Cass to step into the light.

If you have time, please consider leaving a review for WHEN HE GUARDS. Reviews help readers to discover new books—and authors are definitely grateful for them!

If you'd like to stay updated on my releases and sales, please join my newsletter list. Did I mention that when you sign up, you get a FREE Cynthia Eden book? Because you do!

By the way, I'm also active on social media. You can find me chatting away on Instagram and Facebook.

317

Again, thank you for reading WHEN HE GUARDS. Books are my favorite escape, and I hope that they allow you to slip away and destress for a while, too.

Best,

Cynthia Eden

cynthiaeden.com

More Books By Cynthia Eden

Protector & Defender Romance
- When He Protects
- When He Hunts
- When He Fights
- When He Defends

Ice Breaker Cold Case Romance
- Frozen In Ice (Book 1)
- Falling For The Ice Queen (Book 2)
- Ice Cold Saint (Book 3)
- Touched By Ice (Book 4)
- Trapped In Ice (Book 5)
- Forged From Ice (Book 6)
- Buried Under Ice (Book 7)
- Ice Cold Kiss (Book 8)
- Locked In Ice (Book 9)
- Savage Ice (Book 10)
- Brutal Ice (Book 11)
- Cruel Ice (Book 12)
- Forbidden Ice (Book 13)

- Ice Cold Liar (Book 14)
- Ice Cold Christmas (Book 15)

Wilde Ways
- Protecting Piper (Book 1)
- Guarding Gwen (Book 2)
- Before Ben (Book 3)
- The Heart You Break (Book 4)
- Fighting For Her (Book 5)
- Ghost Of A Chance (Book 6)
- Crossing The Line (Book 7)
- Counting On Cole (Book 8)
- Chase After Me (Book 9)
- Say I Do (Book 10)
- Roman Will Fall (Book 11)
- The One Who Got Away (Book 12)
- Pretend You Want Me (Book 13)
- Cross My Heart (Book 14)
- The Bodyguard Next Door (Book 15)
- Ex Marks The Perfect Spot (Book 16)
- The Thief Who Loved Me (Book 17)

The Fallen Series
- Angel Of Darkness (Book 1)
- Angel Betrayed (Book 2)
- Angel In Chains (Book 3)
- Avenging Angel (Book 4)

Wilde Ways: Gone Rogue
- How To Protect A Princess (Book 1)
- How To Heal A Heartbreak (Book 2)
- How To Con A Crime Boss (Book 3)

Night Watch Paranormal Romance
- Hunt Me Down (Book 1)
- Slay My Name (Book 2)
- Face Your Demon (Book 3)

Trouble For Hire
- No Escape From War (Book 1)
- Don't Play With Odin (Book 2)
- Jinx, You're It (Book 3)
- Remember Ramsey (Book 4)

Death and Moonlight Mystery
- Step Into My Web (Book 1)
- Save Me From The Dark (Book 2)

Phoenix Fury
- Hot Enough To Burn (Book 1)
- Slow Burn (Book 2)
- Burn It Down (Book 3)

Dark Sins
- Don't Trust A Killer (Book 1)
- Don't Love A Liar (Book 2)

Lazarus Rising
- Never Let Go (Book One)
- Keep Me Close (Book Two)
- Stay With Me (Book Three)
- Run To Me (Book Four)
- Lie Close To Me (Book Five)
- Hold On Tight (Book Six)

Bad Things

- The Devil In Disguise (Book 1)
- On The Prowl (Book 2)
- Undead Or Alive (Book 3)
- Broken Angel (Book 4)
- Heart Of Stone (Book 5)
- Tempted By Fate (Book 6)
- Wicked And Wild (Book 7)
- Saint Or Sinner (Book 8)

Bite Series
- Forbidden Bite (Bite Book 1)
- Mating Bite (Bite Book 2)

Blood and Moonlight Series
- Bite The Dust (Book 1)
- Better Off Undead (Book 2)
- Bitter Blood (Book 3)

Mine Series
- Mine To Take (Book 1)
- Mine To Keep (Book 2)
- Mine To Hold (Book 3)
- Mine To Crave (Book 4)
- Mine To Have (Book 5)
- Mine To Protect (Book 6)

Dark Obsession Series
- Watch Me (Book 1)
- Want Me (Book 2)
- Need Me (Book 3)
- Beware Of Me (Book 4)

Purgatory Series

- The Wolf Within (Book 1)
- Marked By The Vampire (Book 2)
- Charming The Beast (Book 3)
- Deal with the Devil (Book 4)

Bound Series
- Bound By Blood (Book 1)
- Bound In Darkness (Book 2)
- Bound In Sin (Book 3)
- Bound By The Night (Book 4)
- Bound in Death (Book 5)

Stand-Alone
- Waiting For Christmas
- Monster Without Mercy
- Kiss Me This Christmas
- It's A Wonderful Werewolf
- Never Cry Werewolf
- Immortal Danger
- Deck The Halls
- Come Back To Me
- Put A Spell On Me
- Never Gonna Happen
- One Hot Holiday
- Slay All Day
- Midnight Bite
- Secret Admirer
- Christmas With A Spy
- Femme Fatale
- Until Death
- Sinful Secrets
- First Taste of Darkness
- A Vampire's Christmas Carol

About the Author

Cynthia Eden loves romance books, chocolate, and going on semi-lazy adventures. She is a *New York Times*, *USA Today*, *Digital Book World*, and *IndieReader* best-seller. She writes romantic suspense, paranormal romance, and fun contemporary novels. You can find out more about her work at www.cynthiaeden.com.

If you want to stay updated on her new releases and books deals, be sure to join her newsletter group: cynthiaeden.com/newsletter. When new readers sign up for her newsletter, they are automatically given a free Cynthia Eden ebook.

Made in United States
North Haven, CT
26 December 2025

85798393R00183